Mulliga Revenge

A Peckham Novel

James Court

Mulligan's Revenge

4th (illustrated) Edition

This novel is a work of fiction. Names, characters and locations are the subject of the author's imagination and any resemblance to actual persons, living or dead, locations or objects, existing or existed is purely coincidental.

It is sold subject to the condition that it shall not by way of trade or otherwise, be lent, resold, hired out, or otherwise circulated without the writer's prior consent, electronically or in any form of binding or cover other than the form in which it is published and without a similar condition including this condition being imposed on the subsequent purchaser. Replication or distribution of any part is strictly prohibited without the written permission of the copyright holder.

Copyright © 2016 James Court

All rights reserved.

ISBN:1523262532

ISBN-13: 978-1523262533

To Juliette

Chapter Index

1. A Happy Release?..1
2. The Joy of Freedom...7
3. Piggy's Destiny...12
4. Gaining Gainful Employment..................................18
5. Piggy the Wage Slave..26
6. Piggy Swinton, Cat burglar......................................34
7. Deja Vu for Jason Ponsonby...................................37
8. Streatham, the Sunshine Suburb............................42
9. Money makes the World go Round........................50
10. Too Many Coincidences..58
11. Questions, Questions..65
12. Helping Police with their Enquiries......................69
13. More Police Enquiries...77
14. Piggy in Love?...84
15. Conspicuous Absence...98
16. The Net Closes In..100
17. Piggy in Charge...111
18. Scrumpy and Cream Teas..................................115
19. Boxing Clever..128
20. Sunday, Sunday, So Good to Me.......................134
21. Rainy Days and Mondays...................................143
22. Autopsy..149
23. Piggy in the Middle...163
24. Peace at Last?...168

25. Caught in the Act...176
26. Preparing the Final Account..180
27. Knowledge is Power..183
28. The Wounded Hero Returns..187
29. Tying up Loose Ends...198
30. Business is Business...202
31. Piggy the Protector...207
32. Deception...222
33. Piggy Swinton, Murder Suspect..228
34. All's Well that Ends..231

ACKNOWLEDGMENTS

This book was published with encouragement from the INCA Project.

1. A Happy Release?

Reginald Swinton considered himself to be a career criminal. To date it has not been a very successful career, more like that of a third rate actor who spent most of his time resting. In Reginald's case resting was usually within the confines of one of Her Majesty's Prisons. He is known to his few friends, and many arresting officers, as Piggy: partly because of his surname, but mainly because early in his career he was once arrested whilst attempting to burgle a country house.

In the dark he had fallen through the roof of a pig sty and broken his ankle upon landing. There he was found by a local police officer who was alerted to his presence by his screams, as the short-sighted legitimate occupant of the sty was welcoming him with a slobbering all over lick wash. The motherly old sow had recently seen her piglets off to market and considered him a poor, but acceptable, new companion. It had taken several officers a considerable time to part Reginald from his possessive new friend.

Today Piggy had completed a short period of resting in HMP Brixton after an unsuccessful attempted mugging of the only octogenarian karate black belt in Peckham. As was customary for Piggy he acquired an injury during his attempted crime. In this case a kick to the groin that would have deprived him of much of the enjoyment of female company, even if he was not incarcerated.

He stood in the little car park at the front of the prison and took a deep breath; his first without the dual scents of sweat and disinfectant for the past three months. Having filled his lungs with traffic fumes he exhaled, coughed and spat at the gravel. Then he turned his face toward Peckham and began his weary walk to his mother's council flat where he hoped to spend the next few nights.

Piggy received a decidedly lukewarm greeting from his mother. She had lost count of the number of similar such homecomings her only son had made, and was not particularly anxious to introduce him to her latest paramour. She was not sure that her offspring would get on well with the Reverend Augustus Woods. She also wanted to keep her relationship private, especially from Mrs Woods. She suggested that Piggy seek out Mabel, his girlfriend at the time of his arrest, but Piggy was not expecting much of a welcome there either. Not if the tone of her one and only letter to him during his stay in Brixton was anything to go by. How was he to know that it was her grandmother that he attempted to mug? She had deliberately avoided introducing him to her family and had only herself to blame for his mistake.

Despite her tepid greeting Mrs Swinton was happy to lend Piggy two pounds in order to get him out of the flat before the less than reverent Reverend arrived. So Piggy took the offered notes and adjourned to *The Squinting Badger* for his first pint of beer since his latest arrest.

Sitting in a corner of the public bar he watched the customers come and go, hoping to spot a friend to cadge a second drink from. Given how few friends he had, it was an unlikely prospect and he sipped his beer slowly, savouring the taste as each drop rolled down his throat. There were several people he knew in the bar, but none that he could call friends. Indeed, some might turn openly hostile to him if past events came to mind, so he kept quietly to his corner behind a discarded copy of last week's Peckham Echo, catching up on events in the outside world.

Piggy's love life followed a predictable cycle. He would meet some gullible woman and a sort of romance would slowly evolve. Normally that evolution would get close to the more physically demanding stage just as Piggy got his collar felt for his most recent misdemeanour. About the third week in prison he would receive a letter telling him she had transferred her affections elsewhere and so the cycle was set to repeat from the start with a new prospect when he regained his freedom. None of Piggy's conquests were Hollywood starlet or brain surgeon material, and his most recent attachments were most definitely at or beyond their best before dates.

He had met his latest paramour, Mabel, at the sweet counter in Woolworths. They both lunged for the rhubarb and custards in the pick & mix tubs and Mabel's podgy fist had wedged his relatively small hand against the sticky red and yellow contents. She had apologised profusely and insisted on licking his hand and wiping it dry with a dainty lace handkerchief. Piggy was flattered by her concern for his wellbeing and happily allowed her to steer him across the road to the little café where they sat and talked while she devoured a succession of cream cakes. It would be true to say that she picked him up, as she was clearly physically capable of doing with ease.

He regretted the incident that had caused their romance to flounder, and him roll in agony on the pavement of Rye Lane whilst awaiting being taken into custody.

Having exhausted the contents of the *Peckham Echo* social pages, Piggy sat reflecting on the dismal prospects for his immediate future. It was bleak. The only firm diary entry he had was an appointment with a probation officer and instructions to visit the Employment Exchange. Piggy had made numerous previous visits to the Exchange and they were not happy occasions. They merely emphasized his lack of suitable skills for seeking employment, and the scarcity of employers willing to take on applicants whose only references were a series of good behaviour letters from prison governors.

The door opened and a face scanned the pub, clearly looking for someone. As the woman spotted Piggy she smiled and entered. She went to the bar and ordered a Campari and Soda before settling briefly in a vacant chair a few tables away from him. Piggy took notice of her immediately. She was definitely a cut above the usual customers in *The Squinting Badger*. A full hourglass figure clad in expensive clothes with red high heeled shoes in a shade that perfectly matched her nails and lipstick, and topped with well-groomed long natural blonde hair. The seams of her stockings ran perfectly straight up the backs of her delightfully shaped calves, to disappear under the hem of her cream dress an inch above those cutely dimpled knees. When she smiled, it did things to you, especially if, like Piggy, you had been detained by Her Majesty for the past thirteen weeks.

Piggy had his mind on other things when he first noticed the smile, but it quickly got his full attention. He immediately looked to his left and right to seek out the lucky intended recipient. But his glances about failed to indicate a probable candidate and so he ventured to return the smile himself. He gazed at her for a full minute as he searched his memory for a previous encounter. He was sure he would remember it, however fleeting it had been. Then he attempted to visualise her in police uniform, triggering his mind to wander off into a fantasy which he found hard to control. But his memory refused to reveal any such acquaintance, and so he decided her friendly salutation was a case of mistaken identity.

He sat and feasted his eyes on the delights of her presence for some time until she returned his gaze with another smile. Then his delight turned to transfixed amazement as she gracefully rose from her chair and walked towards him.

"Can I get you another one of those?" she murmured softly as she sat beside him at his table. She lightly brushed his hand with hers as she placed her glass a few inches from his.

"Y, Y, Yes p, p, please!" stuttered Piggy, hardly believing his luck.

The woman rose slowly, turned and walked to the bar. Her hips swung gently as she went, leaving behind a hint of *Evening in Paris* that struggled to compete with the stale beer fumes that filled the air. As she stood waiting to order his drink she turned and gave him yet another of those smiles. Piggy felt parts of his body stirring in response to her presence.

"I'm Tracey!" she said as she arrived back with a full pint glass of best bitter which she set down in front of him.

"Reg," he replied, "but my friends call me Piggy."

"I've been looking for you, Piggy. I'm hoping you can do something for me. I want a man!"

Piggy definitely could not believe his luck. She made the word 'Piggy' sound soft and intimate, but the rest of the sentence resounded with tones of deep unfulfilled passion. He became conscious of other male eyes admiring his new companion and his mind drifted off back into the realms of fantasy.

"Gosh!" he said when he regained the power of speech. He began to hurriedly gulp down his beer in order to get on to the more interesting possibilities implicit in her statements.

Tracey smiled again and stroked her cheek with the back of her hand as she stared intensely at Piggy's eager face.

"The man I want has been very naughty. He stole something from me and I want it back. And I want to teach him a lesson at the same time. I think you can help me. I would be ever so grateful if you can."

She smiled again and Piggy sat captivated. But his expression slowly changed from eager excitement to disappointment as he digested her latest words. It was dawning on him that she did not have any desires for his puny body and prison-pallored face. He should have known from the start that his original assumption of her being drawn to his alluring persona was unlikely. But merely being in her presence was a treat for him, and he could but hope and dream of what his sparkling personality might forge in the future.

Tracey gazed at Piggy as he started on his fresh pint. She said nothing further until he was halfway through it. Then she tossed back her shining golden hair and looked Piggy full in the face.

"I'm guessing that you will be looking for work," she said.

Piggy nodded. His brain had been subject to a multitude of emotions since he had first spotted her, but it was now reluctantly resigned to the fact that she was not about to make his wildest fantasies come true.

Whilst he always went through the motions of seeking work, he really had little intention of looking too hard. In any case he was never high on a prospective employer's wish list.

"You will be seeing your probation officer, John Dillon, at ten o'clock tomorrow morning. He will ask you about what you have done to seek employment. I want you to listen carefully to him. I will see you here again tomorrow lunchtime."

She rose, pursed her lips forward as if to blow a kiss, and turned to leave before Piggy could speak. She was gone long before he could collect his thoughts; leaving him with a dozen unasked questions, and the nagging thought that he had dreamt the whole thing. Only the second beer mug and the lipstick smeared high ball glass sitting on the table convinced him he had been awake.

How did she know about his probation office appointment? He, himself, did not know who his probation officer would be, although the name she mentioned did sound familiar. He eyed the remains of his drink and settled back to sip slowly and reflect on what an odd day it had been so far. Before he could finish it he saw his recent girlfriend Mabel's muscular cousin, Keith Longman, come in and stand at the bar. He had only ever seen Keith from a distance, but knew him from his reputation as a boxer, and as an aggressive defender of the female of the species. He decided to quietly slip away while Keith had his back turned to him, before he sustained any further damage to his body.

2. The Joy of Freedom

Standing in Camberwell New Road, Piggy realised that he had no idea how he was to fill the rest of the day. He was not used to having the freedom to do as he chose. He had the remains of the two pounds in his pocket and a stomach that reminded him that he had not eaten since his prison breakfast that morning. He walked along to Kennedy's and bought himself a family-sized pork pie, and then he headed towards Peckham Rye Park to sit and let the world pass him by.

Halfway down Rye Lane a voice behind him spoke. Piggy froze.

"So they have let you out, have they!" said Detective Constable Holmes from a shop doorway. "How long will it be before we put you away again this time?"

Piggy turned to see the sarcastic grin on Holmes's face.

"I'm not doing anything wrong, Mr Holmes!" he whined. "I'm going straight this time, honest!"

Holmes studied Piggy's worried face and decided that he probably had not yet had time to get into trouble.

"Make sure you do, Piggy, or else I'll make sure you go straight, straight back to Brixton."

Having reminded Piggy of the watchfulness of the Law, Holmes sent him on his way with a cursory nod in the direction that he had been walking. He watched Piggy go and made a note to put an entry in the parade book, just in case Piggy had already been up to his old tricks.

The rest of Piggy's afternoon was uneventful. He sat and ate his pie, over-filling his stomach for the first time in months, and then tilted his head up and closed his eyes to appreciate the warm May sunshine on his face. Small birds scurried about in the adjacent bushes and all was right in Piggy's world. Eventually he decided to return to his mother's flat and got reluctantly to his feet, shaking the odd pie crumbs from his lap as he rose. His route back to his mother's home was circuitous to avoid the area where Mabel and her large family lived. Life in prison might not teach one much, but it does sharpen one's skills in self-preservation.

Back at the flat, Piggy found himself on his own. He would have loved to go straight to bed and stretch out on the soft mattress with a magazine, but his mother had disposed of his library of lurid reading material when she had taken up with the good Reverend. Given the nature of her relationship with the Reverend, Piggy could only assume it was to prevent unfavourable comparisons with the pictures therein.

He sat and watched those programmes on television that he had been deprived of for the past three months. They had not improved in that time, but he was determined not to self-impose the curfew and lights out of his recent incarceration. Eventually he made his way to the bathroom and ran himself a hot, deep tub with half a bottle of his mother's Avon bubble bath. He climbed in and luxuriated in the suds and steam, safe in the knowledge that for once he did not have to keep his eyes open and rush his ablutions. Soon he fell fast asleep and dreamt of grass-skirted dusky maidens swaying to steel guitars. For some reason they all wore red high heeled shoes and bright red lipstick.

It was gloomy in the room when Piggy woke. The small high window, set five floors up a sheer man-made cliff, had not been cleaned outside for years and begrudged every single ray of sunshine that it let in. He was cold, wrinkled and could hear voices in the flat. He rose quickly, but not quickly enough as the bathroom door opened and a man in a vicar's dog collar entered the room. The man turned the light on with the experienced hand of someone who knew exactly where the pull was located.

"Who are you?" the ecclesiastical apparition demanded, as Piggy grabbed for a towel.

"That's my son," came a worried voice from behind him. "He's been away, working for the government."

"Oh!" said the man, clearly not aware of Piggy's existence until this moment. "What line of work are you in?"

Piggy thought quickly. Renovating government office furniture and assembling light fittings would not sound like the sort of work to take one away from home.

"It's a bit hush hush, I'm afraid," said Piggy. "We test the security of government institutions."

Piggy stood there, calf deep in cold foam-topped water, waiting for the man to leave him in peace. It was a while before the interloper decided his call of nature could wait for a few more minutes and left the room.

Once dressed, Piggy joined his mother and her companion in the little lounge. It was an awkward atmosphere, and Piggy realised that his presence in the flat was putting a damper on his mother's plans for the night. Besides he had not had the freedom to come and go as he pleased for some time.

"I'm going out, Mum!" he said, as he got up and headed for the front door. She mumbled a reply as she went to attend to the boiling kettle, but Piggy was already outside. He walked down the five floors to the ground. Piggy was unsure if the lift was working, but in any case it was a confined space, and he had seen enough confined spaces for the time being.

He walked along to *The Squinting Badger* and, having counted his change, bought himself a half pint of beer.

The bar was more crowded than at lunchtime. Piggy sat, sipped slowly and watched the world go by. Yet again he vowed not to go back to prison. He stopped short of vowing to go straight. Simply not getting caught would be enough of a challenge for the moment.

When he could not make his drink last any longer he reluctantly got up and headed down Rye Lane to look in the windows of the closed shops, in case one had forgotten to lock up properly. He was standing admiring the display in a jeweller's window when a dark blue Austin J4 van pulled up alongside him. As he heard the distinctive rumble of the sliding passenger door opening, Piggy did not need to look sideways to know what the van was.

"You there! Stand still!" barked the commanding voice of PC John Walker as he stepped out and walked up to Piggy. Then, as he shone a torch in his face and recognised him, "what brings you out here late at night, Piggy?"

"I'm on my way home!"

"Via the shops?"

"I wanted a bit of a walk," Piggy whined.

"I would not have taken you for a flasher, Piggy. I suppose prison must have been a bit frustrating," said Walker.

"I'm not! I've been in *The Squinting Badger* and am on my way home... What do you mean? Flasher!"

"You'd better come with us. We've two old ladies who gave us your description an hour ago."

Here Walker was stretching the truth a bit. Although two elderly ladies had reported a flasher, and both gave the same detailed description of his lower half, they were both extremely vague about his facial features.

Piggy looked startled. Either it was a mistake, or... For a moment he wondered if Mabel's cousin had spotted him and put up two of her many aunts to nobble him.

Walker grabbed Piggy by the upper arm and escorted him to the back doors of the van. Moments later as the metal doors clanged shut, Piggy was again incarcerated by officialdom. He sat miserably awaiting what fate had in store for him.

But for once luck was on Piggy's side. The van had only driven for a minute or so when it stopped. Piggy could hear the driver speaking on the radio.

"Are you sure? ... And they are both certain that he is the one? ... Half trousers hanging from a suspender belt... Sounds right ... Well in that case we'll let our suspect go."

Again Piggy heard the van's side door rumble open and then PC Walker opened the back door, flooding the gloomy interior with light from Jones & Higgins shop window displays.

"Your lucky day Piggy. Looks like you were telling the truth. Must be a new experience for you. On your way."

Piggy could not get out of the van quickly enough. He jumped onto the pavement and looked around. He was twice as far from home as when they picked him up. But he did not care. He headed off as fast as he could.

3. Piggy's Destiny

Piggy was early for his interview at the probation office. He knew the office well, having had countless uncomfortable past interviews there. He sat for half an hour after his allotted appointment time before his probation officer sought him out. John Dillon was considerably older than most of the young fresh-faced, degree-holding probation officers who Piggy had previously encountered. He beckoned Piggy from the waiting room to the file-stacked office where he worked. He had the air of someone used to being in control, as befits a man who retired from the police force with the rank of Station Sergeant.

Piggy recognised him from an event earlier in his career, when Dillon had run the charge-room of Peckham police station whilst he was being cautioned for shop-lifting sweets from a corner shop. He prepared himself for an uncomfortable half hour.

"Right Swinton, I see you have expressed a desire to leave behind your life of crime and make a fresh start."

Piggy looked puzzled. He had expressed no such desire. He was about to correct Dillon when he realised that it would not be in his best interests.

"And, having learnt furniture repair skills during your recent spell in Brixton, you wish to continue in this, or a similar, line of business if you can."

Piggy's puzzlement turned to mild bewilderment as Dillon steered him in a direction that he had not thought of, let alone expressed a wish for.

"I think you are a most fortunate man, Swinton. Apparently there is a vacancy at Hardcastle & Strudwick which might very well suit you. A junior French polish stirrer."

Piggy was now totally bewildered. The usual probation interview process was to urge him to find an honest job, backed up with threats of further incarceration if he did not comply. Occasionally the probation officer might offer to point him at hostel accommodation or help fill in official forms, but this was quite different. But if he understood it correctly he was being told to apply for a specific job.

Generally there were numerous hurdles to fall over before he ever got close to this point in his half-hearted job searching, but today he had jumped them at a single bound and was being told exactly what he was to do. He began to suspect that the concept of free will was not going to enter into the matter.

Armed with a slip of paper giving him an interview date and time Piggy found himself on the pavement some fifteen minutes after the interview had begun. There had been no mention of further probation service interviews or a contact number in case of need for counselling. He was somewhat dazed by events. Without the ignominy of visiting the Employment Exchange, he had a job interview arranged, and a suspicion that it was a forgone conclusion.

He remembered his appointment with the lovely Tracey and headed eagerly towards *The Squinting Badger*. He arrived ten minutes before the landlord opened up for the lunchtime session and stood queuing with the die-hard alcoholics for the doors to open. As he waited he wondered why Dillon had not gone through the standard set of warnings that he knew by heart. Not to associate with known criminals, to attend all interviews promptly, to report any attempts to involve him in further crime, and not to change his address without first getting the new location approved by the probation service. He was still wondering when the landlord unlocked and the little group of misfits shambled in for another day of intoxication.

Piggy bought himself a half pint and jingled the final change remaining from his mother's handout. He sat in the same chair he had occupied the previous day, and sipped sparingly as he awaited the arrival of the woman of his dreams.

She came in ten minutes later, went straight to the bar, and bought a pint and her usual Campari and Soda. She brought the two drinks over to Piggy's table and smiled her captivatingly radiant smile as she put his glass in front of him. His fellow drinkers, all usually single-minded in their pursuit of alcoholic oblivion, and unaware of all except the liquid filled glasses in their hands, turned their heads as one to admire his companion.

"How did you get on?" she asked.

"I've got an interview for a job at Hardcastle and Strudwick. But I think you probably know that already."

She grinned. "You need to go to Peckham Library and see what you can find out about French polish. You will be interviewed for the job by a Jason Ponsonby and I'm sure you will do well. But if you are thinking of mucking up the interview, perhaps I should remind you that Brixton is not far away, and it would be easy to arrange for your return."

Piggy frowned as he remembered his transient incarceration of the previous evening. He had not reached the planning of a strategy for the interview. He was still trying to absorb all that had happened and work out why. For the first time, he also began to wonder about Tracey. She seemed to wield a lot of power if she could manipulate both the employment and probation services in this fashion.

The woman looked at him intently for a moment, and then she reached into her handbag and took out two sealed envelopes and a folded sheet of foolscap paper.

"You need to read this!" she said as she passed over the sheet of paper.

On the paper was a short neatly typed *curriculum vitae* for a Reginald Swinton. Although he recognised his mother's address and the dates when this person started various jobs as his recent court appearance dates, there was little other resemblance to his own life history. He looked up in disbelief as Tracey handed him the other two envelopes.

"These are your references from your last two employers. Ponsonby might not ask for them, but offer them anyway. Study the CV and improvise anything not covered there. You sent a copy to Hardcastles with your job application form. You will notice that your last employment was as a night watchman. That will explain your pallid complexion, but do spend as much time as possible outdoors before the interview."

Piggy did not remember sending a job application form to Hardcastles, and he was sure he would have remembered if he had. His boring daily routine in Brixton would not have made him forget such an uncharacteristic action. He felt like a pawn on a chessboard. Clearly, despite apparently being at liberty, his life was not his own to do as he pleased. He thought briefly of rejecting the path laid out for him, but the very thought brought the smell of sweat and disinfectant to his nostrils. He glanced at the envelopes. One bore the crest of a well-known City bank and the other had a neatly embossed return address of St George's Hospital. They corresponded to the last two periods of employment on the CV she had given him.

"What if they check up on the references?" he asked, hoping to explore a way out.

Tracey did not answer immediately, but sat scanning his face as if searching for signs of intelligence. Eventually she gave up, and sighed. "Then the people who wrote them will confirm that all is as written," she said wearily. "You were let go from the hospital when they switched from traditional wooden to unit-metal furniture in the wards, and the bank outsourced their security to an external firm. You were not offered a place with the external firm because you do not have a driving licence; hence your need to seek new employment."

Tracey sat back and smiled as she thought of the many favours owed her by so many senior executives, and how a word in the wrong ear could alter their personal futures in a less than fortunate way. She was not generally a vindictive person and would not dream of such malicious actions. Indeed, if either of the two named executives were called upon to perjure themselves in this enterprise, then she would bestow further favours on them beyond their reasonable expectations. She had already given the Employment Exchange manager, Robert Roberts, several evenings of delight for his part in holding back vacancy notifications from Hardcastle & Strudwick until Piggy became available.

Piggy gulped down a large draught of his drink and sat wondering why she was doing what she was. So far all he could see was that he was being forced into behaving in an upright manner. There must be more to it than she was currently prepared to say.

"You should start your new job next Monday. You will need some money to tide you over until pay-day at the end of the week."

She opened her handbag and took out two ten-pound notes, which she handed to him. Piggy could not recall ever previously holding two ten-pound notes at the same time.

"I suggest that you refrain from further visits to public houses. You may come into contact with people you would prefer not to meet, and we cannot afford for you to miss your job interview. In any case you will be too busy reading at the library and getting some sun on your face for the next few days. Spend the money wisely. You will need overalls for work, but not too new looking. I'll see you in the Indian restaurant across the road at seven o'clock on Thursday."

She got up and, as before, was gone before he could say anything. She was good at that, Piggy reflected. Her perfume lingered afterwards as he drained the remains of his drink, and he sat musing for a while before leaving for the public library.

Piggy was not an avid reader, except of the more salacious stories in *The News Of The World*, and was not looking forward to spending time learning about French polish. He had no idea why he was required to learn about the dark finish on period furniture, but suspected that failure to learn was not an option. As he walked up Peckham Hill Street he had the distinct feeling that he had little more freedom than when he was in Brixton prison. He had dreamt of being master of his own life, free to do what he wanted, when he wanted; but it was not turning out that way.

He stepped into the library, with its musty smell and hushed conversations. He had no idea how to go about finding what he wanted so he approached the beige-clad, bun-haired woman behind the counter.

"Can you tell me where I can find a book about French polish?"

"In the building trades books, the fifth section to the right. But if you ask me, you'd be better learning about something else."

Piggy stared at her. He had not expected an opinion on his choice of reading.

"I've got an interview at Hardcastle & Strudwick!" he said lamely.

"Much good it will do you!" she replied tartly. "I used to work there when the Strudwick family ran the place. I wouldn't want to be there now!"

Piggy continued to stare at her for a few moments then turned and followed her directions. He found the atmosphere in the library reminiscent of being shut up in Brixton, and wanted to get a book and leave as soon as possible. He eventually found two books, one on restoring antiques and the other on carpentry with a small section of wood finishes. He returned to the desk with them.

"Library card, please!"

"I've not got a card. Can I join now?"

"Certainly. Fill in this form and give me some identification with proof of residence."

"What proof of residence can I give?"

"Driving licence, rates bill, bank statement or any other official document with your name and address on it."

Piggy thought for a moment. His mother handled the bills and he could not drive. The only official forms he had were summons, copies of charge sheets and letters of reprimand from the probation service. He took the application form and placed the books on the desk.

"I've not got anything with me at the moment. I'll have to come back later to check them out. Can I sit and read for a bit?"

"Of course," she snapped, "that's what libraries are for."

Piggy picked up the books again and found himself an empty chair. She sounded just like the wardens at the prison. Clearly she had missed her vocation and was attempting to emulate the HMP ethos in library services.

4. Gaining Gainful Employment

The factory in Gordon Road could not have looked less factory-like if it had tried. It had started life as a row of terraced houses and had retained much of its original exterior, including more than a dozen front doors. Beside one of these doors was a small brass plate similar to that used by doctors to subtly advertise their presence. Piggy approached this and found it hid a trade counter selling their products. A counter assistant reluctantly gave him directions to the management suite.

Piggy's interview with Jason Ponsonby was a brief event. Ponsonby sat in a large office behind an impressive mahogany and brass desk. But the man himself was less than impressive. He had the look of someone who was only a short step from being committed under the Mental Health Acts. His shirt was creased, much like his brow and unlike his trousers which had lost theirs. He was unshaven, and his shoes, once expensive and highly polished, were scuffed and worn down at the heel. In fact everything about Ponsonby looked down at the heel.

"I see the Employment Exchange has recommended you to us. The manager, a Mr Roberts, sent you I understand. He spoke very highly of you. He seems to think that you would be suitable for polish manufacturing."

The name meant nothing to Piggy, but he thought it unwise to contradict Ponsonby. He was not sure what characteristics he possessed which would make him suitable for polish manufacturing.

"Yes!" he replied.

"And you have experience of both furniture repair and industrial wood finishes."

"Yes," Piggy replied again.

"Well, you can start on Monday on a week's trial. Wages are seven pounds a week, plus subsidised canteen meals. The vacancy is for a trainee junior French polish technician. Report to a Mr Derry at eight o'clock."

Piggy looked stunned. He had never been offered a job before, and took some time to realise that he was being offered one now.

"Thank you," he mumbled.

Despite the briefness of the interview, there appeared to be nothing more to be said so he reached across to shake hands with his new employer. It was a limp handshake, and Piggy was glad to leave the office for the chemically polluted air which dominated the upper floor of the factory.

Ponsonby watched Piggy as he retreated towards the stairs and smiled inwardly. Harry Derry worked in the Stores, and Piggy would find himself spending his days stacking and moving goods about. The title *trainee junior polish technician* carried a lower wage than a storeman, and Ponsonby was always on the lookout for saving a few pounds on wages. If Piggy complained, he would say it was a necessary pre-training period of familiarisation, and eventually sack him as unsatisfactory when a new gullible candidate came along. But Ponsonby wondered how long that would be. He had placed several vacancies at the Employment Exchange, and Piggy had been the only applicant from them all.

As Piggy walked down the stairs his nose was accosted by the twin delights of boiling shellac and boiled cabbage. There had been no maintenance of the ground floor linoleum, which confined the cabbage odour to the basement canteen, since the factory had passed from the Strudwick family's ownership to Hardcastle. The aroma crept through cracks to pervade all corners of the building. Piggy was not sure why he was unhappy about being offered the job, but he knew that someone, other than himself, intended to benefit from his new employment.

Piggy walked home via Rye Lane, and spent some time in the gent's outfitter's department of Jones and Higgins. buying new shirts and a pair of trousers. He had lost weight whilst in Brixton, and his current clothes hung loosely upon him.

When he arrived home his mother was cooking. She stood amazed at Piggy's news of a successful job interview. Typically the probation service would give up insisting he sought work after a dozen or so failed attempts. and his success was far above her expectations for her son. She welcomed the twin facts that he would be out for the duration of each working day, and bringing home a wage each Friday. Being out for the working day was as important as the money. The Reverend Woods visited her religiously every Monday, Wednesday and Friday afternoons, but not for theological discussion.

Her amazement turned to minor irritation when Piggy remembered to tell her that he was eating out. She expressed surprise when he added that he was meeting a woman. She looked him carefully up and down, searching for any slight hint of irony in his voice and demeanour. Piggy's face was deadly serious and he had a slightly stunned expression, as if he did not quite believe what he had just heard himself say. Mrs Swinton was still unsure of the truth of Piggy's announcements when he went off to change. His return in a flowery new shirt and flared trousers went some way to convince her. The hint of Brut, despite him not having recently shaved, finally convinced her that perhaps he was telling the truth.

Piggy was looking forward to meeting Tracey in the restaurant. His life's experience of dining out to date had been solitary ones in greasy spoon cafés and the pie stall on Blackheath. When Piggy arrived at *The Star of the East* he found Tracey waiting, together with John Dillon. What small hope he had that Tracey may have a personal interest in him quickly dissolved as Dillon beckoned to him to sit beside him in the little alcove. Either Tracey or Dillon had already ordered for all three and Piggy found himself eating a very hot curry whilst listening to Dillon.

"So Ponsonby hired you!"

"Yes!"

"And you start on Monday?"

"Yes!"

"Well, do your job for the moment, but build up a plan of what departments are where, and spend some time making friends in the canteen. Keep your ears open for the name Sir Arthur Brain. We'll pick you up from work on Friday week and see what progress you have made."

After this brief exchange the three ate in silence for a while, until Tracey spoke.

"Whatever you do, never speak of either John or me to anyone at the factory. As far as they are concerned, the Employment Exchange sent you. Who did Ponsonby say you are to be working with?"

"I think it was Mr Derry!" said Piggy with his mouth full of naan.

Tracey frowned. She took a brown folder from the seat of the fourth chair in the alcove and leafed through the loose sheets of foolscap that it contained. Eventually she paused at one and turned to Dillon.

"That's the stores!"

Dillon arched his eyebrows.

"Perhaps he's changed departments."

"I doubt it. He's sixty if he's a day, and been a warehouseman all his life."

"Perhaps he's simply an initial contact point."

Dillon looked at Piggy.

"It's important that you find out exactly where all the various clerical departments are. They used to be on the first floor when the factory produced polish and sausages, but that could have changed."

Piggy nodded his acknowledgement of this instruction and helped himself to more rice. Tracey and Dillon appeared to have finished eating.

"How much have you got left from that twenty pounds I gave you?"

The question caught Piggy unawares. Given time to think he would have said most was spent, and hope for a repeat of her generosity. But needing a quick answer he replied truthfully.

"About twelve pounds."

"Good, take your time finishing and you can pay for this. Don't be tempted by the house wine - it's lethal. John and I have things to do."

So saying she got up and, together with Dillon, walked out. A thickset Indian waiter in white cotton gloves carefully positioned himself between Piggy and the door, in case Piggy had any ideas about following them without paying.

Until this point in his life, most of Piggy's thought processes had been focused on who had something worth stealing, and how he could relieve them of ownership. Now, sitting in a restaurant, with a few pounds in his pocket and a job to start on the following Monday, he began to allow his mind to broaden its view. He wondered if this was a new approach to criminal reform. An approach that aimed to fill his mind so full of other thoughts that there was no room left for larceny. Although his mind mulled over this novel idea, his left hand clung to old habits. It unconsciously slid a teaspoon towards the edge of the table and was about to slip it into his pocket when he became aware of the waiter watching him. He smiled at the man and clumsily used the spoon to add some chutney on top of his rice.

After paying the bill, Piggy still had slightly less than seven pounds. He stood outside the restaurant and wondered how to complete his day. The cinema across the road looked inviting, but he never liked going on his own so he turned and headed for home. Walking along he was totally immersed in thought. There was something in that factory that Tracey and Dillon wanted, and it was becoming clear to him that he was going to be the one on the inside. In Piggy's mind there was only one possibility; a wages snatch!

The prospect of being involved in such an enterprise cheered Piggy up. This was the big time, and he was about to embark on a much grander scale of crime than in the past. To be part of a sophisticated gang, planning and executing such a job would set him up and re-establish his tarnished reputation among South London's criminal fraternity. He was still excited by the prospect when he arrived at his mother's flat. He opened the door and went straight for the fridge in the kitchen, where he had previously spotted a six pack of beer.

As Piggy opened the kitchen door he beheld his mother and the Reverend Woods energetically engaged in congress. He slammed the door shut, turned and left the flat, his mind reeling at a sight that no child should ever have to witness. An hour later found him sitting traumatised in Peckham Rye Park, smoking a Woodbine. Piggy was halfway through the packet of ten before he remembered that he did not smoke. He had no recollection of where the cigarettes had come from, but there was broken glass on the pavement up the road from a cigarette machine outside the newsagent's shop.

It was a warm evening and there were a number of passers-by, mostly couples in search of a vacant secluded bench, but also others using the park as a shortcut home from their various evening activities.

"I hope the other night didn't give you ideas, Swinton!"

Piggy looked up into the torchlight as he recognised the voice of PC Walker.

"I'm not doing anything wrong, Mr Walker. I needed some air."

"Well, mind you behave yourself. I see DC Holmes had a word with you as well."

"Honest Mr Walker, I'm going straight. I've even got a job. Start Monday."

PC Walker looked at him incredulously. His past experience of Piggy never included any reference to gainful employment.

"Where?"

"Hardcastles. I'm going to learn a trade. They make French polish."

The mention of Hardcastle got Walker's full attention. He had previous knowledge of the place when the Strudwick family owned it, and occasionally had dinner with the then general foreman and his fiancée. His impression was that under the control of Hardcastle's nephew the place had regressed into a late Victorian work ethic with tyrannical management. He wondered how long Piggy, with his lack of work experience, would last there.

"I'll be keeping an eye on you. But good luck with the job."

PC Walker turned and was about to move away when he had an afterthought.

"Who's your Probation Officer?"

"Mr Dillon."

Walker smiled. John Dillon had been a good section sergeant, with a perfect work record. There was that odd incident when he headed up a raid on a place over a bookshop near the Town Hall. Real odd that was. All sorts of allegations were made afterwards, but Dillon, only eighteen months away from retirement, suddenly got promoted to Station Sergeant with a corresponding boost to his pension, and a cushy job running divisional training to see out his time. Dillon had just one bee in his bonnet, about that mass poisoning at Goose Green some years ago.

Walker gave Piggy a further stern warning to keep his nose clean and continued on his beat. On his own again, Piggy reached for the packet of cigarettes, but decided to leave them in his pocket. In some strange way he had enjoyed his conversation with PC Walker. It was a case of any attention being better than no attention, and Piggy had felt extremely lonely after he had rushed from his mother's flat that evening. Piggy was a placid person and never caused his arresting officers any trouble, but despite the circumstances, he had fond memories of his contacts with the men in blue. He probably had more lengthy conversations with them than anyone else, and Peckham Police Station prisoner breakfasts were better cooked than his mother's.

Piggy got up and headed back towards the flat. He hoped that his mother had completed her evening's entertainment. It was now nearly three hours since he had left them to their table top activity.

Piggy crept into the flat and silently made for his bedroom. He was about to shut himself into his little sanctuary when his mother's voice called him from the lounge.

"Reg! We need to talk."

Piggy meekly turned and entered the room. His mother was in a red dressing gown and pink fluffy mules.

"Since your father left home I've been so lonely, what with you being away so much."

He nodded, but he remembered that she had been comforted in that loneliness by at least a dozen male friends, and if his memory served him correctly then his father left after arriving home from work to an almost identical scene to that which he had witnessed earlier that evening.

"I've had a chat with Augie and we will try to confine his pastoral visits to weekday afternoons. I was not expecting him tonight, but he was in the block and popped in for a cup of tea. We thought you would be out all evening with your lady friend."

Piggy smiled at the thought of Tracey as his lady friend. It was obvious to him that that was definitely not on the agenda.

"I'm tired Mum, I'm going to bed."

5. Piggy the Wage Slave

On Saturday Piggy got up late. He had awoken early but decided that he would stay in bed until he felt he wanted to get up. It was a luxury he had been denied for the past few months and with the prospect of work on Monday would be denied him during the next week. When he eventually rose he found his mother was out and the kitchen table was clear, so he raided the fridge for something to eat.

He ended up with cheese on toast and a mug of tea. He had nothing planned for the day, and was watching children's television when his mother returned with two bags of shopping. It suddenly occurred to him that since she had been home all week, he did not know how his mother supported herself.

"What happened to your job at the bus garage?"

"I left it. We had a disagreement about working conditions."

Employed as a canteen assistant, Mrs Swinton had worked shifts, but her very active social life resulted in her being late for early shift once too often. Since then she had found work as a dispatcher in a mini-cab office, working long Saturday and Sunday late shifts plus the occasional mid-week. She barely managed to get by on the pay. But it was a struggle.

As soon as she had packed away her shopping she announced that she was off to work.

Piggy spent the day lounging about the flat and retired for the night after the nine o'clock television news. On the Sunday he got up early and caught a bus to Greenwich. He wandered the tourist sites and found a little tearoom in Blackheath for a modest meal at lunchtime. After lunch he sat on the grass of Blackheath Common apparently watching kites flying, but really keeping an eye on cars parking, in case a driver forgot to lock one. But he sat without opportunity until the sun lost its power, when he reluctantly rose and made his way home. Despite his fruitless afternoon he felt refreshed and ready for the week ahead.

* * *

On Monday morning Piggy presented himself at the factory at eight o'clock sharp. He had his overalls in a carrier bag, but wondered if he should have put them on before coming to work. After asking several people where he could find Mr Derry he was eventually directed to a ground floor room with rows of metal shelf units stacked with cardboard boxes. He sat in the room and waited until Harry Derry arrived for work at his usual time of eight-thirty. It struck Piggy that none of the people he spoke to were particularly welcoming. He hoped his new boss might be more amiable.

Harry Derry looked Piggy up and down. He had worked the stores on his own for the past five months and welcomed any help that was offered, but Piggy looked rather puny compared with his previous assistant.

"What have you got in the bag?"

"My overalls. Where can I change?"

"Overalls? We don't get dirty down here. A bit dusty occasionally but no need for overalls."

"Oh. I thought making French polish would involve mixing chemicals."

"Making? Nah, we just store it and monitor stock levels."

"But Mr Ponsonby said the job was for a trainee junior polish technician!"

Harry Derry smiled. "Perhaps you are with me temporary, like. Until you find your way around. Put your bag down over there and I'll give you the tour. Then we can get on with some work."

Harry walked Piggy round the warren of converted parlours and kitchens that collectively made up the storeroom. and then back to where he had left his bag. A large ginger cat had pulled his overalls out of the bag to make a nest on the floor, and was fast asleep on them. Harry set Piggy to packing bottles of polish into cartons. An hour later, his arms were aching, having put in more honest labour that day that the previous whole year. Harry noticed his flagging energies and eventually moved him to pasting labels on cartons.

Lunchtime in the factory canteen was a most mixed experience for Piggy. The menu and standard of cooking made him yearn wistfully for the mess hall at HMP Brixton. But the company was, in part, a great improvement. There were a number of women there, some of whom were well worth admiring. In addition he was free to choose which, and as many, items to put on his plate as he desired. On that Monday those around him could have been forgiven for thinking his stomach had earned him his nickname, had he chosen to divulge it.

In the afternoon Harry took Piggy up to the polish production rooms and introduced him to the production foremen. Piggy had never been interested in football, or any other sport. He was not conversant with the badges of affiliation that covered the walls, and were worn by many of the workers, in most of the various rooms. He did, however, recognise the Millwall colours in one room, having been caught in New Cross Road once after a Saturday home match. He had sheltered in a grocer's shop with the shutters drawn as the hordes shambled past looking for rival fans and open public houses. He had left the shop half an hour later, having been sold half a pound of ham carved from the bone and a slab of Genoa cake that the artful shop manager had been plugging all day to rid himself of excess stock approaching its sell-by date.

Harry showed Piggy the dumb waiter that they used to move the finished goods down to stores. Working on his own, it was a slow process for Harry. He had to load the little box, send it down and then walk all the way down to unload. However, with Piggy upstairs sending batches down and Harry downstairs unloading to a set of trolleys they made quick work of clearing this morning's production.

When Piggy eventually came back downstairs, Harry got him to push the final trolley load to the stores. Then, looking at his watch, Harry gave a grunt of approval.

"Time for a mug of tea, lad. Come on!"

Piggy followed Harry towards the canteen. He had only been there once but could have found it on his own by following the strengthening smell of cabbage. Harry generously let Piggy pay for the teas and led him to a table. There were about a dozen other workers sitting in small groups at the motley set of tables that made up the eatery.

"How long have you worked here, Mr Derry?"

"About forty years, on and off. But call me Harry."

"Yes, Harry!" replied Piggy, wondering if he should reveal his own nickname. He thought better of it, and decided that in his new working life he should be called Reg.

"They don't look very happy, some of them, Harry!" observed Piggy.

"We had a change of management last year. The Strudwicks used to look after us, but this new lot must think they are back in the dark ages. I've only got a year to go for retirement so I'm not too worried, but some of the poor sods are stuck with it."

"Why did the Strudwicks leave?"

Harry chuckled. "The old man fell off his perch, or rather fell off his secretary, and cracked his head on the floor. He's still unconscious in some posh hospice, and the family brought in a new man to run things. He made a real mess of it and eventually the managers separated the two halves of the company and sold this part to Hardcastle."

"What happened to the man they brought in?"

"Don't know. I know he got his marching orders though. My previous assistant had the job of seeing him off the premises. Sir Arthur Brain he was called. Half a brain more like."

Piggy became more attentive, but he had exhausted Harry's knowledge on the subject. He sat and reflected on life, while he drained his mug of the oily grey fluid. A grumbling noise started in his stomach.

"Where's the nearest lavy?"

Harry grinned and pointed to the far end of the canteen. Piggy rose and made a dash in the direction indicated. Harry continued to grin as he remembered that it took most people weeks to get acclimatised to Edith's evil brew. Some never did! He had heard of one enterprising polish stirrer who once poured two cups full into a flask to take home for a less than regular relative.

It was almost half an hour before Piggy rejoined Harry in the stores.

"Sit there for a bit and label them bottles!" said Harry kindly.

When the factory hooter signalled the close of the working day Piggy was more than ready to go home. His arms ached, his legs ached and his innards still felt knotted and strained. He walked home and slumped in front of the television. His mother served him spam fritters and chips, cooked in beef dripping, on a tray. Soon the top up of grease in his stomach reactivated the purgative effect of his canteen fare. Piggy had planned to go out that evening, but wisely decided to stay home instead.

By Friday Piggy had grown accustomed to the daily routine, if not the canteen tea, but parts of his body ached and yearned for a day off. He had made little progress in learning about Sir Arthur Brain, but had recorded a number of mental notes on the layout of the building. Harry Derry mistook his interest in where different offices were for keenness to do his job well, and was pleased with his new assistant.

When Piggy left the factory on Friday afternoon he turned toward Rye Lane instead of home. He had his first week's wages in his pocket and he planned to treat himself. He had no idea what form that treat would take, and hoped to browse the shop windows for inspiration.

As he walked purposefully towards Jones & Higgins, a Morris Oxford stopped alongside him. Tracey opened the front nearside door in his path and motioned for him to get in the back.

"Well, you've lasted the week! John here was not sure you would."

Piggy grunted a reply. Sitting in the back seat of the car was the most comfortable he had been all day.

"What have you found out?" asked Dillon without turning round.

"Sir Arthur Brain was escorted from the building when the Strudwicks decided to sell the factory."

Piggy was pleased with his progress.

"And?" prompted Dillon.

"And what?" asked Piggy.

"And where is he now?"

"Don't know. I don't think anybody does. One of the polish stirrers says he thinks he is still employed by Hardcastle. But he's nothing to do with the factory anymore."

In the rear-view mirror Piggy could see Dillon frown. Clearly he expected more about Sir Arthur than he had found.

"We need an organisational chart for Hardcastles, and a list of their other factories." Tracey spoke slowly and deliberately as she thought through how to get more information. "You'll have to get that from the personnel department."

"What personnel department? There's nothing called that in the building."

"Who did you give your National Insurance card to?"

"Ponsonby's secretary took it. She said it had to go to head office."

"Then you'll have to get the information from Ponsonby's office."

"That might be a problem. There's always someone there and there's rumours that Ponsonby is living in the factory."

Tracey grimaced. Getting Sir Arthur's current address had eluded her for four months. He had visited her last Christmas Eve and said that he had an opportunity to buy the factory, but it needed to be a cash deal and he was ten thousand pounds short. It looked like a good investment, though, and as joint owner she could look forward to an income of about two thousand a year, more if she took an active part in management, and she was sure that the bumbling Sir Arthur would be happy to take a back seat and let her shape the company's future. It was a golden opportunity for Tracey. She had tried working in large corporations, and had been passed over time and again in preference for inferior brains simply because no executive would believe that a body that beautiful could contain a sharp business mind. Her present main 'business' was highly profitable, but risky with a very early retirement age - those who lived to retire.

Given the nature of her main occupation, she dealt in cash and stored it safely out of the prying eyes of taxmen and banks. On Christmas Day Sir Arthur had come back and she had handed over a carrier bag of banknotes. That was the last she had seen of him. He had phoned a week later to say the deal was going ahead, but was delayed by lawyers not working over the holiday period. It was late January before she realised she had been conned. She had known Sir Arthur for six years, one of her most regular customers, and she had grown to trust him, even if she was aware of his mental limitations.

Tracey thought long and hard. Then she lifted her head and looked at Dillon.

"We need a diversion while Piggy searches the offices."

Dillon nodded before replying. "There was an incident last year when they found stock was being pilfered. Young Holmes was the arresting officer. They called out the management in the middle of the night to sign the charge sheets."

Dillon still regularly met up with serving police officers to compare notes on villains and mull over old times. He kept himself well informed, especially when he heard that Strudwicks had employed Sir Arthur Brain. He held him directly responsible for his cousin's death in the Goose Green Poisoning Mystery.

It was pure chance that Tracey had sought out Dillon. Unable to report the loss of her money officially without facing tax evasion charges and other issues, she had approached the officer who had overseen the raid on her establishment, and who had dealt with the matter so sympathetically. Knowing he was retired, she hoped to employ him to find Sir Arthur, and was delighted to find he had his own personal vendetta against the man. So far, though, all attempts to find him had come to nothing.

Piggy sat quietly while Tracey and Dillon mused on. He could have gone to sleep were it not for the fact that he knew that they were hatching plans that would involve him in extra-curricular activity at the factory.

"If another person was found flogging stuff in a pub, and the police had good reason to think it was Hardcastle stock, then they would call Ponsonby out long enough for Piggy to search the offices," conjectured Dillon.

"And that would put me right back in prison," bleated Piggy. "Who else are they going to blame?"

"And I've got an uncle who could supply a bottle of French polish with a suitable batch code," added Tracey, ignoring him totally.

Dillon looked at Tracey: his professional 'you'd better get it off your chest and tell me all' look.

"It's a long story!" She giggled as she spoke, then added softly, "there was a gang stealing from them and flogging the stuff in the local pubs."

"But there's other people about. He has three clerical staff working next door to where they think he kips down."

Piggy hoped that this obstacle would squash the plan. He wanted to at least spend the summer in freedom and without injury, and he was becoming mindful of the usual consequences of his criminal activity.

"At two o'clock Sunday morning?"

Piggy was beginning to get the full picture. He squirmed as his seat suddenly became less comfortable.

Tracey and Dillon went over a list of possible documents that Piggy could look for in the offices. Piggy thought of protesting, but knew that it would be useless to do so, perhaps even hazardous to his future freedom.

Eventually he agreed to meet Dillon at midnight on Saturday outside the Town Hall.

6. Piggy Swinton, Cat burglar

It was a warm night, but raining, as Piggy stood in the doorway of the bookshop a few doors up the road from Peckham Town Hall. The Morris Oxford stopped beside him and he got in the empty front passenger seat. Imagine his surprise when he found it was driven by Tracey, and not John Dillon. She was dressed in casual attire, which for her meant a boob tube, hot-pants and flip-flops. They drove off and Piggy's breath came in hot pants as he watched the tube flip flop over the bumps in the poorly maintained road.

They drove to Gordon Road and parked by a telephone box in a position where they would see Ponsonby's Ford Granada come away from the loading bay and down the service road behind the factory. Tracey asked Piggy to wind down his window. Getting rather hot under the collar he was happy to oblige. She turned and stretched between the two seats to reach for a small holdall in the back, her bare arm brushing against him as she did so. Piggy suppressed a squeal of delight as her soft flesh momentarily pressed against him, but only with extreme difficulty.

In the holdall were two flasks and several greaseproof paper bags of sandwiches. She reached in and picked a bag which she dumped on his lap.

"Corned beef and pickle. Mind the pickle, you don't want to leave sticky fingerprints anywhere."

She smiled. Her words and attire had caused Piggy's mind to wander off into the realms of fantasy, and it took him a while to realise that she meant in the factory.

They sat in silence for half an hour before Piggy heard the telephone box ring. Tracey passed him her lipstick stained cup to hold and got out to answer the phone.

"Ponsonby should be coming out soon. Wear these and make it look like a regular burglary once you find what we need."

Tracey handed Piggy a pair of bright yellow Marigold gloves and they both ducked down as they saw headlights shining out of the service road. Ponsonby was on his way.

Piggy slipped out of the car and headed for the service road. During the day he had thought hard about how he was to accomplish his task, and remembered that Harry Derry always left a small high window open for the cat to come and go. There were several wooden pallets on the loading dock and one would be ideal as a short ladder to reach the window. It was a matter of moments before Piggy stood at the window and reached through to open the larger pane below it.

As he slipped to the floor he realised that he still gripped the gloves in one hand. He paused to put them on and then raced through the empty building to the upper floor and the management suite.

Piggy quickly found Ponsonby's address book, and a folder of internal correspondence with various company addresses in it. He continued to search the offices but found nothing with any mention of Sir Arthur. Then he had an idea. He raced along to Henry Fothergill's office and rummaged through the papers there. Yes, a copy of the purchase agreement for the factory, with a role for Sir Arthur in Shropshire. In the drawer with the document was a company cheque book. Mindful of his instructions to make it look like a common burglary he grabbed the chequebook and slipped it into his jacket pocket. Then he rummaged round until he found the petty cash box. With arms full of papers and the box he stepped back and bumped into a set of tall open filing shelves that divided Fothergill's work area from the rest of the room. The shelves wobbled and then fell over with a mighty crash. Piggy stood frozen for a moment, listening for any signs of movement in the building, but heard nothing.

Armed with his loot Piggy made his way back out the way he had entered. After putting the pallet back where he found it he slipped along the service road and across to the car.

Piggy was breathing heavily as he closed the car door and slumped down in his seat. Tracey started the engine and was away before he had enough breath to speak.

"Shropshire!" he gasped as he struggled to pull the Marigolds from his sweaty hands.

"Good boy!" said Tracey as she leaned across and gave him a peck on the cheek. Piggy went bright pink as he realised what she had done. No woman had ever been that spontaneous with him before, especially one who would not look out of place on the cover of *Vogue* magazine, or the centrefold of *Penthouse*.

All too soon Tracey stopped the car a short walk from his home. Piggy hesitated before getting out, but she motioned for him to leave and then sat with the engine running.

"Be in *The Squinting Badger* at seven o'clock on Wednesday evening," she said as he opened the door.

7. Deja Vu for Jason Ponsonby

Jason Ponsonby had not been pleased when he was awoken by a phone call from the police at Tower Bridge police station. But he had brightened up when the night duty CID officer, DC Holmes, explained that they had found a man in possession of a can of French Polish which they believed to be stolen. Ponsonby had heard of the thefts that had happened the previous year and was always pleased to be the instrument by which the lower classes were disciplined to keep them in their place. He agreed to attend and sign the charge sheet, and was further encouraged by Holmes as he explained that he might be able to identify the seller as the man had given him a good description.

Sitting, or rather slumped, in the cells was one Wilfred Makepeace. Wilf was an itinerant who made a meagre living from begging and occasional odd jobs in East Lane market, for which he was usually paid in overripe fruit or other short life foods. Any hard currency which came Wilf's way was usually rapidly converted into hard drink. On wet nights it was Wilf's custom to find a policeman on beat duty near a shop and then to noisily attempt to break a window. His inevitable arrest would lead to a visit to the Magistrate's Court and, in the absence of any monies to pay a fine, seven days in a jail of His Worship's choice. Seven days of warm dry beds, newish clean clothes and three hot meals a day.

But tonight Dillon had found Wilf before he had time to seek his traditional shelter from inclement weather. He had put a proposition to Wilf which he assured him would get him two weeks' respite instead of his usual one. Wilf was to be found in possession of stolen French Polish, and in addition was to be able to describe the man from whom he purchased the article, knowing it to be stolen.

At first Wilf was reluctant to go along with Dillon. He was a man of principle, and larceny was an entirely different matter to simple malicious damage. But Holmes was quick to point out to Wilf the advantages of the scheme. He could claim that the drink had caused him to extend his repertoire, and henceforth he would be suspected of a wider range of crimes. He would be liable to being hauled into the station more frequently, with a dry cell and prisoner's meals as appropriate. Also, Dillon would see him right with a couple of pounds when he came out.

This appeal to Wilf's self-interest made sense to the man. Dillon then went on to give him a detailed description of the man from whom he had purchased the polish. This description was a remarkable likeness of Sir Arthur Brain. Once he was satisfied that Wilf could repeat the description, he handed over the bottle of polish and a can of Tenants, and retired to a distance to observe. As a young PC approached Wilf's chosen doorway, Wilf tossed the now empty can out on to the pavement and turned to carry out his traditional hammering on the glass door.

As soon as Dillon was sure that the PC was going to take him in, he slipped away to find a working phone box.

Unfortunately the duty gaoler at Tower Bridge police station, recognised Wilf as a regular customer of equally regular habits. He failed to initially relieve him of his illicit goods, and by the time he took it from him the can was half empty, with Wilf having consumed the alcohol equivalent of almost a pint of scotch. When Ponsonby arrived at the station, Wilf was too drunk to stand or be charged. Making the best of a bad job, Ponsonby was requested to identify the property and wait until Wilf sobered up sufficiently to be formally charged. Ponsonby reluctantly agreed and waited while a good-natured desk sergeant organised a mug of tea for him.

The whole sorry saga took until four o'clock Sunday morning, by which time Ponsonby was eager to go home to his makeshift pied-à-terre in Gordon Road. As he walked down the steps of the police station he saw his car sitting drunkenly by the kerb. He recognised the effect from a previous such condition in Purley before Christmas. Both nearside tyres has been let down by John Dillon to ensure Piggy had sufficient time for a thorough search.

As he turned and plodded wearily back up the steps of the police station, Ponsonby decided that the world did not like Ford Granadas and vowed to change it for something more sociably acceptable.

When Ponsonby finally arrived back at the factory he found the chaos that Piggy had staged to cover the real purpose of his search. Wearily he dialled 999 and reported the break in.

Given the complexity of the building, and the possibility that the miscreants might still be somewhere on the premises, several police vehicles attended, including a dog handler. An extensive search finally confirmed the building was empty and Ponsonby crawled into his bed a little before ten o'clock on Sunday morning.

At about the same time, Piggy was getting up to face his mother who immediately spotted traces of lipstick on his right cheek. Piggy smiled as she teased him about what he had been up to the previous evening. It was better that she imagined what she wanted to, rather than know the truth.

Also at that time Wilfred Makepeace was woken with the first of a series of prisoner's meals that would sustain him until his court appearance on the Monday. He relished the sausage, beans and fried bread and left the mug of tea until last. As an experienced drinker of methylated spirit based concoctions he knew that when the hot tea hit the residue in his stomach it would again release alcohol into his bloodstream. He was singing drunk by eleven o'clock.

Piggy spent Sunday on his own in the flat. His mother went out for a morning service by the Reverend Woods, and then on to do her shift at the mini-cab office. Piggy knew that her apparent religious conversion had more to do with the deliverer of the sermon than any theological beliefs. He remembered when she took up with an Indian bus driver and developed a passion for curry at every meal. He shuddered at the thought of those curried sardines on toast for breakfast. At least her current interest should not affect her culinary offerings.

As Piggy tidied up and made ready for his second week of honest toil he found the company cheque book in his jacket pocket. He was wondering what to do with it when there was a knock on the door. Thinking it was one of his mother's friends he went to answer, only to be immediately pushed back against the wall by the large hand of John Dillon.

"You've been a naughty boy, Piggy."

"I did what you asked, Mr Dillon," whined Piggy.

"Yes, but you've been holding back on us, have you? You forgot to give us something."

Piggy realised that Dillon knew about the company cheque book.

"Honest, Mr Dillon. I put it in my pocket when I was in there and forgot it until just now. I was going to give it to you. Honest!"

Dillon released the pressure on Piggy's chest and grabbed him by the shirt collar. Then he dragged him into the lounge and pushed him at the settee. Piggy slumped down with a forlorn look on his face.

"You're an idiot Piggy. If the local police were to find it on you then you would be back in Brixton before you could blink, or perhaps The Scrubs if you got the wrong magistrate."

Piggy whimpered. "I never meant to keep it. I just forgot."

Dillon sat down in an armchair opposite him.

"Why should I believe you?"

Piggy started to sob. He knew that Dillon could whisper in the right ear and he would be banged up again in double quick time.

"Honest Mr Dillon. It was a mistake. I just forgot."

"All right Piggy. Calm down and put the kettle on." He held out his hand for the cheque book.

Piggy fished in his inside jacket pocket and handed it over. Then he went out to the kitchen to boil the kettle.

"Well Piggy. Now we understand each other I've some good news for you. Here's the money from the petty cash. Once we take out the twenty quid that Tracey loaned you there is twelve quid for you. Don't spend it all in one go. Hardcastle is known not to pay any more than he can get away with, and flashing money around will draw attention to yourself."

Piggy looked up in surprise. A minute ago he thought he was in trouble, but now Dillon was sharing out the spoils. He heard the kettle click as it came to the boil and went back to make two mugs of tea.

Dillon studied his mug warily and placed it on a little table beside his chair. He looked around the room with a critical eye.

"Looks like your mother has been having a thin time of it. You'd better keep your nose clean and take good care of her for a bit. Make sure you act normally at work tomorrow and keep out of the way of any officers who come to the factory."

Dillon got up and left. Piggy sat drinking his tea, trying to work out how he felt. He wondered why Dillon and Tracey were so keen to find Sir Arthur Brain.

Piggy was in bed long before his mother came home from work, but not asleep. There was too much going on in his mind to permit slumber. Eventually he drifted off, only to be woken by a nightmare where he was back in Brixton sharing a cell with a violent lifer.

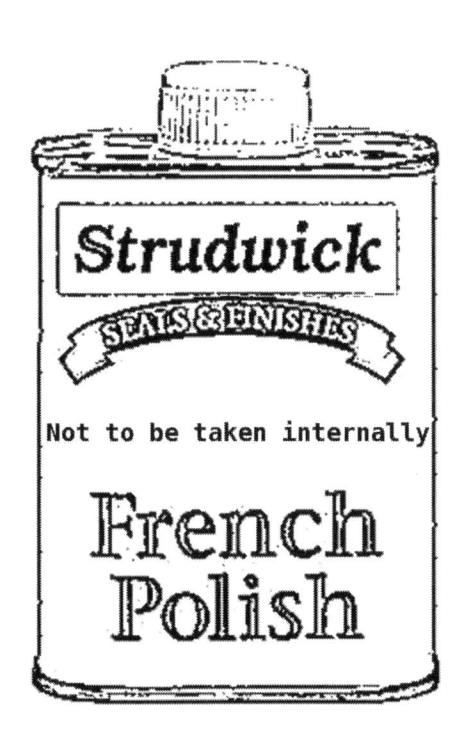

8. Streatham, the Sunshine Suburb

On Monday morning, Piggy stopped off at the newsagents around the corner from the factory and bought himself a Mars bar and *The Daily Sketch*. As a right wing newspaper, it was not the most obvious choice for Piggy, but he felt it would lend him an air of respectability.

Over a mid-morning tea break in the canteen, Harry Derry, in common with many others, wondered who had broken into the factory. Detailed descriptions of the mess in Fothergill's office circulated widely.

"Kids, I expect," said Piggy. "Parents seem to have no control at all these days."

Harry murmured his agreement. He was pleased with his new assistant, although he wondered how long he would stay, on the wages Hardcastle paid him.

Apart from a scenes-of-crime officer wandering around looking for fingerprints there were now no other police in the factory. With no evidence of a point of entry there was speculation as to how they got in. The general consensus was that someone had walked in during the day and hidden in one of the empty rooms that were used for processing and storing German sausage when the Strudwicks owned the place. This shifted the focus of the enquiry towards persons who might bear a grudge against Hardcastle or Ponsonby. The admin staff busied themselves compiling a list of sacked ex-employees and others who bore malice. By lunchtime the list ran to three sides of foolscap.

Up in his office Ponsonby was equally perplexed. He was not convinced of the accepted theory on the shop floor. Why would someone take business papers or his address book? He wondered if the business papers were a smokescreen to cover taking the address book. He became fairly sure that his wife had employed someone to get evidence for a divorce.

On Wednesday evening, Piggy attended *The Squinting Badger*, bought a drink and sat down to wait for Tracey to arrive. At five past seven the barman called out to the room in general. "Is there a Mr Swinton here?"

Piggy walked to the bar and was directed to a telephone on the wall.

"Hello!"

"Piggy. Walk over to the Town Hall. We will meet you there." It was John Dillon's voice that he heard.

Piggy went back to his table, gulped down the rest of his drink and headed out into the warm late spring evening. As he approached the Town Hall he spotted the Morris Oxford and heard its engine start. Soon he was sitting in the comfortable back seat as Dillon drove along Camberwell New Road.

Tracey turned to face him from the front passenger seat.

"We need some more information from Hardcastle. From what you found, he has a little office attached to his home. We need to find Sir Arthur Brain's personnel file, but this time we need to do it without anyone knowing we have been there."

Piggy was aware that her use of the word 'we' did not mean that all three of them were about to break in.

Some while later Dillon stopped the car in a leafy road off Streatham Common.

"There's Hardcastle's house. The office is that extension on the left." Dillon indicated an incongruous flat roofed structure, somewhat bigger than a garage, built onto the side of the grand Victorian four storey house. There were lights on in several windows, but not in the extension.

"Perhaps we should wait a while," said Tracey, "there's a nice fish shop down on Brighton Road."

Dillon gently put the car in motion and they drove for a few minutes before pulling up outside a brightly lit chippy. Its fascia board displayed a smiling top-hatted fish entertaining an audience of crabs. Tracey got out and joined the small queue at the counter.

Piggy enjoyed his unexpected supper. It did much to calm his nerves as he realised that he was about to break in to another building. He was not sure how they were to do it without alerting anyone, but suspected that his controllers had a plan. An hour later they were again parked across the road from Hardcastle's home.

"Here's a notebook and a pencil. All we need is the address where Sir Arthur either works or lives. If you cannot find that then see if you can find his national insurance number."

Tracey handed Piggy the stationery and a torch as she spoke.

"But how can I get in?" asked Piggy, hoping to put an obstacle in the way of this further crime.

In reply John Dillon passed him a bunch of Yale keys.

"One of these should do it."

Piggy saw that he had little choice. He slipped out of the car and across the road. To his surprise the fourth key he tried opened the office door. Once inside he closed the door quietly and began his search for personnel records. A tall grey filing cabinet held them and Piggy soon found Sir Arthur. He laid the file on a desk and, with his back to the door, started to hunt for the information required. He found both a home address and the address of a farm in Shropshire where he appeared to work, or rather had worked for the month of January. In February he seemed to have parted company with Hardcastle.

Piggy was putting the file back in the cabinet when he heard scratching noises at the front door. Then there was a thump and a dull thud as something heavy hit against the door. For a moment Piggy's heart stopped as he stood trapped, not knowing what was going on outside.

"Come on Piggy, time we were going."

Piggy was only too happy to oblige and opened the door to find a man slumped against the wall beside it. Dillon was standing beside the man, and motioned to Piggy to hurry. Piggy recognised the unconscious figure.

"Fingers Fisher!" he said in mock surprise.

Dillon lifted the man and dumped him inside the office then pulled the door shut. They walked quickly back to the car and saw that Tracey was now driving. She started the engine as they approached.

Whilst speeding away Dillon relayed what had happened. Soon after Piggy had gone inside the second man walked up to the house and started to try to open the door. He did not use keys, but a set of pick-locks that Dillon now held in his right hand. Dillon had crept up behind him and laid him out.

"So you know this Fingers Fisher bloke?"

"Yes, I shared a wing with him in Wandsworth once. He works for Big Ernie Ernshaw. But I thought he had another month inside yet."

Dillon frowned. He knew of Ernshaw, but house breaking was not his usual game. Stolen Cortinas cut in two and joined together with bits from legitimate wrecks were his speciality. Fisher was either freelancing or else there was something strange going on.

Given the ad hoc activity of the evening it was some time before Tracey asked about their original purpose.

"Not too good I'm afraid. I've got an address for Sir Arthur, and where he worked but he left in February. Bit of a mystery. He was not sacked and no letter of resignation. He simply disappeared. There was even a note that they reported him missing."

This was not what Tracey wanted to hear, but it made sense. When Sir Arthur had found out the exact role for him in Shropshire he probably would not stay, especially with Tracey's money to play with.

They drove on in silence for some time.

"I wonder why Fingers was there," said Piggy, more to himself than anyone else. "It's not as if the office would have much of value in it. Not compared to all those big houses round about."

"How well do you know him?" asked Tracey.

"Not that well. He lives somewhere in Rotherhithe. Mostly he nicks cars for Big Ernie and occasionally drives getaways. We were on the same landing for a while but Ernshaw got him moved in with a trustee."

Piggy did not elaborate on how a criminal managed to organise the accommodation of his gang whilst they were inside, but he had heard that prison governors always got a new car every time one of Ernshaw's gang got sentenced.

"I think you should go and meet him accidentally Piggy!" said Dillon. "How about next Saturday evening. I believe there is a boxing match arranged at the *Thomas A'Becket*. Ernshaw is partial to a bit of organised brutality."

Piggy shuddered. Mabel's cousin, Keith Longman also frequented the gym at that particular pub in the Old Kent Road. They dropped Piggy off a short distance from his home and he walked through the estate slowly, saving his energy for the five flights of stairs. As he walked past one of the other blocks, he saw the Reverend Woods come out of the lobby looking furtively about as he emerged. Piggy stepped back behind an abandoned van to watch the man. He expected him to head for his block and 'drop in for a cup of tea', but he turned in the opposite direction and walked off. Piggy breathed a sigh of relief and continued homewards.

As Piggy climbed the stairs to the flat a strange thought struck him. He had done two jobs in a week, and not been injured. It almost felt wrong somehow.

* * *

On Saturday night Piggy was glad his mother was at work so he did not have to explain where he was going when he went out. He cut through the back streets and came out by Canal Bridge. The smell of burning fat and scorched meat called to Piggy, and he stopped off for a large doner kebab. As he came out of the shop, Ernie Ernshaw's distinctive yellow Jaguar saloon went past. Fingers Fisher was driving.

Piggy turned the corner into Albany Road and spotted the car again, parked a few yards beyond the pub. Fingers was standing beside it smoking. Piggy walked casually along, chewing on lengths of charred meat from his kebab. He walked past Fingers before stopping, turning and walking back.

"Hello, Fingers. I didn't see you there. But then I wasn't expecting to see you. I thought you were still inside."

Fisher looked Piggy up and down and took a long drag on his cigarette before replying.

"Oh, Hi there Piggy. I'm not really here. I come out at the end of the month. But Ernie wanted me for something special. He got Doc Leachman to write, saying my mother was dying, and I got five days compassionate."

Piggy did a mental sum and decided that Fingers was reporting back in the morning.

"Didn't your Mum move to Spain last Christmas when her rheumatism played her up? I thought she was housekeeping for Ernie in Marbella!"

Fingers smiled. "Nah, she's been promoted. She's running his bordello out there now. Big place with a posh bar and patio for barbecues downstairs, five floors and a roof terrace. Used to be a hotel before Ernie took it on."

"Medical letter! That must have set him back a bit. Leachman never does anything on the cheap."

Fingers broke out into a gurgling laugh. "Nah, Ernie gave him a return flight and a three day pass to the bordello so he could honestly say he had examined Mum himself. He must have made good use of the pass. He could hardly walk when Charlie picked him up at Gatwick."

Piggy joined Fingers in his laugh.

"That's a nasty bump you have there, Fingers. Your Silvia not been knocking you about again, has she?"

Fingers stopped laughing and looked at Piggy for a moment. He took another long drag on his cigarette and studied his casual prison-mate, deciding if he could trust him before saying any more.

"Nah, got it on the job. Bit strange it was. I was just going in when someone clobbered me."

"Nasty! Did you see who it was?"

"Nah! I went out cold."

"You're kidding me. How did you get away?"

"Well, that's the strange bit. When I woke up I was alone in the place I wanted to open in the first place."

"What locked in? Lucky you came to before the old bill showed up. Did you manage to get much before you scarpered?"

"Wasn't like that Piggy. I was looking for information."

Piggy whistled. "Not your usual line Fingers. Ernie after someone?"

Fingers slowly looked left and right and beckoned Piggy closer before answering.

"Little runt who goes by the flash name of Sir Arthur Brain. Owes Ernie big time."

"Never heard of him. Ernie offering a reward if I do hear anything?"

"I should think so. Little sod ran off with twenty grand of his!"

"Wow! There's not many would have the balls to try that, well not for long anyway. How the hell did he manage it?"

"Not sure. Some scam about buying a factory in Peckham. Ernie has been looking to spread his assets about a bit. If the law raided the arches, then he could lose the lot all in one go."

Piggy took a bite of his now lukewarm kebab and chewed.

"Nice seeing you, Fingers. Take care back inside. Perhaps when you get out for real Ernie will give you a three day pass as well."

Fingers laughed again. "Maybe, but I doubt my Silvia will!"

Piggy laughed as he turned and walked on along Albany Road. The laugh died quickly as he got out of earshot. If Big Ernie was looking for Sir Arthur, then they had little hope in finding him, except in the canal or condensed in a squashed scrap car. This put a different complexion on the matter, and Piggy wished he had some way of contacting Tracey.

As Piggy walked, a car drew up alongside him. With a sigh of relief he turned to see Dillon at the wheel. He opened the passenger door and got in. Dillon moved off as Piggy began to tell of his recent conversation.

"We're in trouble Mr Dillon. Big Ernie is looking for Sir Arthur, and I think he would say he has a prior claim. He owes him twenty grand."

Dillon stopped the car abruptly and sat quietly for a while.

"I'd be happy if Ernshaw got him. Not sure Tracey would be though."

After a few minutes Dillon brightened up.

"There might be a way to come out of this ahead of Big Ernie."

Piggy was not so sure. Coming out ahead of Big Ernie would mean getting something that he wanted, and that was always a temporary state. Usually a very temporary state.

Piggy was pleased when Dillon dropped him off. He had done all that he thought Dillon and Tracey could want of him, and looked forward to a quiet Sunday and a peaceful week at work.

9. Money makes the World go Round

The scheme that John Dillon came up with was risky. Tracey wanted her money back and Sir Arthur punished. Dillon wanted him severely, and slowly, punished. Ernshaw wanted his money back and the pleasure of watching Sir Arthur suffer a great deal. To succeed, any plan had to satisfy all three parties.

What Dillon proposed was for Sir Arthur to appear to extract a large amount of Hardcastle company money. Once the fraud was reported the full weight of the Metropolitan Police and other agencies would be focused on finding the man. As long as he could follow the progress of the investigation Dillon thought they could get at Sir Arthur before Ernshaw. It would be more likely if Ernshaw was not actively looking for the man himself. To this end Dillon proposed that they set up a meeting with Big Ernie with an offer to help him.

On Tuesday evening Piggy finished work and was walking along Gordon Road when the Morris Oxford stopped in front of him. Tracey stepped out of the front passenger door and smiled at him. One of those smiles that made your knees go weak and your mind start to project exotic fantasies on the backs of your eyeballs.

Piggy knew it was useless to resist that smile. The small part of his brain which still stored hopeless aspirations did not wish to resist in any case, and he stepped into his now familiar seat in the back of the car.

"We would like you to take a message to Big Ernie." Tracey poured all her charm into that sentence and Piggy nodded his agreement before he had time to work out what she had said. But, given a minute or so to evaluate her words, Piggy became less comfortable with the plan.

"I'm not sure that would be a good idea!" Piggy had heard stories of people going to see Big Ernie, and not coming back.

"Come on, Piggy. We are offering to help the man," said Dillon. "How can he possibly object to that?"

Piggy sank in his seat as if to make himself too small to be seen.

"You don't know Big Ernie! He can take offence at the slightest thing. Even what you are wearing."

Piggy remembered the story of Lefty Fullbright, who once wore lurid red braces with yellow socks on a bank job. Before the job he used to be known as Andy Fullbright. Not quite so handy Andy now! He found many common tasks difficult, including clapping.

"Come on Piggy. We are offering to help the man. What have we got to lose?"

Piggy noticed that use of the royal 'we'. But doubted the plural implication would do him much good when standing on his own under the railway arches that made up Big Ernie's empire.

"Can't we telephone him?"

"Have you got a number for him? Or have you got to look it up? Would that be under C for crime or T for thug?"

Piggy did not appreciate Dillon's irony, but he understood. Big Ernie was jealous of his privacy and would not have a listed telephone number. He liked talking to people face to face. He could work out which features he was going to adjust while he listened.

It was a miserable Piggy who, twenty minutes later, stood in Silwood Street facing the railway arches. He cautiously approached a pair of big metal gates in the chain-link fence that marked the boundary of the Ernshaw empire. A hairy dog, the size of a small pony, came to welcome him and eye him up as a suitable supper dish. A tubby little bald man came out of the caravan parked in the yard and yelled at the dog to be quiet. The dog responded by switching from a series of loud barks to a long continuous low growl. Piggy was not a happy man.

The bald man squinted at Piggy. As he recognised him he grinned. Piggy also recognised the man. Peter something or other. He remembered that his mother probably knew him a great deal better.

"Hello Piggy! How's yer Mum?"

"Hello. She's fine, thank you. Errr, I need to speak to Mr Ernshaw."

Bald Peter again squinted at Piggy.

"Are you sure Piggy? I mean, that can be hazardous to your health?"

"Yes," replied Piggy glumly, "but I do need to speak to him. It's important, and it's something he might want to know."

"You'd better come in then. He's probably got a few minutes before dinner."

Bald Peter unlocked the gate and motioned Piggy forward. The dog growled and Piggy hesitated.

"Don't mind her," said Peter, "she's just being friendly."

Piggy wondered how she acted when she was less than friendly, and stepped gingerly into the yard. The dog trotted up behind Piggy, blocking his retreat, and then followed the pair as they walked across the yard and under the railway arch.

The other side of the arch was a revelation to Piggy. There was a triangle of land about a quarter of a mile long, formed by two merging sets of rail tracks with the canal at the base. He had supposed that the whole area was built up and industrial, but once inside it was more like a country estate. There was a big mock Tudor house facing a lawn hedged in by fruit trees to screen out the ugly brick arches. At the canal end Piggy could see stables and two horses in a small paddock.

But Piggy had little time to take in the sights. Peter walked him briskly up to the house and pulled an iron handle mounted on the wall. Somewhere inside a bell jangled and almost immediately the door was opened by a pretty olive skinned girl in a black servant's dress with white starched pinafore.

"Piggy here wants to see Mr Ernshaw!"

Bald Peter rushed the words out, and turned to go back to the yard. He knew from experience that there was no such thing as an innocent bystander when Big Ernie was displeased. Piggy watched him in dismay as the distance between them grew. Witnesses were always useful, even if they were not impartial.

The girl motioned for Piggy to follow her, and he fell in behind her for what seemed like a very long walk through an ornate hall, a Victorian looking corridor and finally into a large glass roofed room with a swimming pool and paved patio area facing a second, outdoor, pool. On the paved area was a gilt patterned glass and wrought iron table and six chairs. Big Ernie was sitting on one of the chairs. He looked up and scowled as they approached. The girl retired behind Piggy and waited by the door.

"Reginald Swinton, I believe! How's your mother these days?"

Piggy noted the affectionate tone of Big Ernie's voice as he enquired after his mother. She had obviously been more active socially than Piggy was aware of.

"She's very well, thank you, Mr Ernshaw."

"Now then, Piggy. Don't be shy. Call me Ernie. What can I do for you."

"I, I, I've got some friends who have an interest in someone you are looking for. They thought they might be able to help you find him."

Big Ernie pondered on what Piggy had said for some time; long enough for Piggy to become more nervous as he waited.

"Sit down Piggy. What makes you think I need help finding whoever your friends are so anxious to find?"

"No, I'm sure you don't. As you are all looking for the same person, they thought they might save you some time and effort."

"And what do they want in return for me letting them find this person?"

Piggy hesitated. He needed to word this carefully.

"One of them lost a lot of money to him and would like some back if there is any to spare when they find him. The other one just wants him to get what he deserves. They think that you are probably the best person to ensure that happens."

"Ah! So how do they think they can find him if I can't?"

Tracey had warned Piggy not to tell Ernshaw what they planned, but Piggy was having difficulty expressing himself.

"They have contacts, Ernie. With the government and such."

"Ah! So they want to be sure that they are not treading on my toes if they find him, and think they can help themselves to my money when they do!"

"No Ernie. He took ten grand off one of them and she's very upset about it."

Too late Piggy realised what he had said.

"She? Who are we talking about Piggy?"

"Sir Arthur Brain. He conned my friend into parting with ten grand for a factory he didn't own."

"So that's who you're after. But I asked you who she was."

"I only know her as Tracey. I don't know much else about her, except that she has powerful connections, like the Employment Exchange and the Probation Service, and big companies. People seem to do things for her!"

"And your other friend?"

"John Dillon!" said Piggy miserably.

"*The* John Dillon! Recently of Peckham Police Station. The one who nicked my granny for shoplifting when he was a young constable?"

Piggy nodded miserably. This was not going quite as he had hoped.

"Well I never! Strange company you keep, Piggy. I'll have to give this some thought. What makes you think that I'm looking for this Sir Arthur Brain?"

"I heard a whisper that he had conned you as well."

Piggy realised it was a mistake as soon as he spoke. Big Ernie would not want it made public that someone had got the better of him.

"Who's been blabbing, Piggy?"

"Don't know his name. Some bloke in *The Squinting Badger*. Big bloke with a face like a boxer."

Ernshaw nodded. There were a dozen men he knew at the gym who fitted that description.

"Well Piggy, perhaps we can do business. But I want him when you find him, and you've got two weeks to do it. Anything left after I take my money, your friends can have. Now I think it must be time for my dinner. Maria will show you out."

Big Ernie stood up and Piggy scrambled to do the same. As they stood there, Piggy wondered how he had got the label of 'Big'. He was two or three inches shorter than himself.

"Give my regards to your mother."

Maria appeared at the doorway, and Piggy followed her back along the route he had come in by. At the front door she pointed to Peter who was hovering by the railway arch with a spade in his hand. He looked disappointed when he saw Piggy walk out unscathed. Piggy walked back to the arch and followed Peter to the gates. The dog fell in behind them and trotted along sniffing at Piggy. She was not growling. Presumably anyone who came out of the house unharmed was considered a friend.

Piggy was not surprised to find he was drenched in sweat when he got back to the car. He got in the back and wound down the window. Tracey turned in her seat and looked at him for a moment.

"Piggy needs a drink," she said.

Sitting in the crowded bar of the *John Evelyn* public house, Piggy related his tale. He left out the bit about telling Big Ernie John Dillon's name. Both Dillon and Tracey nodded gravely as Piggy told of the two week timetable.

"Best get on it straight away then," said Tracey as she finished her Campari and soda. She got up and made for the door. A sallow looking man of about forty stepped across to block her way and spoke to her. To his surprise Piggy saw her place her hands on his shoulders as if about to dance. Seconds later the man was doubled up on the floor clutching his nether regions and she was smoothing down the hem of her skirt before continuing for the door. A wide path opened up in the packed bar to let her through. Piggy and Dillon hurried to follow her.

"That's the place where the playwright, Christopher Marlow, was stabbed to death. Good to know that a few centuries have not had too much impact on the clientele," said Dillon as they reached the relative safety of the car.

They dropped Tracey in front of the Town Hall and then Dillon drove Piggy back to the flats. Dillon stopped the car, switched off the engine and then turned to Piggy.

"Now Piggy, you can tell me what you left out in the pub."

He gazed at Piggy sternly as he spoke and Piggy wriggled in his seat.

"He made me tell him who you were, Mr Dillon," he whined.

"Never mind Piggy. He had to find out sooner or later."

When Piggy unlocked the front door of the flat he could hear his mother talking to someone. He approached the lounge cautiously and opened the door.

"Ah, there you are Piggy. Your mother was getting a bit worried when you did not show up for your tea. Working late at the factory again?"

Piggy stared at DC Holmes and his throat went dry.

"Don't know what you mean, Mr Holmes," he croaked, "I met some friends and went for a drink. That's all."

"Drink doesn't seem to have helped that voice of yours, Piggy. Mrs Swinton can you put the kettle on and make Piggy a nice cup of tea. I'll call you when he is ready to drink it."

Piggy's mother went reluctantly to the kitchen and shut the door behind her.

"Now Piggy, we need to make sure we understand each other. I'm not sure that you working at the factory and them having a break in are a coincidence. Have you got anything to tell me?"

Piggy sat down on the settee and said nothing.

"You'll have to speak up, Piggy. I can't hear you!"

"I've not done anything wrong," he whined, " I've done exactly what Mr Dillon told me to, and nothing else."

"John Dillon? What's he got to do with this?"

"He's my probation officer!"

Holmes stood and thought for a moment. Apart from the petty cash and cheque book Fothergill had mentioned a number of company papers that had been taken. Ponsonby had been less forthcoming, but Holmes guessed that perhaps papers were taken from his office too. And then there was that incident with old Wilf. It was Dillon who, in his capacity of parole officer, suggested that he looked ill and needed a longer spell in prison to get him off the streets. But why on earth would Wilf want French polish? There was something going on that did not make sense, and there were too many damn coincidences by far.

"You might be in something that's too deep for you Piggy. Come on, get it off your chest. You'll feel better for it."

But Piggy could not be budged. He just repeated that he was behaving himself and had got a job just as his probation officer had told him to.

"Who got you the job?"

"Mr Roberts, the manager of the Employment Exchange."

Holmes gave up. Piggy was firm in his resolve not to incriminate himself.

"Mrs Swinton," he called loudly, "Piggy is ready for his tea now!"

Holmes let himself out and stood on the walkway looking out at the bleak concrete structures around them. Perhaps Piggy was going straight. It was the first time he had got a job, and in double quick time as well. He could see why he would want to improve himself and eventually get out of this dump.

10. Too Many Coincidences

On Wednesday afternoon, DC Holmes was sitting in the canteen writing up his diary when the Superintendent's Clerk found him.

"The old man wants to see you."

"Me?"

"Yes, double quick."

Holmes sighed. The only time he saw the Superintendent was when he had a case that did not go as they hoped, or for his annual appraisal. Neither such events were currently expected. He finished his tea and headed for the Super's office.

"Ah, come in Holmes. I hope you are well."

Supt. Hackworth was not known for social chat with the lower ranks, and Holmes was at a loss to find a suitable reply to his query.

"Very well, thank you sir."

"Good, Good. Have a seat." Hackworth paused while Holmes pulled out the rickety chair and sat carefully down. "We've got a fraud case I'd like you to look after. Go and have a chat with a Mr Wilson at Lloyds bank. Someone has passed a dud cheque for a thousand pounds."

"Shouldn't that be the fraud squad's job, gov?"

"Normally yes, but there are some odd features to this one. The person that they think passed the cheque was reported missing by Shropshire some four months ago. You'll find a file on your desk. Keep me informed of your progress, and ask me if you need any help."

Holmes walked out of the office with his head buzzing. He would have to put Piggy to one side for the moment. This sounded like a serious job. But why had he landed it? Surely it warranted a DS or even a DI if it was that serious, and why report direct to a uniform Superintendent and not to his own DS. Someone was not telling him something, or else not telling it quite right.

Back at his desk Holmes picked up the folder that had found its way there, and scanned through the contents. There was not much. A cheque signed by a Sir Arthur Brain passed at the local bank for a thousand pounds. A brief missing person report of that same name who disappeared from his home and work on a cattle farm in Shropshire. Shropshire police had included a detailed description of the man. Holmes studied it carefully before getting out Wilf Makepeace's statement to compare the descriptions. He then looked at the name of the cheque account - Hardcastle & Strudwick Ltd. He picked up the telephone.

"Lloyds bank? ...May I speak to Mr Wilson? ... It's Detective Constable Holmes from Peckham Police Station ... Mr Wilson? I'd like to come and see you this afternoon ... 3 o'clock? Thank you."

Holmes put down the phone and sat thinking. What was the common link? Hardcastle's factory... where Piggy worked.

He picked up the phone again and dialled the clerk's office.

"Can you get me a warrant for Piggy Swinton's flat? I think he might have been involved in a cheque fraud. I'll meet you in the estate car park at about four o'clock.

Holmes re-read the file and made a few notes in his pocketbook, then he got up and headed out for Rye Lane. He was sure that the bits of information in the file were just the tip of the iceberg, and that there was something altogether more serious involved somewhere.

Mr Wilson was a typical bank manager: immaculate hair, white shirt with an old school tie and a dark pinstripe suit. His accent hinted at origins well away from South London, but with no rural inflections. Mid-Surrey perhaps, via a good grammar school and the City to his current branch.

His story was simple. At three o'clock the previous afternoon, Wilson had received a telephone call from Hardcastle's factory to say that Sir Arthur Brain was down from their Shropshire works and he was to be at an auction next morning buying cattle for the company.

It was a spur of the moment decision, and rather than write a dozen or more cheques to a number of farmers it made sense for him to pick up cash at the bank. He would be in with a cheque for a thousand pounds.

The man had come in with only ten minutes to spare and was anxious not to miss his train, but Wilson had already organised the money. A quick look at the cheque and the transaction was completed. It was only this morning when Mr Fothergill came in with a number of other cheques to pay in, that Wilson had casually asked if Sir Arthur caught his train okay and discovered that something was wrong.

"But surely they reported a stolen cheque book earlier in the day?"

"Yes, and I checked the serial number. It was not in the range reported. At least, not until later when I examined it with a glass. One of the numbers had been skilfully altered to put it outside the range of the book reported stolen."

Holmes asked Wilson for a description of the man. Wilson protested that he only saw him for a few minutes but then, prompted by Holmes, gave an excellent description of Sir Arthur, right down to the monocle and large mole on his left ear. When Tracey had coached him the night before she could have added other markings in less visible locations had it been necessary.

Holmes made detailed notes and asked if any other staff could add anything.

"I'm afraid not. It gets quite quiet as it gets near to closing time, and we cash up all the tills except one at a quarter to. My cashiers were all in the strongroom, reconciling the day's transactions while I manned the one till over here. It means we can get away that little bit earlier of an afternoon."

Seeing there was nothing more to be found out, Holmes bid Wilson good day and headed for the estate to supervise searching Piggy's home. In the car-park was a J4 van with three uniformed officers.

"Anything been happening?" asked Holmes.

"No, quiet as a grave since we arrived. One shifty looking bloke went in about twenty minutes ago. Can't see clearly from here, but I think he went in Piggy's flat."

"Wearing a monocle?" asked Holmes hopefully.

"Couldn't see, only got a quick glance as he slipped round from by the dustbins."

"Well, let's go and get a better look, shall we!"

Holmes knew that a polite knock on the door would give time to flush evidence away, so he took the heavy approach of a swift kick at the flimsy plywood and cardboard structure and they all burst in and ran at different rooms.

One of the uniformed officers charged the main bedroom door and burst through, barely slowing his pace as he did so. He was met by female screams and male oaths as he stopped a yard short of Mrs Swinton and the Reverend Woods lying naked on the bed. A vicar's dog collar and bib hung on one bedpost.

The constable stood watch as Mrs Swinton covered herself with a sheet and Woods scrambled for his clothes. There was a muddy size eleven Dr Marten boot print on his shirt from where the PC had stood on it.

The search continued, and the covered up pair were escorted to the lounge while their love nest was examined. After an hour Holmes called it a day. They had found absolutely nothing relating to their original purpose, only an interesting collection of photographs in the Reverend's jacket pocket. Woods had protested loudly when Holmes began to search the garment, raising Holmes's hopes of finding a monocle. The pictures were a poor substitute. However, Holmes passed them round the team and was rewarded with several of the ladies being identified by one of the older officers, although how that was possible from the unfamiliar angle at which some were taken was beyond Holmes's comprehension.

Holmes advised Reverend Woods that he was keeping the photographs for further examination and consideration of criminal action. He would return them when they were no longer needed. Holmes made a mental note to ensure that Mrs Woods was present when he returned them. Reverend Woods did not look a happy man as the officers withdrew. Loud voices were heard from above as they returned to the van.

Piggy made a special effort to get home after work. His mother had given him much grief over breakfast about not letting her know if he was not in for tea. He was surprised to find her in tears sitting by a buckled front door. As soon as he came in, she set about him, accusing him of lapsing into old habits and lying to her about his whereabouts. Clearly he had ruined her chances with the good Reverend. She ignored the fact that Reverend Woods was obviously also taking his chances with several other ladies at the same time.

Piggy protested that since the police had found nothing, she was blaming him unfairly, but in her current state Mrs Swinton was not amenable to logic. Piggy went off in search of an old chap on the second floor who did odd jobs, to see if he could secure the door. He took his time, hoping his mother would cool off in his absence.

Back in Peckham police canteen the photographs were displayed to a wider audience, in an effort to identify the few remaining subjects. When they had named the full set, a WPC was briefed to go and see the ladies, and accidentally advise them that they had competition for their paramour. Strictly speaking it was not a police matter, but Holmes had crossed paths with Woods before and had been subjected to his sanctimonious lecture on the subject of marriage and fidelity. He objected to the double standards of the man.

PC Walker came in to write up a few traffic process books over a mug of tea, and joined in the debate. After listening to Holmes as he outlined the details of the case, Walker got up.

"Let me make a phone call. I might be able to add some information."

Downstairs in the reserve office, Walker phoned Stanley Capes, general foreman of the defunct Strudwick French Polish and German Sausage Company.

"Hi Stanley. I wonder if you can help me. Sometime last summer I was in your office when a man came in wearing a monocle. Was that Sir Arthur Brain?"

Intrigued by the question Stanley confirmed and asked why he was asking.

It was a long conversation, covering Sir Arthur's incompetence and his greed at using the petty cash as his personal property, and also mentioning his role in the Goose Green Poisoning Mystery.

"Thanks Stanley. Incidentally, we've got a dance organised for Saturday week. Are you and Gloria doing anything that evening?... Great I'll pop in one evening with some tickets."

Walker trotted back to the canteen and drew Holmes to one side.

"I thought you'd got called out. Any luck?"

Walker beamed. "I think we need some more tea."

After a few minutes Holmes held up his hand to pause Walker.

"God, you're right. I never saw the man myself. Who did I see?.. Mr Capes, Mr Cortina and the lovely Gloria. Did Stanley say if Sir Arthur had any associates outside of the company?"

"Only one that he remembered. A Tracey Mulligan. Ran some sort of business training company called Executive Services. Had an office somewhere near the Town Hall."

Holmes grimaced as he searched back through his mind. Something, about four years ago or more. A complaint from a stuck-up lady councillor about a house of ill repute. He summarised what he knew of the case for Walker.

"Good looking woman?"

"The councillor or Mulligan?"

"Mulligan, of course. If it's the councillor I think you mean she has a face like a prune sucking lemons."

"The way Stanley described her, good looking would be a gross understatement."

Holmes smiled. It was all coming back to him. What came back most forcefully was the fact that Sergeant Dillon had organised the raid, and when the dust settled there were no charges and Dillon got promoted. It was Hackworth who had subsequently pushed so hard for Dillon to get the job in Training, although there were other good candidates who were already ranking station sergeants.

There was something else. Yes, the councillor divorced her husband and stood for parliament against him, switching political parties to get a nomination. They had to quell a small riot at the result declaration. Both stood on the platform accusing each other of splitting the vote and letting in an independent. The brawl ended with the returning officer sporting a black eye and five arrests for disorderly conduct.

Holmes sighed. It was beginning to look like Piggy was just a small cog in something large, and that Dillon and Mulligan could give him some answers, although it occurred to him that he might prefer to not ask the questions. Given Dillon's known bitterness about that Goose Green affair, he might not like the answers.

11. Questions, Questions

It did not take Holmes long to find Executive Services. The flashing pink fluorescent sign was a dead give-away. Holmes ambled along the alley and clumped up the external metal staircase. He found the pink door at the top of the stairs held open by a brick. Inside Tracey had anticipated his visit and set the scene to look much like what you would expect of a secretarial agency. Apart from the preponderance of pink on every conceivable surface it looked very different to how it had been described in the report that John Dillon had submitted.

Tracey smiled at Holmes as he knocked on the open door and walked in. That smile, and the way she matched Walker's lurid description of her, immediately told Holmes that he had found his quarry.

"Can I help you?" she asked.

"Tracey Mulligan?"

"Yes!"

"I'm Detective Constable Holmes. I'm making enquiries about the whereabouts of a Sir Arthur Brain."

"Oh! Yes, Sir Arthur. How is he?"

"I was hoping you could tell me? I understand that you know him socially."

Tracey laughed. "No officer, not socially. We did some consultancy and training for him. Let me think. It was sometime last year. Autumn if I remember rightly. I'd have to check the dates to be sure."

"Consultancy? What sort of consultancy?"

"Industrial production, quality assurance, that sort of thing. We also did some company management coaching for him. I'm afraid he was not ideal management material. He needed a lot of support. But

I've not heard from him since... let me see... must be a few weeks before Christmas last year. I expect he has been busy since Strudwicks merged with Hardcastle."

Holmes was at a loss for further questions to ask, at least for the moment until he could eliminate her as a suspect. If he could do that then he might have several more questions for her, like 'what are you doing this evening?' or 'fancy joining me for a meal at that nice Indian restaurant?'

"He's been reported missing, Miss, but he is also possibly involved in fraud."

"Oh dear, and he seemed such a nice man. But then I suppose that seeming to be nice is probably the stock-in-trade for a fraudster. What has he done?"

"I should not really say Miss, but suffice to say a local bank reported a crime yesterday, and from the description, Sir Arthur was involved."

"Good heavens officer, I shall certainly keep an eye out for you. If I do hear anything I'll be sure to let you know. Do you have a direct telephone number or must I call the station switchboard?"

Her tone implied that she would go out of her way to please Holmes, and she made the question sound as if she would be disappointed if such an important officer did not have his own telephone. Holmes eagerly gave her the CID office number and got ready to leave. As he got up she put her hand on his arm.

"Just a minute. There is something. He used to talk about having a country seat in Hampshire, but I believe he had money problems and lost it. I've no idea where in Hampshire."

She paused, as if thinking, and then continued.

"And the last time I saw him he was talking about team building exercises for the company managers on Dartmoor. He was asking us if we could develop some motivational skills courses, but nothing came of it. I believe he had made contact with a rundown holiday camp as a base down there. I'm sorry it's a bit vague, but if you knew the man you would realise that most things about him were a bit vague."

She smiled and left her hand on his arm for somewhat longer than was necessary. Holmes made a mental note to find an excuse to come back sometime. Sometime soon!

As he clanked down the metal steps of the external stairs, a Morris Oxford slowed down across the road, but the driver changed his mind and sped off.

Holmes plodded back to the station. It certainly sounded as if Sir Arthur Brain had some questions to answer, but it seemed that the tricky part would be finding him to ask them. The one thing Holmes could not work out was where Piggy fitted in with all this! He knew in his bones that Piggy was in there somewhere. It was just too much to believe that he wasn't involved, even if it did feel like whatever was happening was way beyond Piggy's league. However, when he last saw Piggy, he looked a picture of health, and Holmes had never known him to commit a crime without being injured.

Over the next two days, Holmes was busy. He put out a general alert for Sir Arthur and contacted Hampshire police to see if they had anything on the man. But apart from some old debts, including five years' rates on a country house and various unpaid tradesmen's bills, they had nothing to help him.

Then he had an idea. He approached Henry Fothergill and asked if he had the telephone bills for the factory from the previous year. In particular he was looking for listed numbers dialled from Sir Arthur's private line.

Henry shook his head. "Sorry. Before we owned the place! The Strudwicks might have something, but I doubt it. But he went to Shropshire from here. He was making a real mess of it up there and disappeared a couple of days before Mr Hardcastle could sack him."

Henry reached for his address book and found a number for Lionel Dee.

"Have a word with this man. He used to be the Company Secretary, and from what I can make out was the main force in dumping Sir Arthur on us when we bought the factory."

"Dumping on you? Did you not have a say in it?"

"Hardcastle handled all negotiations," he replied bitterly. "He thought he was fleecing a bunch of innocents but instead he got stung and was landed with a failing industry. Then to cap it all he put his idiot nephew in charge to make a further hash of it."

Henry Fothergill became aware that there was someone behind him as he spoke. He turned to see said nephew standing behind him.

"Fothergill, you're fired!"

12. Helping Police with their Enquiries

As Piggy returned from work, he found his path across the estate obstructed by two heavy men. He stepped onto the scrubby grass to walk round them, but they moved to block his way forward. One of the men took him by the arm and spun him round, then they walked back the way he had come towards the yellow Jaguar saloon that was parked up the street. Piggy recognised the car and struggled, but the man gripped him tighter.

"Big Ernie wants to have a word." he whispered, as if it was a secret not to be shared by those who did not need to know.

The statement was surplus to requirements, Piggy was already wondering what word it was he wanted to say, and how long he had to consider it after it was said.

The big gates opened as the car approached and they drove in under the railway arch with barely a slackening of pace. Piggy was unceremoniously dragged out, and the hairy dog came bounding up to him. Piggy had visions of his weeping mother standing at the graveside as the animal approached, but relaxed a little as he felt a hot wet tongue slap against his face and two paws press down on his shoulders.

"Thank God for at least one friend here," he thought.

One of the men pushed Piggy through the arch and towards the house. The door opened as he approached, and Big Ernie came out. The maid walked a few paces behind him carrying a wicker basket. Piggy wondered what was in the basket, but the part of his brain that managed his survival did not really want to know.

"Piggy, how nice of you to accept my invitation. Let's have a walk."

Piggy waited for Big Ernie to come alongside and turned to follow him as they headed towards the paddock that fronted on to the canal. The dog followed a few paces behind them.

"Your friends have been busy, Piggy. I'm impressed. Every policeman in the country looking for Sir Arthur. Now that's real clever of them."

Piggy had no idea what Big Ernie was talking about. He had not seen Tracey or John Dillon. But he wondered how Ernshaw knew what was going on. He also wondered why he was telling him. Big Ernie had a habit of telling people things they did not need to know, and then ensuring that they were not around to repeat it. Piggy looked ahead at the pitchforks stuck in the top of a pile of horse manure and suddenly the warm summer evening felt decidedly chilly.

"Yes, very clever indeed. I could do with brains like that working for me. I'm surrounded by Neanderthals. Have to do all my thinking for myself."

Piggy's brain was racing! He began to feel very damp under the armpits, amongst other places. But Big Ernie was beginning to sound content, even pleased with himself.

"I was sorry to hear about your poor old Mum and that rat Woods. I sent a couple of the boys round to have a quiet word with the Reverend Woods. He's decided to seek a change of air. Missionary work on a Pacific island. A new challenge converting cannibals to Christianity, I believe. I also understand that Mrs Woods has decided not to go with him, on account of her being allergic to tropical fruit."

Piggy began to relax as Big Ernie turned and called to Maria.

"Be a good girl and see what you can find for Piggy to take home to his dear old Mum. Bit too early in the year for the fruit but there should be plenty of eggs, and that bloody cockerel that woke me this morning can go as well."

Maria walked smartly on ahead into a large hen run. Once there she put down the basket and took a hatchet out of it. She made a quick rush at a large bird and with one grab snatched it off the ground before dashing it back down on a block of wood and swinging the hatchet down on its neck. She then threw the head to the dog and attached the bird to the wire fence by its feet to drip whilst she sought some eggs from the nest boxes. The bloody hatchet stayed where it was embedded in the block.

"Real useful girl that," said Ernshaw, "but you should see her mother. Best looking knife fighter in all of Malaga before she took on three gypsies at once. She helps Fingers's mother out now. You know Fingers Fisher don't you? I believe you were in Wandsworth together."

Piggy shuddered. Big Ernie was making a point, as only he could. He turned towards the hen-house.

"That should be enough, Maria. We don't want to overload poor Piggy do we?"

Maria came out and carefully emptied a dozen eggs from her turned up apron into the basket. Then she pulled the dead bird from the wire fence and laid it on top. She brought the basket to Piggy, curtseyed to him and held it out for him to take.

Ernshaw turned to the two thugs who were walking a dozen paces behind them.

"See Piggy out, lads. And make sure no little old ladies attack him on the way to the bus-stop. We don't want Mrs Swinton's eggs to get broken do we? Give my regards to your mother Piggy, and thank your friends for what they are doing. I do appreciate initiative in people."

Two thugs and the dog escorted Piggy out into Silwood Street and watched as he headed home, his progress marked by the occasional drip of chicken blood as he plodded along. There was no point in trying to catch a bus, not with the slow drip of blood from the basket.

As Piggy approached the flats he steeled himself for another stressful conversation with his mother. He climbed the stairs and stood on the walkway for a while to get his breath back before the coming confrontation. Standing there he could hear his mother talking inside through an open window. The voice that answered her was female, but only made occasional short replies and Piggy was not able to identify it. He pushed his key in the lock and quietly opened the door so he could slip in and put the basket in the kitchen sink before joining whoever was in the lounge.

As the door opened his mother's visitor was talking, and Piggy was sure he knew the voice. But, muffled by the closed lounge door, he still could not place it. He deposited his bloody load and walked back towards the lounge as if unaware of the occupants.

"Hello Reg, how are you?"

Piggy looked at his mother's companion in surprise.

"Hello Mabel!" he replied.

"I just popped in to see your mother," said Mabel, "and she has been telling me the good news about your job. My cousin Keith used to work at that place when the Strudwicks owned it. He's doing ever so well for himself now. He's in charge of security for Strudwick & Wouters at Goose Green and he has just got engaged. You remember Keith don't you?"

Piggy nodded. He certainly did. The man had muscles in places where most people did not have places, and an obsessively protective attitude towards female family members. It was rumoured that he flattened a man sometime before Christmas for insulting his sister.

"You're late Reg. I expected you home an hour ago."

"Sorry Mum. I stopped off on the way home to see a friend. He sent you a present, but I'll tell you more about it later."

Mrs Swinton looked at Piggy and wondered. He had few friends, and none whom she thought likely to send her presents. She was in half a mind to go and see what it was, but Piggy anticipated her move.

"You stay and chat with Mabel and I'll go and make us all a cup of tea. Would either of you like a sandwich, or a boiled egg?"

"We haven't got any eggs, Reg. I used the last of them this morning."

"Yes we have Mum, I brought some in."

Mrs Swinton looked quizzically at her son. Ever since he had got a job he had behaved rather strangely at times: normal behaviour for other men perhaps, but strange for Reg. Never had he done any shopping unless specifically asked to, and even then he often forgot. Perhaps the job was making him more responsible.

Having not got a reply to his question, Piggy went and busied himself in the kitchen. Given the content of the letter Mabel wrote to him in Brixton, he wondered why she was now sitting in the lounge with his mother. He made a plate of cheese sandwiches while the kettle boiled.

As Piggy came back into the lounge, bottom first to push open the door which had swung to, he heard his mother laugh. Mabel was recounting some story about her grandmother and a peacock.

"I'm really sorry about your grandmother, Mabel. I wouldn't have done it if I knew who she was!"

"Oh, that's okay Reg. She enjoys a good workout and the club won't let her spar these days in case she hurts herself. Fat chance of that! The only time she manages to build up a good sweat now is when she and Keith get together."

Mabel smiled at Piggy and he returned the expression, with a dash of puzzlement thrown in. There was something going on and, just as with Tracey and Dillon, he just knew it would involve him in doing things that he did not want to do.

"Walk Mabel home, Reg," said his mother once all the sandwiches were gone and the teapot was dry. "Take your time. You might like to stop for a drink on the way."

"Okay, Mum."

Piggy got up, held out his hand to assist Mabel to her feet and picked up the angora cardigan that she had lain on the arm of the settee.

"Are you going to be in when I get back, Mum? I really need to talk to you."

"Yes, Reg. I'll be here."

As Piggy closed the front door behind him and stepped out onto the walkway he heard a shriek from indoors. Mrs Swinton had found her present!

Piggy and Mabel walked along in silence for some time before he spoke.

"I didn't expect to see you again Mabel. Not after your letter to me."

"Silly boy. My mother made me write that. Didn't you see the little heart that I made the last full stop into?"

"I thought that was a blot."

Mabel gave Piggy a playful push on the arm and he toppled over a privet hedge. Mabel could never have been described as lithesome, as like many members of her family she was built on substantial lines, like a battleship. Since they last met before his incarceration she seemed to have been promoted, from heavy cruiser class to aircraft carrier. She pulled him back upright and grasped him in an embrace that most gorillas would have found too forceful. Piggy was back in the bosom of his beloved one, and finding breathing difficult. Eventually she released him, grasped his hand and guided him towards the public bar of *The Squinting Badger.* Piggy checked his jacket pocket as they approached that hostelry. Yes, he had his wallet. Mabel had been known to down six pints of an evening and still carry him home afterwards.

Piggy was late getting home, and none too steady on his legs as he climbed the stairs to the flat. Inside, his mother was sitting in the lounge in her pink nightgown and fluffy pink mules.

"Have you got something to tell me Reg?" she asked.

"Yes. I, err, met Big Ernie this evening."

"Nobody just meets Big Ernie. He does not just wander about the streets looking for people to chat to."

"No, Mum. He sort of sent for me. But he was real nice and he sent you that chicken and those eggs. He also said that Reverend Woods would not be about as he was going abroad."

Mrs Swinton smiled. She had a brief dalliance with Big Ernie some years ago, and unlike her son she knew exactly why he was called Big Ernie. She was flattered that he should still take an interest in her well-being, until she realised that he had probably also had a similar attachment to some of the other ladies in the Reverend's photographic collection.

"You're not involved in any of Big Ernie's shady deals are you, Reg?"

"No Mum. But some friends of mine are looking for something that he has lost. It's a long story and I'm tired Mum. I'll see you in the morning."

Mrs Swinton frowned. That was the second time that her son had referred to friends that evening, and in the plural at that.

Piggy went off to bed and, despite having had a worrying day, was asleep as soon as his head hit the pillow. Around three o'clock he woke from a dream about the film King Kong. As he lay there soaked in sweat he realised that he had been playing the part acted by Fay Wray, and he had a sneaking suspicion about the ape's identity as well. It was wearing an angora cardigan and sucking rhubarb and custard sweets.

It seemed like ages before he drifted back to sleep, and all too soon he was awakened by noises in the kitchen. His mother was singing to herself and, by the smells drifting in, making a cooked breakfast. Piggy got up and dressed quickly.

Mrs Swinton did not hear Piggy as he entered the kitchen. She was singing the Doris Day song *Que Sera Sera,* and putting a lot of enthusiasm into the line 'whatever will be, will be', as if it had some particular significance for her.

The table was laid and a teapot sat on a mat under a cosy. Piggy lifted the cosy to pour himself a cup just as his mother turned and transferred two eggs and a slice of bacon from the pan to his plate. She had already buttered several slices of bread for him.

"I thought I'd return Mr Ernshaw's basket this morning. I'll walk with you as far as the factory."

Piggy was not used to seeing his mother so happy, especially this early in the morning. He chewed and nodded. As he ate he noticed that his mother was wearing her best C & A dress and high heels. His walk to work was going to be slower than he would wish.

When Piggy got home from work that evening he again saw the yellow Jaguar parked in the road beside the estate. One of the two men standing by the car walked over to him. Piggy steeled himself for another trip to the arches.

"Big Ernie sends his regards," said the man, "and says your Mum will be staying with him for a while. I've got a list 'ere of things she wants you to send her."

The man fished in his pocket and pulled out a crumpled sheet of notepaper.

Dear Reg,

Ernie has asked me to keep him company for a few days. I'm not due at work until Saturday so I think it will be a nice break. Can you send me the things below. There is a holdall on the top of my wardrobe,

love Mum

toothbrush ~~nightdress~~ slippers swimsuit(blue) undies from the drawer   long blue dress and shoes   yellow shell suit   little red wash bag

Piggy looked at the list with mixed feelings. It crossed his mind that Ernshaw might be holding her against the possibility of anything going wrong in the search for Sir Arthur, but that ~~nightdress~~ seemed to tell a different story. He climbed the stairs to the flat and searched around for the items requested. Having stuffed the bag, Piggy walked down to the car. One of the men grabbed the bag and put it in the boot. It was clear that Piggy was not to be invited to join his mother.

As the Jaguar sped away Piggy realised that for the very first time in his life, he would be alone in the flat for the night. He returned home and sat wondering how to pluck the bird that still sat fully feathered on the draining board.

13. More Police Enquiries

DC Holmes stood at the iron gates of Strudwick and Wouters and held up his warrant card for the man behind them. Holmes recognised the battered features of the man but could not put a name to him. The man grinned and opened the gate. Once Holmes was inside the man then carefully locked it again and beckoned the policeman to follow him.

Lionel Dee looked up from his desk as Keith Longman brought Holmes into the room.

"Visitor for you Mr Dee," said Keith. He then waited a few moments to ensure the policeman was welcome before turning and leaving the room.

"Mr Holmes!" exclaimed Lionel Dee, "How are you? We've not had the pleasure of your company since you kindly arrested those thieves for us last year."

"I'm looking for some help, Mr Dee. We are hunting for a Sir Arthur Brain."

Lionel Dee opened his eyes wider in surprise as Holmes spoke.

"Now that's a name that should only be spoken when in close vicinity to a spittoon or gutter," said Lionel. "But I'm not sure how we can help. I last saw the man at a meeting of the shareholders in December, after which we escorted him off the premises."

"We've got reports of where he was until February this year, but then he disappeared."

"Disappeared?"

"Without trace. Nobody will say anything, but I suspect he may have taken something he should not have with him. Apart from us I believe a local criminal is also looking for him. What I need is any information you have about his social contacts."

"He was not the sort of person we mixed with socially. As soon as we realised what an idiot he was we spent a good deal of time rescuing the company and staff from his clutches. What information do you think we can give?"

"Do you have Strudwick's phone records for the time he was with you; trunk calls from his phone line?"

Lionel Dee grinned and looked across the room.

"Stella, can you join us?"

Stella got up and smiled as she crossed the room. Lionel introduced her with great pride, as befits a man presenting his bride-to-be to a friend. He then outlined their conversation to date and Stella went off to find the archives.

"These are the phone records. I need to filter out the sales lines, although they are mainly incoming calls and won't show much. Give me half an hour."

Lionel looked at his watch. "That can wait for a bit Stella. Why don't we go and get some lunch."

Holmes was in two minds about this offer. He remembered the dire fare of the Strudwick factory menu in Gordon Road, where they had a hundred ways to serve mince, and rarely told you what they had actually minced to make the grey sludge on offer. But he need not have feared. The canteen was on the side of the building, facing on to the yard. It had a set of French doors to the yard and a number of tables outside with parasols shading them. Roos Wouters's influence on the new canteen had given it a continental feel that went beyond the furniture. The menu included salads, recognisable meats in red and white wine sauces, delicate pastries and small Paris goblets of table wines.

Lionel ordered lunch for the three of them, while Stella led Holmes to one of the outside tables. They had a pleasant half hour or so, talking of how the company was doing and all the things that had happened since Christmas.

"Why don't you stay down here for a while and have some coffee," said Lionel, "and we will go and see if we can find anything. Come up when you are ready."

Lionel went inside to the counter just as Stanley Capes and Gloria Ford arrived there. He quickly told him of the purpose of Holmes's visit. Gloria immediately went out to renew her acquaintance with the man who had helped her sever her connection with her domineering mother. A few minutes later Stanley came out with a tray holding a pot of coffee for three and an oval tray of rolls and pastries. Holmes put away the expenses form that he was writing on.

"Nice to see you, Holmes. If we can help catch the blighter it will be our pleasure."

It was almost an hour before Holmes made his way back up the stairs to the row of offices. As he entered the room, he saw Stella and Lionel, highlight pens in hand, working their way through the phone bills. Ivor Cortina had joined them and was checking marked entries against his list of customers.

"Only the trunk calls are itemised, I'm afraid, but there are a few worth thinking about: these two in Devon for a start. He was talking about setting up a company team building programme, sending us all down to Dartmoor to pothole and swing down cliffs. He might have a contact down there."

It was not long before Stella escorted Holmes downstairs, armed with five possible leads, a packet of Belgian sausage and a newly inflated expenses form.

Back at the police station, Holmes contacted the Post Office Investigations Branch to get addresses for the telephone numbers he had brought back. But something was still nagging at him. If Sir Arthur was hiding out somewhere in rural England, then how come he had been sighted twice within the past week in the borough of Southwark? And why would a man who stole a thousand pounds bother to flog bottles of polish in a pub. Everyone who he contacted about Sir Arthur referred to him as an idiot. But were they right? He seemed to have displayed a certain degree of cunning.

While Holmes was waiting for the Post Office to call him back, he sat trying to sketch out a sequence of events. As he stared at the paper he realised that his instincts were right. Something was wrong!

Wilf Makepeace must have acquired the polish during the day on Saturday, and he was in custody before the factory was broken into. Wilf's arrest appeared to be a decoy to ensure the factory was empty. That would mean Sir Arthur knew Ponsonby was sleeping there and wanted to lure him out.

If Sir Arthur was an idiot, then he was a very clever idiot.

Then another thought struck him. Was the factory really broken into? They had not found a point of entry. What if Ponsonby got someone to impersonate Sir Arthur at the bank and roughed up the factory before he came out to sign the charge sheet. He looked as if he could do with some money. His clothes had seen better days and he was about to lose his home in a divorce if Lionel Dee's source of information was correct.

If Ponsonby was behind it all, then blaming Sir Arthur would only work if he was not found. If he was somewhere else he might have an alibi for the time of the crimes. Ponsonby would only be safe to do it if Sir Arthur was missing permanently: if he was already dead and buried somewhere where he would never be disturbed!

Holmes picked up the telephone and dialled Lionel Dee's number.

"Oh, hello again. Lionel, what can you tell me about Jason Ponsonby?"

"Not much I'm afraid. He was not directly involved in the factory handover process. But he was involved in an underhanded attempt to get information about Strudwicks by coercing one of our lady staff. He went so far as to promise to marry her, despite already being married and having absolutely no intention to honour his promise. He's quite a seedy character. Why do you ask?"

Holmes thought for a moment. It certainly made the case against Ponsonby stronger.

"Just trying to get the full picture, Lionel."

"Why not have a word with Hardwick's accountant, Henry Fothergill. I've known Henry on and off for years, and although he is a bit of a cold fish he's dead straight."

"Okay! I'll have to tread carefully getting in contact with him. I was talking to Fothergill on Monday when Ponsonby fired him."

"What! Hold on a tick, I'll give you his home address and telephone number. And when you speak to him ask him to call me at home tonight."

Holmes wrote down the number, then he phoned the criminal records office at Scotland Yard. While he was waiting for them to answer he thumbed back through his notebook a few pages to find Ponsonby's car details.

"Hello! I'd like an all index search for a Jason Ponsonby. Start with the vehicle index for a Ford Granada...Telex the results for the attention of DC Holmes at Mike Delta."

Holmes got up and went to get a cup of coffee while he waited for a reply. The more he thought of it, the more Ponsonby looked like a good suspect. A man like that must be guilty of something! He lifted the phone and dialled Henry Fothergill's home number.

"Mr Fothergill? ... Hello, I'm DC Holmes. We spoke on Monday. May I come and see you? ...Yes? ... Good! ... May I come to your home address or would you prefer to see me at Peckham Police Station?"

DC Holmes rang the doorbell at Fothergill's home in Forest Hill and stood back. There was a blue Rover and two children's bikes on the drive. Henry answered the door, with his wife Jane hovering behind him.

"Hello Mr Holmes, come on in. We were about to make a cup of tea. Will you join us?"

"Thank you, if it's no trouble," he replied, as he made a mental note to add a line to his expenses. "I want to talk to you about Jason Ponsonby."

Henry stepped back as Holmes spoke, revealing several newspapers on the table behind him, all open at the situations vacant pages. Holmes nodded at the papers.

"Mr Dee asked me to ask you to phone him. You might not need those."

Fothergill smiled. He had not had a lot to smile about recently and the mention of Lionel's name gave him hope.

"What can I do for you?"

"Tell me all you can about Jason Ponsonby."

"Where can I start? He's incompetent and making a hash of running the factory. True he was short staffed at the beginning, but he's put the backs up of everyone he's dealt with, and several people have quit. His wife kicked him out after she found he was having two affairs simultaneously, and his uncle, Sebastian Hardcastle, has put him on productivity related salary. He was living at the Brixton factory until it closed and moved into the Peckham factory straight away."

"So he's possibly short of money?"

"Almost certainly. He has a gambling habit and, given his nature, I suspect that he only manages to find partners in his affairs with his cheque book."

Holmes smiled as Fothergill spoke, but suspicion was not enough. He needed some proof of the man's crimes. He needed to keep Ponsonby under surveillance, but Ponsonby knew him. Besides, he seemed to spend most of his time in the factory. He needed someone in there to watch him, but the Superintendent was unlikely to sanction it from his budget without some evidence to begin with.

Holmes thanked Fothergill for his time and left, nearly tripping over a discarded roller skate as he went. On his way back to the station he applied his mind to the problem of watching Ponsonby. Then he chuckled to himself. Piggy Swinton!

Back at the station there was a telex on Holmes's desk giving the results of his request to the records office. Ponsonby had two arrests for drunkenness, one for assault and an unproven allegation of sexual assault. In addition there was a note saying that the file was flagged by the Lambeth Weights and Measures officers.

Holmes was still reading the telex when his phone rang.

"Hello!"

"DC Holmes? Hello, Fred Holdsworth here. Lambeth Council. I understand that you have an interest in a Jason Ponsonby. I think perhaps we should have a chat."

"Why?"

"We've been building a case against him for contaminated meat products."

"Contaminated meat products?"

"Yes, beef pies that contain things not listed on the label."

"What, other meats?"

"Horse, donkey, you name it!"

"Members of the minor aristocracy?"

"I don't follow you."

"We are looking for a missing person, a Sir Arthur Brain. He was last seen working on a cattle farm for Hardcastle."

From the other end of the line there was a long silence.

"I think I need to get on to our food lab right away. Can I come and see you tomorrow morning? About ten o'clock?"

As Holmes put the phone down he glanced at his watch. 'Just time to go and have a chat with Piggy before I sign off for the day,' he thought as he reached for his overtime card.

14. Piggy in Love?

Piggy was not looking forward to going home after work. The flat was empty except for a dead chicken in need of plucking. He had no idea how to go about it, but he suspected that it was a time-consuming messy business. Still, he had nothing else to do this evening and he might as well get it over with. At least once he had cooked it he would have solved his menu for most of the week.

But Piggy was in for a surprise. As he turned his key in the door he could smell cooking. Roast chicken if he was not mistaken, and his heart leapt as he rushed into the kitchen to see his mother safely returned home. But the bulky figure that he saw bending down to put something in the oven was not his mother. It was Mabel!

As she heard him come she straightened up, turned and smiled.

"I heard your mother had gone off for a few days so I came round to look after you."

Piggy stared. How had she heard that? He appreciated a nice roast dinner, but suddenly the thought of being left alone with Mabel filled him with foreboding. She was not a girl who would take no for an answer, or even ask the question before acting in the first place.

"That's good of you," croaked Piggy. "I'll pop down to the shops and get a couple of bottles of beer to go with dinner."

"No need, my precious, I brought a Party Seven in with me."

Piggy gulped. A Watneys Party Seven Red Barrel held seven pints. If Mabel behaved true to form then that sounded suspiciously like six for her and one for him. He might need rescuing before the evening was over.

"Dinner in fifteen minutes. Go and make yourself comfortable in the lounge while you wait. I've put a stack of records on the deck. It just needs starting. I've got a little something to show you later on."

Piggy went to the lounge and gazed at her choice of music stacked on his record player. It was a mix of James Last, Perry Como, Frank Sinatra and Sacha Distel: music to seduce by, none of which came from his own collection. Mabel had brought them with her, and Piggy had a fairly good idea of what she had in mind when she talked about 'a little something for later', although little was not the adjective he would have used to describe anything about Mabel.

To be fair to Mabel's dinner, it was excellent: more like a full Christmas dinner with all the trimmings. Dessert turned out to be a treacle sponge with far fewer lumps in the custard than his mother had ever achieved. Mabel watched Piggy with glowing eyes as he lingered over the last few scrapings of pudding from the side of his bowl. But eventually she lost patience and got up from the kitchen table to switch the kettle on before dragging him to the settee in the lounge.

"I won't be a moment!" she crooned sweetly as she returned to the kitchen, leaving him sprawled on the settee, heavy with food and a bit weary after an unaccustomedly hard day at the factory. Piggy closed his eyes as he heard the clatter of crockery. He concentrated on the music and began to doze a little as he wondered how long he could make a cup of coffee last, and at what time he could excuse himself on the grounds of an impending hard day's work.

It was some while afterwards, in that long silent pause while the auto-changer sweeps the record player arm back and drops another LP onto the deck, that Piggy realised that Mabel had been gone longer than he expected. He assumed she had started on the washing up and relaxed a little. Shortly after, with eyes still closed, he heard movement in the lounge and felt her sit down beside him. He reached out an arm and found himself holding bare flesh where he had expected to find the voluminous sleeve of her dress. He opened his eyes wide to see that the C&H Fabrics curtain material smock had been shed in favour of a skimpy baby doll pyjama set in sheer red nylon. Her earlier reference to 'a little something' was right! The outfit would have been immodest on a much more slightly built person. On Mabel it struggled to establish any authority at all.

Mabel was making her intentions extremely clear in a non-verbal way! Piggy gulped as he took in all that he saw sitting beside him. It took a while as there was a lot to take in. Mabel smiled beguilingly and took his hand. Piggy dreaded to think where she was going to take it to.

At that moment the doorbell rang. Piggy jumped up and headed for the sanctuary of whoever it was calling.

"Hello Piggy. I was hoping to find you at home. May I come in?"

Without waiting for an answer DC Holmes stepped over the threshold and passed Piggy towards the lounge.

"We'll be better in here, Mr Holmes," said Piggy loudly, as he steered the detective towards the kitchen. "The kettle has boiled."

Holmes stopped and looked at the closed lounge door for a moment before he changed direction and followed him. As Piggy shut the kitchen door behind them he heard the lounge and his bedroom doors also moving and banging to.

"I hope I'm not disturbing anything, Piggy?" asked Holmes as he saw the remnants of the meal for two on the table.

"No, Mr Holmes. Nothing that can't wait. Do you want me to come to the station?"

"No Piggy. It's just a friendly chat."

"Oh," said Piggy disappointedly.

"I want you to do something for me."

"I'm not a grass, Mr Holmes!"

"Oh, it's nothing like that. It's just that I think there is a problem at the factory where you work, and I would like you to keep an eye out for me. In particular, I want you to let me know if you see this man about there."

He took an identikit picture of Sir Arthur Brain from his pocket and handed it to Piggy.

"Never seen him, Mr Holmes. But I'll let you know. Do you want a cup of coffee?"

Holmes shook his head, he wanted to get home early for once.

"It's no trouble Mr Holmes."

"Very kind, I'm sure, Piggy. But I must get on. Oh, by the way, can you also keep an eye open for anything odd going on at the factory. Especially anything involving Jason Ponsonby."

"Sure, Mr Holmes. Anything you say Mr Holmes." Piggy searched desperately for something to prolong the conversation. "Mr Ponsonby has a room in the factory that he keeps locked. Is that the sort of thing you need to know?"

Holmes smiled at Piggy. "What's in it Piggy?"

"How would I know, Mr Holmes. It's locked. Do you want me to find out?"

"I can't ask you to do that Piggy. I mean, that would mean breaking in when the man was not there and searching the place. I couldn't condone that, could I?"

"I could go tonight," said Piggy hopefully.

"Oh, I can't put you out like that. Besides you have company and I've kept you away from them for far too long already. I'll come and have another chat some other time when you are not so busy. Oh, and Piggy, don't take any chances! "

With that Holmes turned and let himself out, leaving a crestfallen Piggy to rejoin Mabel: wherever she had got to. Holmes's last words echoed in his head, but not with reference to the factory. Piggy steeled himself for what was to come.

Piggy found Mabel in his bed, but six pints of beer and a heavy meal had taken their toll. She was snoring heavily and being chivalrous, Piggy declined to wake her. He tiptoed around picking up the garments he needed for work the next day and returned to the lounge settee. As he curled up, he wondered what DC Holmes thought he had on Ponsonby. Soon Piggy was fast asleep himself. For the second time since his release he dreamt of scenes from the film *King Kong*, but this time the beast was drinking a Party Seven as if it was an individual can of cola. Some splashed on Fay, and Kong wiped it off with a dainty lace handkerchief. He woke up saturated in sweat and lay there listening to Mabel snoring loudly the other side of the thin wall.

Next morning Piggy was standing in the kitchen, hovering over the kettle to switch it off the moment it boiled, when Mabel found him.

"Good morning," he said blithely, "I hope you slept well."

Mabel snarled. None of her family were at their best first thing in the morning. They tended to be monosyllabic until hot drink and food had a calming effect on them.

"You looked so peaceful last night. I thought it would be a shame to wake you. Not after all the effort you put in to making dinner," he said. 'And all the beer you put away as well,' he thought.

Mabel took a gulp of hot tea and smiled at him. Simply because he was up when she woke did not necessarily mean that he had not been by her side whilst she slept. And that was most thoughtful of him. Some men would have taken advantage of her, she thought, although she could not think of anyone in particular at the moment.

Piggy crunched on the remains of a piece of toast and drained his mug.

"Must dash. Mr Derry is showing me how they crush shellac this morning," he lied. "Take your time and let yourself out when you are ready."

Piggy escaped to the walkway and down the stairs. It was not until he had cleared the estate that he asked himself the question he should have asked when he arrived home the night before. 'How did Mabel let herself into the flat in the first place?'

Piggy arrived at work long before his boss and set to tidying up and sweeping the floor. The cleaners were not allowed in the stores in case they pilfered the stock, so Piggy usually did a bit of sweeping in the mornings. It was mainly paper and cardboard dust from assembling cartons. Harry Derry walked in as he was persuading a pile of dust into a box before tipping it out the window.

"You're early Reg. A lump in the bed stop you sleeping?"

Piggy looked at him. No, it's just an expression, not an insight. He laughed.

"I thought I'd get it cleaned up before you came in, Harry. So the dust would settle before you arrived. I know how it makes you cough."

Harry Derry nodded. His assistant was turning out to be a real treasure.

"That's very thoughtful of you, Reg. You're a good lad."

Piggy picked up a clipboard and went along the rows of shelves writing down the stock levels of the various sizes and shades of polish. Harry smiled again. He had been really worried when Strudwicks sold out, taking Keith Longman with them, and he had a most trying few months running the stores on his own, but young Reg was turning out to be just fine.

"When you've done that, take the figures up to Tom Dawes, the general manager. You know where he is, don't you?"

Piggy nodded.

"Then join me in the canteen for a cuppa."

Piggy rushed the last two shelves and left as Harry picked up his newspaper and headed for the canteen. Upstairs he chose his route carefully so that he walked past the suite of rooms used by Ponsonby on his way to Dawes's office. He noted the doors, and especially their locks, as he walked: all old simple three lever internal mortices; the original fittings from when the houses were built.

Tom Dawes had been foreman in the polish manufacturing area, and got his current job on the basis that anyone who could keep the peace between twelve gangs of rival football supporters could manage the rest of the workers easily. He was not an insightful man, but so far the works had run relatively smoothly during his five months in office.

Piggy found Dawes coming out of his office.

"Stock figures? Put them on my desk, lad."

Piggy nodded and entered the converted box-room of an office. He scanned about and soon found what he was looking for. An Oxo tin full of mortice keys.

Down in the canteen Piggy bought a bacon sandwich and a mug of tea, then sought out Harry.

"Eating already, Reg? You need a good woman to look after you. Have you got a girlfriend?"

Piggy began to wonder if the world and its wife knew all the details of his home life, but guessed that it was Harry's way of making polite conversation.

"I live with my Mum, but she's away for a few days."

"Never mind lad. My last assistant had lots of female cousins. If I see him perhaps I'll ask him if he can fix you up."

Harry laughed at his little joke. Keith Longman had a fearful reputation for looking after the honour of his female relatives.

"Mind you, Keith Longman would need to be sure you were a gentleman before he let you near any of them, even with a chaperone. You should have seen what he did to the union man who trifled with his sister."

At the mention of Keith's name, Harry had Piggy's full attention. He doubted that he could convince Keith that it was Mabel who was doing the trifling! He gulped and then coughed violently as a lump of bacon stuck itself to the back of his throat.

"Steady lad, you'll do yourself a mischief!"

If anyone was to do Piggy a mischief then it was not likely to be himself. With Mabel, he was damned if he did, and damned if he didn't. The thought of his complicated love life sent Piggy back to the counter for a second conciliatory bacon sandwich.

For the rest of the day Piggy worked diligently, but his mind was elsewhere as he mulled over how he was to get into the locked room without Ponsonby knowing. Obviously it had to be out of normal hours, and after the evening cleaners left. But how could he make sure that Ponsonby was out of the way. He had either to be out of the building or else so soundly asleep that he would not hear anything.

Piggy still had no idea how to find out what was in the locked room when he trudged home that evening. He put his key to the door carefully and opened it as quietly as he could. He stood and listened but there was no sound from inside. He stepped inside and shut the door. A quick look round assured him that he was alone. He began to have pangs of guilt as he noticed all his shirts freshly washed and ironed and carefully folded on his chest of drawers. Even his underwear from the linen basket had been washed and ironed. He had never had creases down the front of his Y-fronts before. As he walked around the flat he saw evidence everywhere of Mabel having cleaned and polished. He was reproaching himself for his resistance to her advances when he heard a key in the lock.

"Coo-eee Reg! It's only me. I popped home to get a few of my things. I'll start dinner in a minute."

Piggy could not bring himself to reply. Mabel took his silence to be awestruck appreciation as she dragged in a huge suitcase and headed for his bedroom.

"Won't your parents be worried where you are?" asked Piggy anxiously.

"No, they have gone to Margate for the fortnight. We have all this week, and next week provided your Mum don't come home before that. You'd better get another key cut so I can leave hers here for her."

Piggy's brain was racing, but try as he might he could not think of a way to avoid the inevitable, and for Piggy he felt the inevitable would include crushed ribs tonight, and various other orthopaedic injuries when cousin Keith got to hear of the night's events. He traipsed into the lounge and sat to await his fate.

Mabel again surprised him with an excellently cooked dinner of lamb chops in a tangy tomato sauce with new potatoes and peas, followed by gooseberry fool. Piggy slowly ate his fool and Mabel whipped the bowl away as soon as she had judged him to have finished. She then hastened to carry on from where they had been interrupted the previous evening. She appeared in the lounge doorway in her baby doll set at the same time as someone knocked on the front door.

The visitor did not bother to use the doorbell, but hammered on the flimsy door with a force that shook it on its weak hinges. Piggy rushed to answer it. As he opened the door a large hand grabbed him and pulled him outside.

"Mr Ernshaw wishes to see you Piggy."

Piggy reached the yellow Jaguar that Big Ernie had sent to collect him a good ten yards ahead of the thug who had knocked on his door. He clambered into the relative safety of the back seat of the car and waited for his messenger to join them.

Big Ernie was waiting for Piggy in the paddock of his empire.

"Hello, young Reg," he gushed as Piggy was pushed towards him.

Piggy frowned. Ernshaw always used his nickname, and Big Ernie gushing was not a common sight.

"Well lad, I thought it best if we had a bit of a chat before things went too far."

Piggy did not like that expression. To Big Ernie 'too far' had irreversible possibilities way beyond the limits of Piggy's imagination.

"We're doing our best, Mr Ernshaw. We've got the police to put out a countrywide hunt for him, and I'm sure he'll turn up soon."

"Oh, it's not that I want to talk to you about. I'm sure you are all doing all you can. It's something else entirely I want to talk about."

Piggy's mind raced, and came to a rapid conclusion. Big Ernie frequented the gym at the *Thomas A'Becket*, along with Keith Longman and several of his family. It began to sound as if Mabel had not been too discrete in her movements over the past two days.

"Honest Mr Ernshaw. I never tried anything. She moved in with me. She didn't wait to be asked, and I've not done anything wrong. She's forcing herself on me."

"What are you burbling on about, Reg?"

There it was again. Calling him Reg instead of Piggy. Piggy was really confused.

"Your Mother and me are going to get married."

Piggy's eyes opened wide as he took in what Big Ernie was saying. No, he must have misheard.

"Aren't you going to congratulate me? I wouldn't want to do it without your blessing. We thought that we would have the wedding at the end of August. The motor trade is a bit slack then and we can have a couple of weeks in Spain afterwards. Perhaps you could join us."

"Gosh, Mr Ernshaw. Yes, congratulations." Piggy frowned. "But Mum would need to get divorced first. I've not seen Dad for years. I've no idea where he is."

"I'm afraid your mother is a widow, Reg. Your father died in an accident at Harwich docks. He fell off a shipping container into the path of a truck."

Piggy, who had no real feelings for his absent father, nodded. Nobody had told him about his father's death and he was amazed that Ernshaw knew of it.

"When did it happen, Mr Ernshaw?"

Big Ernie paused and looked at his watch before replying.

"Just about now!" he said solemnly.

Piggy stood and stared at his future stepfather. All sorts of ideas floated through his mind, but one dominated all the others. Keith Longman would probably think twice before harming the stepson of Big Ernie.

"I expect you want to have a chat with your mother while you're here. Pop along to the house. I'll be back after I've had a look at the horses."

As Piggy approached the house the door opened to reveal Maria, impeccably attired in her black dress with a freshly starched pinafore. She gave Piggy a little curtsey as he stepped over the threshold. Clearly she now considered him a favoured son of her employer. She led Piggy to a rather gaudily furnished room filled with elaborately carved furniture and gold fittings. She motioned him to a Regency chaise longue, upholstered in a vile striped material that no self-respecting deckchair would wish to be seen dead wearing.

"Madam will be with you in a moment, sir," she said in that quiet respectful tone that servants learn at their mother's knee. "She is in the tanning parlour at the moment." She looked at her watch before continuing. "She is due out in two minutes."

Piggy nodded his acknowledgement and then gazed around the room at the collection of tasteless *objet d'art*. Maria coughed to regain his attention.

"Can I get you anything? Mr Ernie always has an Amontillado at this time of day."

Piggy had no idea what an Amontillado was, but nodded his agreement. Maria walked over to what appeared to be a writing bureau and pulled down the flap to reveal a dozen or more bottles and a set of gold decorated crystal glasses. She poured a drink from one of the bottles and reached in the lower shelves for a silver salver and a tin of biscuits.

Maria was standing beside Piggy, having silently deposited the salver containing his drink and several Amaretti biscuits on a small occasional table beside him, when Mrs Swinton walked in. She was wearing one of those thick fluffy white robes that cannot be bought, but only stolen from West End hotels. She held her left hand forward to Piggy, ostensibly to shake, but really to show off the huge diamond and ruby ring she was wearing. Piggy looked at the ring. He was sure that in that first week home when he was watching interminable television programmes he had seen Shaw Taylor hold up a picture of it on Police Five.

"Hello Reg," said his deeply tanned mother, "it's nice of you to drop by. You really are a thoughtful son. Can you stay for dinner?"

"I've already eaten Mum. Mabel came round and cooked for me."

Mrs Swinton narrowed her eyes and looked at Piggy for a while before replying.

"You want to be careful there Reg. You know I'm not one to interfere, but your probation officer might not like you seeing too much of Mabel. I believe that some of her family are not particularly honest."

Piggy stared at his mother. Of course they are not honest, he thought, half of them work for Big Ernie! In any case his mother's advice was a little late. In that bright red nylon attire he had already seen too much of Mabel. Far too much!

Ernshaw came in as Piggy bit into his third biscuit to balance the dry taste of his sherry.

"Your mother tells me you cannot drive, Reg. Perhaps one of my men could teach you. It would be useful if you could as I might not always be available when your mother fancies a ride, or wants to do a bit of shopping."

"I wouldn't want to put you to any trouble, Mr Ernshaw," said Piggy.

"No trouble, Reg. Half an hour round the block and a word with the examiner is all it takes."

Piggy tossed back the rest of his drink and reached for his fourth biscuit.

"Well if you are not staying to dinner I'll get one of the boys to drive you home. I'm glad we've had this little chat."

"I'd rather walk if it's all the same to you, Mr Ernshaw. I need the air after being in that factory all day."

"Well, please yourself, Reg. Incidentally I've two spare tickets for Saturday's boxing. Perhaps you would like to bring your lady friend. Mabel isn't it?"

Piggy nodded. He was being drawn in to the Big Ernie empire, whether he liked it or not. He wondered what John Dillon would say.

Piggy walked home slowly, via a circuitous route. Although he was soon to become a favoured member of the Ernshaw family he wanted to be sure the news was public knowledge before he ventured anywhere near the haunts of Mabel's large clan.

As he arrived home he saw the Morris Oxford parked on the edge of the estate. He walked towards it and opened the front passenger door.

"Evening, Mr Dillon!" said Piggy with excessive enthusiasm. Any excuse for not going home was a good excuse.

"I've been looking for you, Piggy. Some woman up in your flat said you had gone out. She seemed a bit annoyed that you had not told her where you were going. Is there anything I ought to know?"

Piggy sat in the security of the car and glanced up at the flat.

"It's complicated, Mr Dillon. My Mum is getting married."

"What's complicated about that?"

"To Big Ernie Ernshaw!"

"Ah. Still you cannot be held responsible for that. I presume she will move out when she ties the knot. I'll have a word with the Housing Department and get the tenancy transferred to you. That way we can show that you are doing your best in difficult circumstances to avoid criminal contacts. Don't worry Piggy. By the way, who was that up at the flat?"

Piggy took a long while to answer. "Mabel Longman. She's moved herself in to look after me."

Dillon looked at Piggy. It was clear from his tone that Piggy had not encouraged this habitation arrangement, and from the brief conversation that he had with Mabel, Dillon could see that Piggy was not up to persuading her to leave.

"Could you talk to her, Mr Dillon? Tell her that I must keep myself legal and upright and her being there would risk me being recalled to Brixton."

John Dillon thought for a moment. Certainly a few of the clergy nominated members of the parole board would take a dim view of co-habiting.

"Come on Piggy. We'll go and see her together."

Piggy followed Dillon up the stairs and opened the door of the flat.

"I'm home," he called, "and I've got someone with me."

There was a blur of red nylon as Mabel dashed from the lounge to the bedroom. She returned shortly afterwards wrapped in a long blue wool dressing gown.

"This is Mr Dillon, my probation officer," he said. "Mr Dillon is a bit concerned about us being alone together. The parole board takes a very dim view of unmarried couples sharing accommodation unsupervised. We need to assure him that all is proper and respectable, otherwise I could go back to prison."

Piggy hoped the dictates of officialdom would deflect Mabel's wrath from him, but felt a twinge of guilt about pointing the blame for her eviction at John Dillon. Still, Dillon was a big, strong man who should be capable of taking care of himself.

Mabel looked at Piggy and then at Dillon. For a moment she stood there staring at Dillon. Piggy glanced nervously about to ensure his path to the front door was clear. Eventually, she turned back to Piggy and her face lit up with pure delight. Her eyes shone as she rushed towards him and clasped him to her ample bosom.

"Oh Reg,! Yes! Of course I'll marry you."

15. Conspicuous Absence

Tracey Mulligan sat with Superintendent Hackworth on a pink Chesterfield and sipped her Campari and soda. Hackworth was on his third Scotch and was recounting their progress in their search for Sir Arthur Brain. When Sir Arthur had left Shropshire he had gone to the little cottage on Dartmoor which he had intended to lure Tracey to. He stayed for a month before moving on. Having learnt from Tracey that the man's apparent recent activities in London were merely a ruse to start an official search for him, Hackworth had admonished her for a few minutes. However, her conciliatory attitude, and hint of delights to come, soon overcame any scruples he had about the matter.

But Hackworth was concerned. Tracey had told him that Ernie Ernshaw was also keen to find Sir Arthur, and why. Hackworth knew that Ernshaw was not a man who would be satisfied with Sir Arthur simply returning his money. If Ernshaw found him first then there would be a new vacancy in the peers of the realm, and virtually no chance of Tracey getting her money back. Indeed, Hackworth wondered if Ernshaw had already found him, and his currently expressed desire was simply a smokescreen to establish a defence against any future criminal investigations. He had seemed unusually open to accepting help in his quest.

Hackworth was intrigued by his recent progress meeting with Holmes. Jason Ponsonby was a new, and promising, aspect to the enquiry. Holmes was almost convinced that the man was involved somehow, and with a cattle farm in Shropshire he certainly had plenty of space to hide a body. Holmes had hinted that he had a man inside the factory who would make some discrete enquiries. Tracey had raised her eyebrows as he mentioned this. She had not told him of Piggy's involvement in searching for clues, or how she came to

Mulligan's Revenge

know of Ernshaw's interest. She would have to have words with Piggy. Strong words!

"Are there any other ways you could find him, Chopper?" she asked, using the nickname that was commonly used by his PCs to refer to him, but not necessarily for the same reason as she did.

"I had hoped that his personal bank account might help, but he left Peckham with an overdraft of two hundred pounds and seems to have only used cash in Shropshire."

"What about before he came here, where did he bank then?"

"Several banks! He would run up debts with one and then move to another."

"But surely the banks circulated a list of such debtors?"

"Only to their own branches! They were only too happy to off-load bad customers on to their competitors"

Tracey smiled at Hackworth.

"So if we make a list of all the banks he has used so far we can eliminate them from his potential safe havens for my money."

"But what if he does not use a bank? He won't want all that money sitting around not earning five percent."

Hackworth thought for a moment. "What if he put most of it in a building society and only kept a little with him for daily use? There are hundreds of them. We could take years to contact them all."

"Perhaps we should look at where he is likely to spend it, rather than where he is keeping it. I've an idea that I'll try out tomorrow."

Tracey got up and held out her hand to Chopper. He gulped down his drink and hurried to follow her.

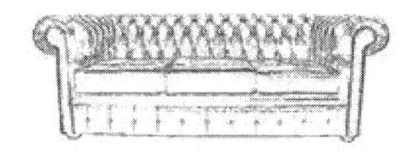

16. The Net Closes In

Stanley Capes was pleasantly surprised when Keith phoned him from the little lodge by the gates to say that a Tracey Mulligan wished to speak to him. He wondered if she was touting for business for her office management schemes. But she would be a pleasant diversion from work for half an hour or so and he asked Keith to bring her up.

"Good morning Mr Capes. I'm hoping you can help me in a personal matter. It's a bit of a long shot, but I'm running out of options."

Stanley looked up at Tracey and smiled. She was modestly dressed in the same business suit that she wore when she first came to see him, and despite her attire, her charms and eye-pleasing character shone through.

"You're welcome Miss Mulligan. What can I do for you?" asked Stanley, with little hope that her reply would invite him to do what was uppermost in his mind.

Tracey returned his smile and launched into the reason for her visit. Sir Arthur had gone missing and she was anxious to find him. Stanley expressed little hope that he could help her. He had already had the police visit him on a similar quest, and since Sir Arthur moved to Shropshire from Peckham he was not sure how he could contribute. Besides given how the man had nearly wrecked all their futures, he was not keen to help unless finding him involved some unpleasantness befalling the man.

Tracey decided that honesty was the best policy, with some slight distortion for the sake of her reputation of course.

"I'm afraid that Sir Arthur was not totally honest. When he left Peckham he was in possession of a large sum of money that rightfully belonged to my company. I know the police have made enquiries, without success, but I thought a different approach might be more fruitful."

Stanley nodded.

"Can you tell, from your invoices what his preferred drink was?"

Stanley thought for a moment, then he picked up his telephone.

"Carol? Could you come and see me for a moment, please."

Stanley grinned inwardly. Most of the male staff would give their soul to spend time squashed in a small room with the twin delights of Tracey and Carol.

"Ah, thank you for coming. I believe you met Tracey Mulligan on the Quality Initiative training course."

Carol nodded. Unlike many male attendees she had concentrated on the subject matter of the course, but she remembered Tracey very well.

"Miss Mulligan has her own reasons for wanting to trace Sir Arthur Brain. Do you remember what his favourite drink was?"

"Scotch!"

"Can you be more specific?"

Carol thought for a long time. "Tobermory!"

"Are you sure?"

"Yes! It's the same name as a character in a book I bought for my niece last Christmas."

Stanley smiled and lifted the phone again.

"Grant, could you join us in my office for a few moments, please?"

He put the phone down and turned to his delightful audience.

"If anyone here can help you any further then Grant De'War is your man."

Grant De'War bounded into the little room and smiled at its occupants. Grant had been an employee of the ill-fated Goose Green Liquor Company, and had lost a number of good friends in the poisoning incident. He had as much interest in revenge on Sir Arthur as anyone. Tracey introduced herself and he stood spellbound as she explained what she hoped she could get from the meeting.

"If you have an idea what part of the country he is in then I might be able to narrow it down for you. There's not many distributors who stock Tobermory, and a sudden increase in sales would not go unnoticed. Single malt drinkers tend to be rather regular in their habits, and any sudden change in consumption is rare. Let me make some calls and then perhaps Miss Mulligan would care to join me for lunch," he said hopefully.

"I would love to," replied a smiling Tracey.

Grant De'War could not believe his luck. He bounded off to his cubicle in the warehouse and reached for his address book. Starting with the distillery itself, he soon had a short-list of distributors who had increased their orders since March. Concentrating on the South West Grant soon came up with three likely areas. One distributor in Newton Abbot looked particularly promising. Grant racked his brains for a contact name there. He had been in the whisky trade for a long time before the demise of the Goose Green Co-op. During that time he had meticulously noted the names of contacts he made at trade events. Eventually he found what he wanted.

"Hello, may I speak to Nathan Nathaniel?"

After a few minutes of general chat to re-establish rapport, Grant launched into what he really wanted. Nathan was delighted to assist. The Goose Green poisoning had harmed sales of spirits and liqueurs throughout England for a while.

"Let me see what I can find, Grant. I'll call you back in ten minutes."

Grant put the phone down and spent the time straightening his tie, polishing his shoes on the back of his trousers and combing his hair as he waited for the call.

"I think we might be in luck. There be a hotel in Torbay that has doubled its order since April, and an off-licence not far from it that ordered an extra case in March."

Grant took details of the two customers and thanked Nathan for his help. He made a note to send him a complimentary Belgian sausage and rang Stanley's phone.

"I think I might be on to something," he said.

It was a sunny day and Grant had lunch with Tracey on the patio of the staff canteen. He could not help noticing that suddenly all the porters had decided to have lunch there at the same time, and that they chose to all crowd round the most adjacent table to his. Several of them paused with their laden trays as they passed his table, and greeted Tracey with obvious affection in their voices.

Despite the interruptions, Grant enjoyed his lunch. The continental atmosphere of the staff canteen and the delightful company made a most enjoyable hour. He was sad to see Tracey go, as he escorted her to the gates. She promised to call him in a few days to tell him of any progress in her search.

Back at her Executive Services office she called Hackworth and gave him the information she had got from De'War. Hackworth was most impressed. A nationwide search turns up nothing, yet she comes up with precise information in a morning. He wondered what she would look like in uniform and felt the need for a cold shower as he visualised a scene that included relieving heavily strained tunic top buttons and handcuffs. In the absence of such a facility in the station he went down and ordered a mug of tea. On his way back to his office he left a message for Holmes to come and see him as soon as he came into the station.

"Ah, Holmes. I've a little trip for you. You are to go down to Torquay and liaise with a PC Rudge. There is a possibility that Sir Arthur is at the Scrumpydown Hotel on the Totnes Road."

Holmes, who was of the opinion that Sir Arthur was more likely to be occupying a corner of a Shropshire field, asked Hackworth where the information came from.

"You're not the only one with contacts Holmes. But we do need to tread carefully on this one. I understand that Ernie Ernshaw is also anxious to get hold of Sir Arthur. I use the words 'get hold of' advisedly in this case. We need to be wary. We don't want Ernshaw getting to the man before we do. There wouldn't be much chance of interviewing him afterwards if he did. Take the unmarked Hunter and make your own arrangements for accommodation once you are there. You can trust this officer to help. But tell nobody else. I don't want any leaks at this end about where you are heading."

Hackworth passed Holmes a slip of paper with a name and telephone number on it.

Holmes left the Superintendent's office and, after phoning to make arrangements, went home to pack a bag. He wondered how long he could make his trip last, but was concerned that it took his eye off Ponsonby. He was still convinced that the man was guilty of something: even if Sir Arthur was alive, and living on pasties.

Piggy was not a happy man. It was true that after Mabel had accepted his unintentional proposal last night she had switched from carnal desires to talking about wedding plans, but that was merely a temporary reprieve from what was now clearly to be a life sentence. Suddenly Brixton and slopping out seemed an attractive alternative.

Harry Derry was quick to pick up on his assistant's change in mood. Over a mug of canteen tea he taxed Piggy on what was ailing him.

"But if you got engaged then you should be full of the joys of Spring, lad."

"I never meant to get engaged, I wanted to throw her out of the flat, but it all came out wrong."

Harry looked puzzled. How could giving her her marching orders be interpreted as an invitation of marriage. He looked at Piggy with crinkled eyebrows.

"You had to be there," mumbled Piggy unhappily. He realised he was too close to revealing his true past life and concentrated on his tea.

"Mabel Longman," mused Harry, "not related to Keith Longman by any chance?"

Piggy nodded and Harry shook his head. To break off an engagement to a female Longman was not a trivial matter. Harry realised it could deprive him of his assistant for a long time, or possibly permanently.

"The only way out is for her to dump you. Preferably in favour of another man, that way you will be the aggrieved party and safe from any repercussions."

Piggy brightened up for a moment before realising the odds were against it. He had more chance of winning the pools without sending in his coupon. For the rest of the day he looked intently at the other workers in the hope of spotting a suitable mug. He did not find a likely candidate, but did get some funny looks when people noticed him staring at them. He also found other men giving him extra space in the canteen queue. However, he did cling to one hope. Perhaps she would see something she liked at the boxing on Saturday night.

That evening after work he headed for the railway arches instead of home. He had decided to take up Big Ernie's offer of teaching him to drive. At least it would keep him out of the flat and take his mind off his problems.

Piggy found Ernshaw in a sombre mood. Despite a long separation Piggy's mother was upset to hear the news of her husband's demise. Ernshaw had wisely not given her any details, and especially not the date of his departure from this world, but she grieved for him who suddenly became the most wonderful man she had ever known. She thanked Ernshaw for finding out for her, and mourned her loss in the only way she knew how: with a bottle and a half of gin.

When Piggy arrived she was well past intelligent conversation, but Big Ernie was more than happy to have an excuse to get out of the house.

"I thought you might change your mind, Reg. Every young man should be able to drive these days. I'll get Peter to give you a lesson."

With that he went off to consult with his gatekeeper about a suitable vehicle from the yard. A few minutes later, Peter came back to see if Piggy was ready. Piggy had dreamed of gliding about at the wheel of the Jaguar, but parked in the yard was a battered Transit van. Despite its tatty bodywork, the inevitable result of frequent rapid departures from various banks and post offices into heavy city traffic, the vehicle had a highly tuned V-eight engine and uprated brakes.

Peter talked Piggy through the various controls and then left him to get familiar whilst he went off in search of a pair of number plates. Once these were installed, he suggested that they drive round the yard for a while before going out onto the road.

"Do I need 'L' plates?" asked Piggy.

"You're better without them," replied Peter, "they only encourage other drivers to take liberties with you."

Piggy sat in the driver's seat and put his foot on the clutch. It too had been uprated and was so heavy that he nearly had to stand to depress it. He pushed the gear stick into first and stamped on the accelerator. To his surprise the vehicle did not immediately rush forward, but noise and smoke from the rear wheels indicated that the tyres were warming up and about to grip the asphalt. Eventually contact was re-established and the speedometer climbed rapidly toward fifty miles per hour: just as the brickwork of the distant arches became considerably less distant.

"Brake!" shouted Peter.

Piggy obliged and was rewarded by the sound of four tyres screaming as they locked and slid along the ground. The arch still continued its rapid progress towards them.

Eventually the vehicle slowed and Peter grabbed the wheel and pulled them to the left. They stopped less than a fag paper's width from the wall. Once Peter had recovered, he spent some time getting Piggy to practise gently pushing down the various pedals before letting him restart the stalled engine and drive off at a more sedate pace. Ten minutes round the yard gave Peter the confidence to point Piggy at the open road.

After an initial few minor mishaps that relocated keep left bollards and a telephone box, Piggy began to get the hang of driving. He found that other vehicles kept a healthy distance from the rusty dented beast that he hurtled in their direction. After half an hour he had not hit anything for the past fifteen minutes, and Peter decided he was now a seasoned driver ready for anything that the traffic could throw at him. He directed Piggy back to the yard where an anxious Big Ernie awaited the return of his favourite getaway van.

Peter got out beside Ernie and motioned Piggy to park the van under an open arch.

"If you're thinking of using him on a job forget it, at least for a while. He might be okay at the stock car track though."

Ernie grinned. "Give the lad a chance. I remember your first drive. You rammed a baker's wagon instead of the security van."

Peter chuckled. Instead of twenty five grand they got two hundred doughnuts and a wedding cake. Piggy walked back to join them and Ernie reached in his jacket pocket.

"I think I've got the hang of it now, Mr Ernshaw. I'll put in for my test as soon as I get a provisional licence."

"No need for all that, Reg. I had every confidence in you, so I got Little Alf to take your test for you yesterday. Here's your licence."

Piggy took the little red booklet and looked at it. It was the first time he had seen his name in print other than on police and prison stationery.

Big Ernie looked at his watch and frowned.

"I'm afraid I must be off. I've a delivery of cigarettes due soon. I'll see you at the boxing on Saturday. I presume you'll be bringing Mabel."

Piggy mumbled his thanks and turned to go home. He wondered if he dared take a more direct route yet. He erred on the side of caution: it would mean less time with Mabel.

When Piggy got home he found the flat empty. There was a ham salad on the kitchen table, under an upturned plate, and a note scrawled in eyebrow pencil on the back of the electric bill final demand.

'Gone to see Cheryl, back late. Don't wait up.

XXXXX'

Piggy searched his memory for the large area storing the names and relationships of Mabel's family. As he came to Cousin Cheryl he found her brother, Keith, stored alongside her. Cheryl's finely chiselled porcelain doll features and petite figure were a marked contrast to Mabel's slab-like appearance. He dug a fork into a slice of ham and put it in his mouth to chew while he pondered the ramifications of her note. Provided Cousin Cheryl approved of Mabel's choice then he should be safe from harm. But if cousin Cheryl did not approve then he would probably get a visit from Keith Longman in a day or so, and he probably would not enjoy that visit.

* * *

After a quick call on her cousin to discuss wedding dress designs and potential bridesmaids Mabel had met up with a number of her family in *The Flatulent Fox* off the New Kent Road. Her attendance at such gatherings was usually a cause for dismay, initially as she cadged drink after drink from aunts and uncles, and subsequently as the effect of her consumption made her mood more and more belligerent.

However, on hearing her news, many were pleased to buy her a celebratory drink. Most had given up hope years ago of her ever getting married and, on hearing of her intended nuptials, realised that in future her betrothed would be financing her legendary alcohol consumption. That fact alone was worth a celebration.

It was gone midnight when a minicab stopped in the forecourt of the flats. Mabel lurched out and, after a loud argument with the driver who disputed her addition and assertion that there were two half-crowns to the pound, she swayed towards the foyer of the block. She stumbled as far as the lift and pressed the call button.

By pure chance it was at the ground floor and the door opened immediately. She lurched in and looked at the block of numbered buttons. There was not a number forty two, Piggy's flat number, so she pressed the four and the two instead. After stopping at the second floor, the lift groaningly hauled her bulk up to the fourth where she got out.

Mabel walked along to the third door on the right and noted approvingly that Piggy had not been idle in her absence. The door was a delicate shade of blue, instead of the tatty red it was when she went out. After struggling for five minutes trying to jam her key in the lock she gave up and looked for the doorbell. It was on the other side of the door to where she expected it. She pressed it and waited. Nobody answered her. She pressed it again and kept her finger on the button for a full minute before a light came on somewhere in the flat.

The door opened and a woman in curlers demanded to know why she had been disturbed in the middle of the night. Mabel, who still had not realised that she was on the wrong floor, slowly came to the obvious conclusion. In her absence Piggy had been two timing her with a trollop who was almost old enough to be his mother. She pushed the woman, known locally as Mrs Butler, to one side and charged into the flat, calling Piggy any number of colourful but unprintable names as she went.

In the second bedroom she came upon the sleeping form of Mrs Butler's son. The boy, Dennis, was a big lad who had a fruit stall in Lower Marsh. But he was no match for the enraged Mabel, who did not bother to turn the light on before she hauled him to his feet and started pummelling him about the chest with her fists.

Meanwhile Mrs Butler, whose husband worked nights at the gas works, was knocking up a neighbour who had a telephone and screaming for someone to call the police.

By a stroke of good fortune, a police car with two officers was attending an accident nearby and, given the choice between a jumped traffic light and the attempted murder of a local resident, they leapt at the opportunity to attend. One of the officers handed over the partly written process booklet to a bemused driver, and told him to fill it in and hand it in at Peckham Police Station.

Then they roared off, lights flashing and two tones blaring to rescue the besieged resident. On route they called for reinforcements and within minutes half a dozen men in blue were pouring into the flat. Two dragged Mabel away from Dennis, and once she was restrained two others began to assess his injuries.

As a precaution, because of suspected internal injuries, they called for an ambulance and Dennis was quickly removed to King's College Hospital. Mabel, handcuffed but still attempting to head butt anyone who came within range, was dragged out and down the stairs to a waiting police van.

Piggy, finally woken by the noise from the flat below him, peered out of the window to see a struggling figure being hauled into the back of the van.

"Hmm, looks a bit like Mabel," he thought sleepily, and went back to bed.

17. Piggy in Charge

Next morning Piggy woke up to find himself alone. He hoped that Cousin Cheryl might have talked Mabel out of the engagement, and hummed cheerfully as he made breakfast for himself. He wondered what the neighbours had been up to in the night, but it was none of his business, so he made no attempt to find out.

At the factory he set to work happily, whistling as he swept the dusty floor. Harry quickly noticed his change of mood.

"Beginning to appreciate the advantages of being a couple, eh, Reg?" he asked jovially.

"Not quite, Harry, but she didn't come home last night and that's almost as good as being single again."

Harry frowned. He really could not make head or tail of Reg's love life.

They had only been back from lunch for a few minutes when the general foreman, Tom Dawes, rang the stores and asked to speak to Piggy.

"Reg, I've a policeman with me and he wants to have a word with you. Can you pop up to my office?"

"Right away, Mr Dawes" said Piggy. On his way he feared numerous possibilities related to his activities over the past two weeks or so, but he had no idea why the policeman wanted him.

"Ah, Piggy!" said PC Walker as he walked in.

Piggy stared at him in despair. Those two words should have told Dawes that he was not only known to the police, but known sufficiently well for them to have a nickname for him. Dawes did not appear to appreciate the significance of the greeting.

"Can we talk somewhere else, Mr Walker?" asked Piggy.

Walker nodded. "What's the canteen like these days? It used to be a bit grim when Strudwick owned the place."

"Double grim," said Dawes. "Use my office. I've got things to do in polish production."

Dawes left them and Walker sat down in his chair. He motioned Piggy to also sit, but he remained standing.

"I understand you know a Mabel Longman."

"Yes!" replied Piggy.

"And she gave your address as her address also."

"Gave her address to who?"

"To us when we arrested her last night."

"Arrested her! What for?"

"ABH, GBH, assault on police, criminal damage, drunk and violent with it. You name it Piggy. There's a man in hospital, Sergeant Gladworthy with a black eye, and a bedroom on the floor below you that looks like something from the blitz."

"Gosh!"

"When she eventually began to sober up this morning she still claimed that you were two timing her, and she was glad that you were in hospital."

"Me?"

"Yes, it seems she went back to the estate last night well and truly plastered. She got the wrong floor, and somehow jumped to conclusions. Your neighbour's son got a real hammering."

"Why do you need to speak to me?" asked Piggy, "I knew nothing about it."

"Well, Piggy, I'm just here to confirm her real address. Is it right that you and she are engaged?"

"Yes!" he replied miserably.

"Oh dear, Piggy. What have you got yourself into?"

"A mess, Mr Walker."

"Too right, Piggy. Still you probably won't see much of her for three months or so."

"Three months? For a first offence? Surely that's a bit harsh, Mr Walker."

"Who said anything about a first offence? She's got a string of convictions for drunkenness and violence as long as your arm. Didn't you know?"

Piggy shook his head miserably.

"No. I thought she was a bit keen on the beer. I never knew about her record."

"Well, I mustn't tell you the details, even if I could remember all of them. I suggest you try and find some way to put her off you. One man who turned her down spent six months in hospital and he still can't eat fish and chips."

"Can't eat fish and chips?"

"Yes, he feels too much sympathy for anything that has been battered," said Walker with a laugh.

Piggy did not find it funny at all, but refrained from saying so.

"Can you confirm that she is living at your address?"

Piggy brightened up. "She's not on the voters' register there Mr Walker. So I suppose her parents' address is her proper home. And the Council would have to agree before she could move in to the flat officially."

Walker pondered on Piggy's reply. He felt sorry for him, but could not see any way to help.

"Would you be prepared to have her stay at the flat if she gets bail this afternoon?"

Suddenly Piggy realised he had a way out.

"I can't, Mr Walker. Now that I know she has a criminal record, I would be in breach of my parole terms to let her stay with me. In fact now you have told me I'll have to report her to Mr Dillon straight away."

Walker smiled. Perhaps that was the legal position, but he would hate to be the one to explain it to Mabel Longman.

"I tell you what, Piggy. I'll make sure her parents' address is the one on the charge sheet and push for an order that she must not go within 500 yards of the Butlers' flat as a condition if she gets bail. That would also exclude your mother's flat as well, and put the blame for an enforced separation on the beak."

Walker smiled inwardly. If Mabel turned her wrath on the magistrate, then it would not bother him. Not after he left off that upper class yob with a caution, just because he recognised the old school tie the man wore to court.

"Would you, Mr Walker. That would help a lot. Incidentally it won't be my mother's flat for much longer. She's getting married and moving out. Mr Dillon said he would help to transfer the tenancy to me."

"Well, I must congratulate her sometime... That's a bit quick though isn't it? I thought after that incident with the Reverend Woods she might have gone off men. Who's she marrying?"

"Ernie Ernshaw!"

"Big Ernie? Oh dear! Oh dear! I'm beginning to think you were better off in Brixton, Piggy!"

"So do I, Mr Walker. So do I!" said Piggy glumly.

18. Scrumpy and Cream Teas

DC Holmes enjoyed his drive down to Devon. Every mile driven took him further away from the dust and dirt of London, and made it harder for Hackworth to check on his overtime claims. He soon found the B&B that Hackworth's contact in the local force had recommended. It was in a hamlet called Longcombe. There was not much of Longcombe: a few cottages, a garage and pub at the crossroads and a patchwork of hilly little fields surrounding it.

The B&B was a low slate-roofed cottage with massive cob walls. The south facing wall was covered in trellis up which grew vine-like plants with showy pink and white flowers. On close inspection they could be seen to be runner beans. An old collie lay in the red dust outside the gate. If he was supposed to be a guard dog then he was not taking his duties very seriously. He barely opened his eyes as Holmes stopped the car a few feet from him. The landlady was a contrast to her sleepy surroundings. She was a trim, suntanned woman in her mid thirties who bustled about and listened attentively as he told her the bare minimum of the reason for his visit.

It was a short walk up to the crossroads to a country pub that served meals like 'chicken in the basket' and 'pasty and chips' for half the price he would have paid in Peckham. Having checked in Holmes walked to the pub for a well-earned lunch. The beer was unfamiliar, with 'Flowers Keg Bitter' being the main brew, but they also had draft scrumpy in old oak barrels behind the bar. A drink made from apple juice, now that should be nice and easy on the stomach, thought Holmes as he ordered a pint. He picked up his glass and held it up to the light. It had the opacity of a thick soup, and when he tasted it the sharp tang on his pallet gave little hint of its original fruit.

Whilst waiting for his food, Holmes phoned Torquay Police Station to make contact with PC Rudge.

"He's up on the moor investigating a bit of poaching at the moment," said a Sergeant Holdsworth, "but I'll radio him to tell him you've arrived and get him to contact you as soon as he can. Have you got a radio in the car? ... OK I'll get HQ to give you a call sign and a channel number."

Holmes thanked Holdsworth and decided there was nothing he could do until he had made contact. There were strict protocols when working in another force's area. Besides, he had plenty of admin to do while he waited, especially his overtime and expenses claim forms.

After his lunch he slowly walked back to his digs, wondering why his legs did not seem to be fully under his control after a single pint of the quaintly named Foxes' Piddle. The old dog raised his head as he approached, but upon recognising him dropped it back on his outstretched paws and closed his eyes. Holmes found a pleasant spot in the garden and collapsed in a deckchair to look out on a field of sheep. Soon, despite not attempting to count the animals, he was fast asleep.

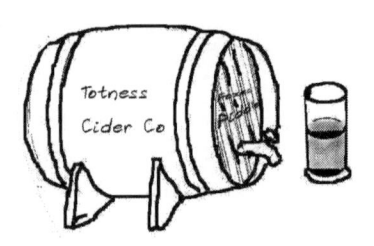

He was woken sometime later by the sound of cattle down the lane as they protested at being disturbed in their grazing for evening milking. Now awake, and with the whiff of cow manure wafting up the lane from the farm, Holmes got up and wandered round the garden. Many of the pretty flowers he had noticed from a distance turned out, on closer inspection, to be vegetables or fruit. Only the front hedge of small-headed fuchsias remained purely decorative. As he meandered his landlady came out with a pot of tea and a plate of scones with cream and strawberry jam.

"I prefer the raspberry jam myself, but it's too early for them yet. Enjoy your tea Mr Holmes."

Holmes returned to the deckchair and rustic table and stretched forward to the plate of scones. As he did so he heard a distant drone. A rasping hum that steadily kept on getting louder. The dog also heard it and jumped to his feet. As his brain cleared the remnants of sleep, he realised it was not a bee, but a fast approaching two-stroke motorcycle. The dog started barking, running repeatedly between the gate and the front door.

The sound grew louder until it filled the air and a mud caked scrambler bike came down a track that he had assumed was a path in an unkempt garden opposite and stopped at the cottage gate. The coarse tread of its tyres threw mud to left and right as it approached, including covering the bonnet of his car. The heavily splattered rider dismounted and came through the gate and across the lawn towards him.

"Stay right there Martin Rudge!"

It was the cottager's voice as she came round from the back of the house with a hosepipe in her hand. The mud coated rider held his hands up as if to surrender, and Holmes got ready to intervene in a domestic dispute. She turned the hose on and, starting at the top, sprayed him from top to toe; the dark red mud running down and across the lawn.

The rider wiped his goggles, removed his helmet and advanced on Holmes, dripping as he walked.

"DC Holmes? Welcome to Devon. I'm PC Rudge!"

Holmes looked at the wet, stocky figure in front of him and cautiously held out a hand. Rudge pulled off a gauntlet and grasped Holmes in a vice-like grip.

"So, you're looking for a fugitive by the name of Sir Arthur Brain!" said Rudge as he plonked himself down on a garden chair and continued to drip on the grass below.

Before Holmes could reply, his landlady approached with another plate of scones and a second cup and saucer.

"You never said 'e was a friend of yorn, Martin," she said as she put down her load, "if I'd of known I'd 'ave put him in the big bedroom."

"I'm sure he'll be fine where he is, Aunt Milly. We will be out most of the time. He's not here on holiday."

Aunt Milly did not look convinced. She hurried back to the house and returned with a fresh pot of tea and jug of milk.

Holmes spent the next half hour filling Rudge in on the background to the case. Rudge nodded and shook his head as appropriate.

"Might be difficult to find him: there's lots of monocled old men in Torquay, mostly ex-army, and they all drink scotch in one form or another. The Scrumpydown Hotel is one of them fancy eating places. I doubt he's staying there unless he's loaded."

"It's a bit vague as to how much money he started with. The charges relate to one thousand pounds. But if rumour is correct he's got about thirty thousand, and most of it belongs to a villain from Peckham."

Rudge thought for a moment.

"When you're ready, llow me home to get changed and then we'll go pay the Scrumpydown a visit."

Holmes was not sure he was up to driving far, but the tea and the soft tap-water of South Devon was beginning to flush him through nicely and he assumed he would improve as the evening went on.

When Holmes and Rudge walked into the hotel there was a middle aged woman vacuum cleaning the carpet in the entrance hall, and a man in the bar polishing and arranging glasses. There were few customers in the bar, but there was the hum of a considerable number of people from the other side of a door marked 'Dining Room'.

Holmes went up to the barman, took out the identikit of Sir Arthur and placed it on the bar.

"Have you seen this man?"

The barman quickly shook his head. "No, never seen him."

Rudge, who had been standing back watching, now stepped forward and beckoned to the man to lean towards him over the bar.

"The man asked you polite, like, Thomas Hudson. Now I'm asking you again, and if I don't get the answer I want, I'll be telling your wife where you were on Tuesday night, and who you were with. Now that we understand each other, have you ever seen that man?"

Hudson grimaced and looked at the picture again.

"It's not a good likeness, but it could be the Major. He usually comes in about eight o'clock of an evening."

"Now, that was not too difficult was it? Go and make us a cup of coffee and we'll mind the bar for you until you get back."

"Nice work," said Holmes. "It's handy knowing who is doing what with whom."

"Just a lucky guess. Tuesday is his night off, and the randy little git is always up to something. Don't know who his current attachment is though."

Holmes laughed. "If you ever want a change of scene, I'm sure we could find you a place at Peckham."

Holmes and Rudge sat in the bar for three hours, but although it became busier as time went by, their quarry did not show up. Some of the customers who came in took one look at Holmes and Rudge and walked out again. For each one who did so Rudge made a short note on the back of an envelope. At about nine-thirty they decided to call it a day and Holmes dropped Rudge off on his way back to Longcombe.

The cottage was in darkness when he arrived, so he quietly let himself in and made his way up the creaking stairs to his room. On his bedside table he found a note, written in Aunt Milly's hand, detailing his temporary call sign and channel number. In his bed was Aunt Milly herself!

The next morning Aunt Milly excelled herself, exactly as she had the previous night. As Holmes dozed afterwards he began to smell breakfast cooking, and roused himself to wash in the china basin and hot water jug that had appeared on the dressing table. Then he stumbled downstairs to be greeted by a smiling Milly, and a breakfast that would keep an army going for the day. There was little hint of the more intimate familiarity of their time upstairs.

About nine o'clock, feeling overfull and somewhat weary, Holmes went out to his car. He turned on the radio, switched to channel nine and automatically reported in to wherever the local information room was.

"Right you are, me 'andsome," came the less than formal confirmation in a rich girlish voice, "and I've a message from a Superintendent Hackworth for ee. Ee says that two of Ernshaw's men were seen coming your way in a blue Cortina. Now you take care out there."

Holmes frowned. How had Ernshaw got to hear so soon? He went over all that he had done. He had gone home and stopped the milk. Then he had picked up the car and filled it up at the contract garage. He had bought a Devon and Cornwall map and put it on the petrol account and then pointed southwest. He had approached the local police via a contact Hackworth had made on a course at Bramshill. It had to be the garage or the police switchboard!

As he parked up outside Rudge's house, he spotted a blue Cortina that had been following him drive past and park a hundred yards down the road. Steady he thought, you're being paranoid! But just in case he noted the registration plate and called it in for an index check. Almost before he had finished speaking the letters he realised that the last two denoted a local registration, and he felt foolish as he waited for a negative search response.

"Papa two two, are you receiving?"

"Go ahead," said Holmes as he waited to be embarrassed on air.

"Papa two two. I've got that index recorded as a cattle transporter from Newton Abbot. Can you verify the registration please?"

Holmes screwed up his eyes and repeated the distant plate very carefully.

"Ok, my lovely, I'll send a TD unit to investigate. Will be about fifteen minutes. Can you maintain visual?"

"Yes. Can you phone PC Rudge at his home and let him know I'm outside?"

"Right you are me 'andsome."

A few minutes later Rudge slipped out of his house and into the passenger seat of the Hunter.

"What made you suspect them?" he asked.

"Co-incidence. I got a message to watch out for a blue Cortina and then noticed one follow me for the last three turns."

Holmes paused for a moment and then continued on a different topic.

"How close a relation is your Aunt Milly?"

Rudge looked at him for a long time before replying, studying his face for clues as to the reason for the question. Then he laughed.

"No relation at all! She was married to a sergeant at Brixham. He died in an accident at the harbour. Tragic it was, late twenties and only recently married. She gets a pension, of course, but to help her out whenever other officers come down here we lodge them with her. I guess you ask because she has taken to you. Relationships are difficult with locals at her age and in her position. All the good ones are married, and all the available ones are dodgy. So once in a while she hits it off with one of her lodgers for a day or two, especially at this time of year round the anniversary of his death."

Holmes thought of what Rudge had said for some time as they settled back in silence to watch the Cortina.

Eventually Holmes broke the silence by talking about the case.

"He would probably put the money in a local building society. I think he's running out of banks to use."

Rudge thought for a moment.

"There's five in Torquay, and one in Totnes. Does he drive?"

"There's no record of him doing so."

"From Scrumpydown there are buses each way, but Totnes is the quieter. I don't understand why he would drink at Scrumpydown, but not stay there. There's nowhere else within walking distance to stay unless he knows someone who lives down here."

Two police solos pulled up alongside them and one officer leaned towards Holmes's window.

"Morning gents. Can you say which house they went into?"

"I didn't see any movement. I think whoever was there is still in the car."

The solos moved off and stopped, one in front and one behind the Cortina. A man made a break for it from the driver's side and Rudge was out of the car and waiting for him before he realised he was running the wrong way. The man stopped and turned but now two officers were either side of the road behind him. Rudge beckoned to him.

"Well, well, Sammy. Not in a hurry are you? We could do with a chat."

Rudge grabbed the man by the upper arm and turned to Holmes.

"What we have here is one of the Blackmoor brothers. Sammy here specialises in housebreaking when young mums are taking the kids to school. And I expect we will find his other brother's prints all over the motor. Sammy don't have the brains to steal cars. Too complicated for him. Ain't that right Sammy?"

One of the traffic officers came back to join them.

"Not very clever Sammy. A nicked Cortina with plates copied from a lorry. Your Harry do that for you? And a bag of housebreaking stuff on the back seat. Looks like it's time for another visit to the magistrates for you my lad... Martin, can you two take Sammy into Totnes. Pete will wait for a truck to bring the car in and I'll follow you to sort the paperwork out."

Once Sammy was deposited in the cells, Holmes and Rudge walked up the hill to the Totnes Mutual Building Society to make their first enquiry of the day. The manager was a cousin of a cousin of Rudge, but they drew a blank on recent large cash deposits. The manager obligingly phoned their other three branches and a few contacts in Paignton, but without result. A pretty blonde girl on the Deposits Desk listened as they chatted to the manager. She got up and came round to look at the identikit.

"I knows 'im, Mr Rudge," she said. "Ee was in Torquay Sunday afternoon. Walking along the front with a big brassy woman."

"Are you sure?"

"Course I am. Making a right exhibition of themselves they was."

"Can you describe the woman?"

"About my height, with dyed blonde hair. About forty-five with a really eye catching figure provided them corsets kept things in place."

"Big earrings?" asked Rudge.

"Gold dangling things, like little wind chimes," she replied.

"Bugger!" said Rudge as he turned and made for the door.

Holmes chased after him. "You know her?"

"Maggie Sullivan, the owner of the Scrumpydown Hotel!"

They went back down the hill considerably faster than when they had plodded up, and were soon headed along the A385 towards Collaton St Mary where the Scrumpydown stood.

"I'll have Hudson's guts for garters," said Rudge. "The reason our man always came in for a drink at eight is because Maggie Sullivan always has dinner at seven o'clock before her restaurant gets too busy. He must be with her and I bet that little sod tipped her off while we sat in the bar."

Rudge reached for the radio mike and called the information room.

"Put out a watch for a Maggie Sullivan of the Scrumpydown Hotel, Collaton. She has a file, so you can get a description from that. She drives a white Volvo sports car. If seen, then observe and report to me."

"Right you are, my lovely."

"Five one two, this is six eleven. I saw her driving out of Torquay railway station about forty minutes ago."

Holmes slowed the car to a more moderate pace and took the radio mike from Rudge.

"Thank you, six eleven. Information room, this is Papa Two Two. Can you telex the Met at Mike Delta to inform a Superintendent Hackworth that his target is on the move by train. And let the Transport Police know they probably have the target on their patch."

"Will do, me 'andsome."

Rudge was out of the car almost before it slid to a stop on the gravel at Scrumpydown, and by the time Holmes had caught up with him he had cuffed Hudson and was reminding him of the penalty for conspiring to aid a fugitive.

"Where's Maggie?"

"She's out."

"Be a bit more specific. Your last attempt at withholding information from me is likely to put you inside. You don't want to add to your spell on the Moor."

"She went out with the Major. He had a suitcase with him, and she was going on to the cash and carry afterwards."

"The Major. What room has he been staying in?"

Hudson hesitated and Rudge squeezed the cuffs tighter. Holmes remembered that vice-like handshake and grinned.

"Do you want me to leave, Martin?" he asked nonchalantly.

Hudson's face turned white. "He's been staying in Maggie's flat this last week. Before that he was in fifteen."

"Well I guess we need to search her flat then, keep an eye on him while I go out to your car and organise some help and a warrant."

As Rudge walked back through the lobby, a man in cook's whites was coming in. He saw Rudge, turned and walked out again. Rudge appeared not to notice him, but when he returned to the bar he grabbed Hudson and propelled him towards a door at the far end of the room.

"Let's start with the kitchen, shall we?"

Hudson protested loudly, but Rudge pushed him through the swing door into the kitchen preparation area. The room was empty, but the half-prepared food on the worktops suggested that it had not been empty for long.

"What have we got here then?" Rudge asked as his gaze landed on the carcase of a large animal hung up and skinned ready to be butchered.

"I know nothing about that," whined Hudson.

At first Holmes could not make out what the animal was. Skinned and headless it looked too thick jointed for a deer, but the wrong shape for a cow. Eventually he realised he was looking at a horse, probably a Dartmoor pony. The evening before whilst sitting waiting for Sir Arthur to make an appearance they had noticed the bar meal specials board advertising steak sandwiches.

"Oh dear, Oh dear. Looks like we need to bring in the public health people to have a look round here, and the wildlife crime team will need to join us as well," said Rudge.

Holmes nodded. All good police work, but it was delaying him in his quest to find Sir Arthur.

Before long the hotel was a hive of police activity. Two vans arrived, each with four officers, plus a duty inspector who waved a warrant at them. Shortly afterwards more individual specialists arrived, filling the hotel car-park.

"Let's get on with it shall we? Looks like you've made a good start already Rudge," beamed the duty inspector.

The owner's flat was a suite on the top floor. In the absence of an available key, an obliging officer built like the proverbial brick outhouse took a run at it and sprang the lock as the flimsy door bowed under his weight. Inside it was clear that the occupants had left in a hurry. Dirty breakfast crockery sat on a table and despite the summer heat there was the remains of a fire in the grate. The thin stratified ash suggesting that it had been mainly paper.

Holmes hunted through all the waste bins he could find. A mucky job, but eventually he found a receipt for five thousand pounds from a Babbacombe Building Society. It was made out to a Major Pilkington-Smythe. After consulting with the duty inspector, Rudge called for a fingerprint man. Holmes began to wonder if they had stumbled on a lookalike who was also on the run.

There were several other items of interest to the local police, including two shotguns, a crossbow, and a hunting rifle in a coat cupboard, but nothing further of interest to Holmes.

"We don't seem to have got your man, but you've certainly turned over a few stones for us," joked Rudge as they walked back to the car.

"Let's go into Babbacombe and have a chat with the Building Society," said Holmes. "We might learn something from the money."

The Babbacombe Building Society was housed in two rooms above a laundrette. The manageress, and part-owner, greeted the two policemen as if she expected them.

"I suppose you are here about Major Pilkington-Smythe," she said as soon as they had introduced themselves. "I did wonder about him when he came in this morning. Waiting outside when I opened up and withdrew all his money. Fair cleaned me out he did!"

Over a cup of tea they got the full story of the man. He arrived in February and deposited twenty-nine thousand pounds in cash, claiming he had recently sold his business to a consortium who always dealt in cash. Then three weeks later he came in and deposited a cheque for four hundred pounds from a Shropshire estate agent. This morning he had taken seventeen thousand in cash and the rest as an uncrossed draft.

"I wonder why seventeen thousand in cash," mused Rudge.

"Because that was all I had and he was anxious not to wait!" replied the manageress.

"And you just handed it over?" asked Holmes.

"You'd be surprised how many folk round here only deal in cash. Some of the farmers walk around with several thousand in their pockets, in case they see something they like."

Holmes laid the crumpled identikit on the table and smoothed it out.

"That's him! I wondered why with all that money he did not get that mole removed," she said as she pointed to the left ear.

It was clear that Sir Arthur was no longer soaking up the Torbay sunshine, so Holmes dropped Rudge off at his home and then drove back to Longcombe. On the way he stopped off to buy a bottle of perfume and the most expensive box of chocolates he could find. He also made a telephone call to Peckham and left a message for

Hackworth. The message said, 'Have two days of extensive enquiries to make in local banks, and interview female suspected of assisting Sir Arthur. Will be back Sunday night'.

Back at Longcombe the old collie welcomed him like a member of the family. By the next morning an exhausted Holmes was really enjoying the benefits of country living, and wished he had said he needed longer to complete his enquiries.

19. Boxing Clever

Luck was on Piggy Swinton's side. The magistrates took a dim view of Mabel's assault on her innocent victim and remanded her in custody for seven days for medical and mental reports. Piggy packed all the belongings into the giant suitcase. Then making use of his new skills as a driver he borrowed a van to take the suitcase back to her parents' home, and dumped it on the doorstep. On his return he carefully parked the van almost where he had found it, and hoped that the unwitting donor would not notice the additions to its collection of dents, or the missing wing mirror.

Despite Mabel's secure accommodation at the government's expense, Piggy was still nervous. He had little doubt that iron bars and locked doors would be little deterrent to Mabel if she wished to be in the arms of her true love. But as the week, passed he was comforted by the absence of red nylon and Party Sevens from his flat. On the Thursday morning he mentioned to Harry Derry that he had a spare ticket for the boxing and wondered if Harry would like it. Harry, who was a widower, was not over-keen on boxing, but enjoyed an occasional outing so he accepted eagerly.

On Thursday evening Piggy was attempting to prepare his dinner when there was a knock on the flat door. His first instinct was to hide, but he realised that the knock was too gentile for Mabel or Big Ernie's thugs so he cautiously opened it. Outside was John Dillon.

"Official business, Piggy!" said Dillon, as he pushed his way into the flat. He handed Piggy a letter. Piggy read it carefully. It started by stating that it had come to the notice of the probation service that he was keeping company with a known criminal, one Mabel Longman. It went on to say that if he did not desist from such association then his parole licence would be terminated.

"Don't worry too much, Piggy. John Walker told me of your predicament and it's as much for your protection as anything. If Mabel attempts to contact you then you can quote the letter, and say that the neighbours downstairs are watching you to ensure you conform."

Piggy wondered how successful such an action would be. But it was better than nothing, and in any case Mabel should be out of circulation for some time to come. He wished he could be more confident of the security of the prison system.

On Saturday night Piggy met Harry Derry outside the *Thomas A'Becket* half an hour before the start of the boxing, and they had a drink in the bar before finding their seats. Piggy, in line with his general expectations of life, assumed that they would be back seats some distance from the ring, behind a pillar or next to a noisy extractor fan. To his surprise they were second row seats a few along from the official timer. Harry was equally surprised at the well-upholstered, armchair-like seat that he sank his weary bones down into. In front of them were Big Ernie and his mother. She was wearing a new maroon evening gown and a string of pearls. Sitting directly behind her, Piggy was convinced he could see traces of brick dust and minute fragments of jeweller's shop window glass on the clasp of the necklace, but it might have been a trick of the light.

Big Ernie turned in his seat to acknowledge Piggy and to comment that Piggy's friends seemed to have been most active on his behalf. Harry was puzzled by the way this well-known local villain spoke to his young assistant. He knew Ernshaw from the frequent photographs in the Peckham Echo, but had no idea his upright young assistant kept such company.

The first bout was a pair of flyweights. They energetically rained blows on each other's puny bodies with giant gloves that put one in mind of a pillow fight. The bout went the distance and one of the men won on points, although Piggy could not for the life of him work out how the judges decided.

The second bout was a pair of heavyweights: one Keith Longman against a modestly named Killer McGrath. The action was more ponderous, but punches when landed accurately had much more power and were clearly effective. On balance, Longman was landing much more than he received and in the fourth round his opponent was beginning to tire. Half way through the fifth Longman spotted Piggy and for a split second his attention was distracted. It was just long enough for McGrath to land a blow to Keith's already disfigured face. Once landed, the blow stunned Keith long enough to allow McGrath to finish the job and put him on the canvas.

Piggy could not help but be alarmed as he realised his small part in the outcome of the match, but in that instant he also saw something else. On the other side of the ring, five rows back, sat Jason Ponsonby.

Piggy turned to Harry. "Guts ache," he said, "I'll be back shortly."

Piggy walked slowly to the exit, but once there he raced outside and searched for Big Ernie's car. He spotted it, with the driver leaning on the front wing smoking.

"Quick. Take me to Gordon Road!"

The driver looked disdainfully at Piggy and shook his head. Piggy, knowing it could be a long time before he got another chance like this one, gambled on Ernshaw being agreeable once he explained what he was up to.

"Big Ernie said it's important!" he said with fingers crossed behind his back.

The driver nodded for him to get in and they demonstrated to the empty streets the enormous power of the Jaguar engine. Piggy wondered how long it would be before he could drive in such a fashion. The man was a wizard behind the wheel. He never hit a single thing in the five-minute drive to the factory.

"I'll only be a few minutes," Piggy gasped as he jumped out onto unsteady feet.

Piggy's route was a repeat of his previous nighttime entry to the place. But this time he went to Dawes's office and grabbed the Oxo tin. The seventh key from it opened the locked door of Ponsonby's room. Inside it was a disappointment. The room mainly housed Ponsonby's clothes and other personal effects. On a table was a case of peppermint cordial and two tins of rat poison. Other than that there was nothing unusual about the room.

Piggy locked up and retraced his steps. The Jaguar drove more sedately back to the Old Kent Road, but still Piggy was back in his seat long before the end of the third bout. He was deep in thought, and not paying attention to what was going on when he heard a voice beside him.

"Hello Harry. I didn't expect to see you here."

Piggy turned to see the freshly bruised face of Keith Longman standing beside Harry.

Harry smiled. "My young assistant here had a spare ticket." He turned to Piggy. "I don't think you have met my previous assistant Reg. This is Keith Longman. Keith this is Reg Swinton."

At the mention of Piggy's name, Keith's eyes, already puffy and half-closed, narrowed further. Piggy wished he had not already used the guts ache excuse as he might need it for real in a moment.

Keith moved along the row so he was directly in front of Piggy. He blocked several people's view, but no one was about to complain. Piggy suddenly realised that it was not he who had distracted Longman, but the presence of Harry at the ringside.

"You the man my cousin Mabel has got engaged to?"

"Yes!"

"And the one she thought was doing her wrong?"

"Yes!"

"Well, best of luck. Mabel has always been a bit wild. Not like the rest of the family at all. The only reason her parents had not thrown her out long ago is because they thought nobody would take her in. Perhaps you're what she needs to quieten her down."

Piggy grinned a foolish grin and held his hand out to Keith's giant paw to shake it. At the same time he realised that Keith had not heard of his legal device to rid himself of his betrothed, and also that Keith now knew his face. His blessings were very mixed indeed.

At the end of the evening Big Ernie turned to Piggy.

"Why don't you and your friend join us for dinner? I fancy Italian tonight."

Piggy realised it was not an invitation, but an order. Big Ernie was going somewhere and he wanted an entourage. He looked at Harry and then nodded to Ernshaw. He wondered how he could get round his use of the car. It certainly would not do to tell Big Ernie that he was working for the local police. He motioned to Ernshaw to drop behind and let his mother lead Harry out.

"I got your driver to take me to the factory earlier. I hope you don't mind. I saw Ponsonby sitting across the ring and thought I'd take a look in a locked room in the factory. Nothing in there but his clothes and personal stuff."

"It would have been nice if you had asked first, young Reg. But I suppose time was of the essence. I understand the local flatfoots traced Sir Arthur to Devon, but he gave them the slip."

Piggy was always impressed with how much Ernshaw knew, but now he wondered if he knew about his conversations with Holmes. And if so, then how?

Squashed in the back of the Jaguar between his mother and Harry, Piggy watched the world go sedately by as they made their way to Deptford. Instead of going to a restaurant, the car pulled up outside an ice-cream factory. Big Ernie got out and stood by the open factory door for the other members of his party to join him. A short, black-haired man with a walrus moustache came out and kissed Ernie on both cheeks.

"You a come in. Everybody, you a come in and meet Mamma. She say you a come tonight and she a do her special ravioli for you."

They were ushered through a workshop into an unexpectedly domestic looking large dining room. A long table covered in a lace-edged tablecloth was set for about twenty people for dinner. Silver candlesticks held burning dark wax candles that made the silver cruets and cutlery sparkle. Several flasks of Chianti stood on a sideboard and the whole effect was of a Mediterranean family home.

Their host shouted a few words through a door and five solidly built young men and two young women came into the room.

"First we a eat and then we talk a business," said their host.

Mamma appeared from the kitchen and greeted them excitedly. Piggy watched as the rather short Big Ernie stooped so she could kiss him on both cheeks. His mother disappeared with Mamma, back into the kitchen, from which was subsequently heard the crashing of pots and pans and the sizzling of meat on hot metal.

Dinner was a real treat, especially for Harry Derry who ate many of his evening meals straight from the tin. It finished with their host's own special variation of tutti frutti, laced with Strega.

The family ran both the factory and a fleet of ice-cream vans. Intense rivalry on the streets had escalated into virtual warfare and a number of their vans had been wrecked recently. A tie-up with Big Ernie would ensure a high level of protection for the family, but at a price. It was the sort of protection policy that the man from the Prudential could not offer.

While their host and Big Ernie went off for a private discussion, the rest of the party were taken for a tour of the factory by one of the sons. Brought up in South London he spoke in that curious mix of English and Italian that schooling had failed to modify.

Eventually they all squashed back in the Jaguar and drove back to Peckham. Harry Derry was conspicuously quiet on the way back. He was wondering how he had become on nodding terms with the infamous Big Ernie, and what the implications were of having Reg Swinton as an assistant.

20.   Sunday, Sunday, So Good to Me

DC Holmes was reluctant to part from his cosy billet in Longcombe. It most definitely had all the comforts of home, certainly more than his police flat in Stockwell. He began to wonder if putting his heart, soul and every hour God made into the job was the best way of using up his allotted span. It was past noon when he finally drove up to the Jet filling station at Longcombe Cross and converted two pounds into eight gallons of four star and several sheets of Green Shield Stamps.

As he cleared Exeter he called the information room to sign out and relinquish his temporary call sign.

"Cheerio m' dearie. You come back and see us again soon," came the response.

Holmes needed no such cajoling. He had already arranged to come back for a week in October and possibly another over Christmas.

They had not yet been able to trace Maggie Sullivan, and Sir Arthur had slipped through their fingers. From a Met point of view the trip was a failure, even if Devon and Cornwall were happy to have broken a poaching gang, seized illegal firearms, arrested a car thief and would-be burglar and found a stash of bonded export spirits at Scrumpydown. It was amazing how cases of glass bottles fell from the backs of lorries with virtually no damage, other than losing the freight information labels.

Traffic was light as he reached the A303 and he began to let his mind play over what little they had established. Certainly Sir Arthur was alive, so Ponsonby was no longer a suspect. It was a pity as he had taken an instant dislike to the man and really did want to find something to arrest him for. Sir Arthur was not only alive but also aware that the police were looking for him so he would probably go to ground somewhere else, and be wary of showing himself. From

Torquay the railway could have taken him anywhere, and buying a ticket to a place from Torquay was no guarantee that he did not get off at an interim station and go on by bus or some other method. Also, they now knew that he was not using his own name.

As he approached Honiton, a blue Cortina passed him. The driver obviously had his foot flat on the floor and the car cut in close in front of him to avoid hitting an approaching coach on a day trip. Holmes swore and was about to reach for the radio when he recognised the narrow head and elephant like ears of the driver: Little Alf, one of Big Ernie's getaway drivers.

He encouraged the Hunter to go a little faster, but despite his best efforts the Cortina slowly edged further away from him as it thrashed along. Holmes watched it for as long as he could before it disappeared past another group of slower moving vehicles.

It was half an hour later when he almost missed the Cortina, parked at a Little Chef. He braked hard and turned into the exit of the car park. A quick look through the window of the cafe found Little Alf and another man sitting with their backs to him watching the young girl behind the counter.

Holmes slipped back to the Cortina, lifted the bonnet and swapped the spark plug leads about. Then he returned to the Hunter and headed on towards London. He felt a bit better knowing that they would take a considerable time before they realised what had happened.

Holmes was tired as he parked the car back at the station and walked up to his desk to see if there were any messages for him. There was one. Shropshire police had added another crime to Sir Arthur's growing sheet. Before leaving Shropshire he had put the farm cottage up for sale and taken a deposit of four hundred pounds from an estate agent who was eager to get the property at a knock down price, and failed to ensure he was dealing with the rightful owner. Holmes smiled. It's nice when little predators get bitten by bigger ones.

Holmes looked through the crime book to see if there was anything interesting there. But there was nothing serious for him, except a sudden increase in failing to stop accidents. They were mostly unwitnessed damaged traffic bollards and other street furniture, but one amused him. A van that smashed a phone-box and knocked a vicar off his bike had two reliable witnesses, but when subsequently traced and questioned, the owner swore that it was parked at the time and he was visiting a lady friend in the council estate.

The 'lady' in question also begrudgingly supported his story. As did several neighbours who complained of the thin party walls and the noisy way in which the man conducted his visits. At the very moment when the accident was happening, one neighbour was actually banging on the wall to complain about the sound, and heard the man interrupt his grunting to swear at her. However, neither the man or his companion could explain how the van's missing wing mirror could have found its way into the vicar's basket on the handlebars of the bike. Holmes made a note to go and interview the vehicle owner next day.

With nothing else that needed his attention he went home and tumbled into bed. Suddenly, after all these years, it seemed cold and lonely there. He fell asleep wondering what the possibilities were of transferring to Devon and Cornwall Constabulary.

* * *

If Holmes had had a good day, then Piggy had not. One of Big Ernie's thugs had woken him at seven o'clock and told him he was expected for Sunday lunch. After the late night the day before, Piggy had intended to have a lay in, with breakfast about noon. Now he found himself summoned to attend the arches and, according to the thug, 'to dress proper for it'. Piggy had no idea what proper dress was for lunch with a local crime boss, but decided it at least needed a collar and tie and clean shoes.

So instead of going back to bed Piggy set about cleaning his shoes, pressing a crease in his best trousers and ironing a shirt. He began to have a small feeling of regret about his decision to separate himself from Mabel and her domestic skills when sober, but the feeling passed as he reminded himself of the downstairs neighbour still in King's College Hospital.

Piggy presented himself at the arches after a rather warm walk that had brought puddles of sweat to his armpits and recoated his shoes in a fine layer of dust. Upon arriving he found that the thug had failed to mention that lunch was around the outdoor pool and the order of the day was shorts and a soft shirt or only swimming trunks. His mother wore a crinkly material one-piece swimsuit with an abundance of frilly additions and flip-flops. Big Ernie was in a Fred Perry tennis shirt over a pair of long trunks with leather sandals.

There were three senior thugs present, each dressed in the uniform of soft shirts and shorts, except for Bald Peter who also took the precaution of wearing a straw hat. Piggy ditched his jacket and tie on a chair and rolled up his carefully pressed shirtsleeves. The telephone rang and one of the thugs answered it before coming and whispering in Ernshaw's ear. Big Ernie scowled at the man.

"I didn't realise you don't swim, young Reg," said Ernshaw. "I find it an excellent way to keep fit."

Before Piggy could reply Ernshaw turned his gaze to Piggy's mother, whose subtle smirk confirmed that Big Ernie was indeed very fit. Piggy had never seen his mother smirk before.

Maria appeared with a tray of tall glasses each containing what looked like a drowned fruit salad. Piggy noted that whilst he and the others sat baking in full sunlight, the glasses each had their own parasol to shield them. Maria approached him and handed him a glass.

Piggy looked at the concoction for some time, wondering how he was supposed to drink it without the pointed top of the parasol removing one of his eyes. Hot and thirsty as he was, he waited until another took their first sip and revealed the technique. Apparently the little umbrella was simply removed to drink and replaced afterwards. Piggy managed the removal but when he replaced the thing afterwards it automatically folded up and floated on the surface, bleeding its purple colour into the tawny liquid. Piggy fished it out and shook it dry, transferring a series of purple spots to his shirtfront and trousers in the process.

It is said that the art of being a good servant is to anticipate your master's needs before he is aware of them himself. Maria was an excellent servant and almost before Piggy had become aware of his deteriorating appearance she was behind him and she gave a discrete cough to attract his attention. As he turned towards her she handed him a pair of swimming trunks and nodded towards a little candy striped changing room on the far side of the patio.

Piggy gratefully accepted the garment and strolled nonchalantly across the patio. Once inside he removed and folded his clothes on the wooden bench and slipped into the swimming trunks. As he tied the cord at the front of the garment a hand that he recognised as Maria's reached through a slit in the canvas material and removed his trousers and shirt. She was gone before he had time to protest.

Piggy stepped out of the changing room onto the patio. It was not a grand entrance. The trunks, long legged Bermuda patterned things in a lurid pattern, were obviously a spare pair of Ernshaw's and were two sizes too big for him. Bunched together at the waist to keep them up he was best described as 'a sack of spuds tied up ugly'. His lily-white puny body and spindly legs did nothing to enhance his appearance.

Bald Peter sniggered as he came out, and Piggy decided that as he had now been humiliated he might as well enjoy the rest of his day. He dived into the pool, only to find that it was considerably colder than he had expected. He gasped for breath as he came to the surface and quickly doggy paddled to the side. As he put a foot on the bottom rung of the short ladder he turned to look across the pool to see what all the merriment was about. Halfway between his seriously amused audience and himself a pair of shorts floated on the surface of the water. He took a moment to recognise the pattern and confirm that they were the same ones as he entered the water in. He then paddled his way across the pool to retrieve the wayward garment before continuing on to attempt a clumsy redressing in the partial privacy of the sidewall of the pool. Eventually he clambered shivering from the water to thunderous applause from the onlookers.

"I'm sorry," said Ernshaw, "I assumed you did not swim, otherwise I would have mentioned that we usually wait until late afternoon when the sun has heated the water. I do hope it was not too cold for you, especially as you seem to prefer to swim without the impediment of clothing."

"No, n,n,n,not at all," replied Piggy through chattering teeth.

As if by magic, Maria appeared behind him. He recognised the gentle cough and turned, just as she held up a thick fluffy robe for him to slip into.

Piggy found lunch to be a novel experience. He only recognised about half of the ingredients of his main course, and the selection of desserts all had names that sounded like those of obscure Mediterranean islands. He settled on something resembling a crusty topped custard and a small, strong, bitter cup of black coffee. It was only after he had drunk it that someone passed him a jug of cream. After lunch Big Ernie and his mother walked down to see the horses, but Piggy felt self-conscious straying too far from the house in what he considered to be a dressing gown. Maria had again disappeared, and there was no sign of his clothes!

Piggy sat in the afternoon sun with Bald Peter and gazed around him. Except when a train rumbled along the top of one of the arches it was difficult to imagine that they were surrounded by industry, and were only a few miles from Central London. After a while Peter got up, walked to a cold box on a side table and came back with two small bottles of beer. He passed one to Piggy.

"I hear you were busy last night. Anything interesting in the factory?"

Piggy did not answer immediately.

"I thought there might be something to lead to this Sir Arthur geyser, but all I found was some clothes, rat poison and some bottles of peppermint."

Bald Peter nodded. "So who's he trying to do in?"

"Sorry?"

"Who is this Ponsonby bloke trying to snuff out?"

"What do you mean?"

Peter sighed. "Look, you take a strongly flavoured drink, like peppermint, and pour some rat poison in. You give it to the mark as a cure for their indigestion, but over a period of time the stomach starts to bleed. If you do it nice and slow, starting with a weak dose then it will be mistaken for an ulcer or something."

Piggy stared at him. It had never occurred to him that the two items were related, they simply happened to be on the same table. He wondered who Ponsonby was planning to poison. He was a mean sod and had no friends in the factory. The only one who he was ever mildly pleasant to had been Fothergill, and Ponsonby had recently sacked him. He was living in the factory because his wife had thrown him out. That left his equally mean and miserly uncle or his wife as potential victims.

Piggy sat and reflected on this revelation all afternoon, right through afternoon tea of cucumber sandwiches. He was still pondering on the facts during a light buffet supper as the sun was sinking and the world was taking on that quality of light that makes everything seem somehow more peaceful than during the bright harsh light of noon. As Piggy balanced a plateful of cheese flan, potato salad and radishes on his lap, he realised that in his pre-occupation with Ponsonby he had forgotten he was still wearing a white bath gown instead of his clothes. He looked round for Maria, but she had disappeared.

"Mum, where's Maria?"

The widow Swinton looked at her watch before replying. "You've just missed her. She finishes at eight o'clock. Did you want her for something?"

"My clothes!" whined Piggy.

"I expect she's washed them for you, dear. Do you need them right now."

"But I need to go home soon, Mum."

Piggy's mother nodded her head before replying."

"Of course dear. You have to get up in the morning don't you. I keep forgetting that you have a job to go to. I'm not used to it you see. Well, I must visit the little girl's room so I'll say goodnight now in case you're gone before I get back."

Piggy looked at his mother in disbelief. She clearly had no inkling that he was referring to walking home in a bathrobe. As soon as she had excused herself one of Ernshaw's men came up and whispered in Big Ernie's ear. He smiled, the big broad smile of a man who had been informed of a forthcoming treat. He watched a blue Cortina drive through the arch and down towards the paddock. He turned to Piggy.

"I'm sorry but business calls. I'll leave Peter to see you out."

Then he got up and walked off towards the stables, humming to himself as he went, and leaving Piggy alone with his minions.

"Time to pack up! The boss won't be back 'til gone dark now!" exclaimed Peter.

Piggy took this as an invitation for him to leave immediately. He took a last look in the changing hut and found his jacket, pants, socks and shoes. He put on his jacket and stuffed the pants in a side pocket. Then he bent down and put on his shoes and socks before plodding self-consciously to the gates.

Piggy did not enjoy his twenty-minute walk home. Dressed in flapping Bermuda shorts and a formal jacket with no shirt he was conscious that no one would believe he was making a fashion statement. He felt, quite rightly, that everyone stared as he passed and was glad to eventually reach the safety of the stairwell to his block of flats. His relief was short lived, for when he stood catching his breath on the fifth floor landing he realised that his front door key was in his trouser pocket, not his jacket!

He brightened as he remembered that a friend of his mother had a spare key two floors above him. He clambered up another two flights of stairs and knocked on her door.

"Hello Mrs Brompton. I seem to have left my key with my mother. Can you lend me her spare?"

As Piggy spoke he suspected that his mother may not have told her friend of her new romantic entanglement and change of address. His suspicions were soon confirmed in Mrs Brompton's face.

"Why? Where is your mother young Reg?"

"She's staying with a friend for a few days. I've been over to see her but had a mishap and forgot to bring my key back with me."

Mrs Brompton eyed Piggy more closely, starting with his bare chest peeking from his buttoned up jacket and travelling down his luridly patterned long shorts to his bare spindly legs. She could not envisage what sort of mishap would have caused the result that stood before her.

"I wondered why I'd not seen her about. Which friend is that dear?"

Piggy took a chance. "It's the Ernshaws. Up near the Bricklayer's Arms."

"I don't think I know them, dear. The only Ernshaw I've heard of is that gangster who runs most of the crime around here. Any connection, dear?"

"I don't know," lied Piggy.

"Then I'm probably mistaken. I thought I saw your mother the other day, riding in that flash Jaguar of his. Just shows how wrong you can be dear. Mind you, he's not the only troublemaker round here. What with them on the fourth floor being carted away by the police and her above me and her man friend having the police round for something or other. There's only your mother and me who are behaving themselves respectably these days. I'll get you that key dear."

Piggy stood on the doorstep while she went for the key. He wondered how Mrs Brompton would take the news of his mother's engagement when she eventually found out. One thing that Piggy was determined of was that he was not going to be the one to tell her.

21. Rainy Days and Mondays

DC Holmes was having an uncomfortable time in the Superintendent's office. Hackworth was not a happy man. He had a three page expenses form to sign, and little to show for it.

"What's this entry here? Meal for informant while pursuing financial enquiries?"

Holmes thought quickly of a way to reword the pub lunch he had provided to Rudge as they went over the evidence, which had expressed itself on paper as the 'chicken in the basket' for two and two pints of Foxes Piddle he had shared with Milly on Saturday night.

"It was a long observation and my informant would have stuck out if she had sat there all night without it. Would have put her at risk, guv."

Hackworth looked up from the form. It crossed his mind that the man was entertaining a woman at the force's expense, but Holmes was one of his few officers who did not rank chasing skirts as their main hobby. He also had on his desk a glowing letter of commendation from the Deputy Chief Constable of Devon and Cornwall for Holmes's assistance in solving several crimes while on their ground. Reluctantly he initialled the form and put it in his out-tray.

"Bit of an expensive do all round, Holmes. So much for your early theory about the man being dead and buried. You missed him by a few hours and now we know he is on to us and using false names. Doesn't look like we will catch him now. And while you were away there were several odd crimes on our own ground. Any idea about that hit and run? The owner of the van seems to have a cast iron alibi."

"I've got it on my list, guv. Personally I think the van was nicked and put back. I suspect a gang of kids joy-riding. Probably the same gang as those driving around knocking over traffic signs. I was thinking of doing some evening overtime observing some of the likely places where they might take the cars from."

Hackworth exploded. "No you don't. You've used up your quota of overtime for the next three months, unless I specifically authorise it. Now go and catch some criminals!"

Holmes left the office and returned to his desk. There were a couple of possible sighting reports from the British Transport Police: one in Bristol and the other in Reading. But they both seemed to be within half an hour of each other so neither seemed to be worth pursuing. Holmes was still racking his brains for a way forward when his telephone rang.

"A Mr Swinton for you at the front desk."

Holmes grabbed his jacket and wandered downstairs.

"Well, Well, Piggy. This must be a first. You coming voluntarily to the Nick. Are you feeling poorly or something?"

"I had a look round like you asked, Mr Holmes. And I think Ponsonby is trying to kill someone."

Holmes stared at Piggy for a moment and then ushered him into a little interview room.

"I think I said the opposite, Piggy," Said Holmes as he formally disassociated himself from Piggy's action. "I distinctly remember telling you not to look in that locked room. But since you have been snooping you had better tell me everything."

Piggy stood silently with a pained expression on his face.

"All right, forget how you came to be in the room. Tell me what you saw there."

Piggy brightened up. "It was mainly just his clothes and stuff. But on a table was a box of bottles of peppermint cordial, and two tins of rat poison. One of the tins had been opened and one of the bottles was out of the box."

Holmes smiled. So he was right about Ponsonby. But who was the intended victim?

"Well done, Piggy. I suggest you do not mention this to anybody else. I owe you a favour and I won't forget that. Any ideas as to who he intends it for?"

"His wife chucked him out and his uncle has him on short money until the factory makes a profit. And if canteen gossip is right he blames a Lionel Dee for the mess the factory is in."

Holmes smiled. Possession of the family home, inheriting the business or revenge. Three motives, but which one was it? He thanked Piggy and showed him out with his usual caution not to speak to anyone else about it. He would start with Lionel Dee. It should be easy to eliminate him as a victim.

"Mr Dee? ... It's DC Holmes. May I come and see you this morning?"

Holmes put down the phone and looked at his diary. He'd make his enquiries about the hit and run first and get to Goose Green about eleven-thirty. He should complete his enquiry about lunchtime. He pencilled in expenses for lunch with an informant. If he was going to be short of overtime for a while then he needed all the expenses he could get.

Back at the council estate Holmes drew a blank. The van owner had a cast-iron alibi, or rather a creaky cast-iron bedstead which gave him an alibi. The more he asked, the more witnesses came forward to assure him that the man was otherwise engaged at the time. His initial suspicion of joy-riders seemed the obvious one, and since they put the van back where they found it, they must come from the estate, or somewhere near it. He would have a word with the collator, but since the owner had been driving it again there was now little chance of fingerprints, and no likelihood of catching anyone, especially not without overtime.

Lunch with Lionel Dee and Stella also drew a blank. No anonymous gifts of peppermint cordial, or anything else. He asked a mystified Lionel to check his milk bottles for punctures in the foil cap and left to visit the estranged Mrs Ponsonby.

Sonia Ponsonby was a bitter woman. Jason had kept her ignorant of his true financial position, and had appeared to work long days at the Brixton factory while she was tied to the home with two small children. Her suspicions had been aroused in October last when she found lipstick on a shirt, but Jason had passed it off as carcass marker used on animal hides when grading them. Similarly he passed off hairs on his jacket collar as from particularly shaggy cattle.

It was only when she spoilt a new coat by sitting on a lipstick in the front passenger seat of their car that she found irrefutable evidence. A particularly lurid, tarty shade of lipstick at that. A further search of the car also turned up a cheap earring squashed in the passenger seat. The lipstick was not the same shade as that she had found on his collar. Under questioning with the aid of a rolling pin Jason had admitted to an affair, but claimed it was only to learn about another company.

Sonia, who having seen the new James Bond film knew that such behaviour was only sanctioned at government level, not in the pie making business, threw him out and dumped his clothes on the front lawn from an upstairs window.

No! Nobody had sent her any peppermint cordial.

Holmes left the woman with the distinct impression that if there was a murder planned within that family, then it would be Sonia Ponsonby facing charges - provided anyone had the heart to prosecute.

That left only Ponsonby's uncle as a potential victim. Holmes started the car and was heading toward Streatham when he got a call.

"Mike Delta eight three, please attend at Surrey Commercial Dock. Unidentified body recovered from the water."

When Holmes pulled up there was a Thames division launch and crew with a body pulled onto a rubber dingy behind the boat. The body was on its right side and wore an Abercrombie coat with a monocle hanging from the top buttonhole. There was a large mole on what remained of its left ear.

A rubber gloved PC was removing possessions from the coat pockets. They included a train ticket from Torquay to Reading and a chequebook in the name of Major Pilkington-Smythe. The PC looked up as Holmes peered down from the wharf.

"Looks like he had a nasty accident. Lost all the fingers on one hand and his face is none too tidy. Could have got trapped in a lock gate, perhaps."

Or a bolt cutter and a lead pipe, thought Holmes. He looked along the dock towards the lock-gate that led to the Grand Surrey Canal.

"Is that gate ever opened?"

"Twice a day to flush the water in the canal and prevent it from becoming stagnant."

Holmes nodded. He guessed that Sir Arthur Brain had attempted to return Big Ernie's money and not appreciated how the man could harbour a grudge. He smiled at the play on the word harbour.

There was a slim possibility that the man had fallen in by accident, so Holmes asked the Thames unit to scout around for a holdall or any other luggage. They left the dingy for a crane to lift and went off steering a zigzag pattern across the expanse of the dock. They later radioed him to say that their search was fruitless.

Holmes arranged for the body to go to the mortuary and returned to Peckham. After contacting the bank that had issued the Major Pilkington-Smythe chequebook, he went to the canteen for a cup of tea. Once he had turned things over in his mind he knocked gently on Superintendent Hackworth's office door.

"Come!"

Holmes opened the door and stepped inside. He stood in front of the desk where Hackworth sat surrounded in paperwork.

"Well?"

"I'll need a positive identification, but I think we have found Sir Arthur Brain."

Hackworth looked up sharply.

"What do you mean by think you have found him? What has the man got to say for himself?"

"Nothing. Thames fished a body out of the dock and it matches our description of Brain. He even had a chequebook in the name of Major Pilkington-Smythe. I've not had time to get a formal ID yet. The bank tells me the account for the chequebook was opened with a cheque from the Babbacombe Building Society and then was emptied this morning for cash."

"No valuables on him, I suppose?"

"Thames are looking, but nothing in the dock. I suppose a bag of money would float, but if it sunk then it's lost."

Hackworth sucked the end of the pencil he was holding. Tracey was not going to want to hear this, which meant that he did not want to hear it either.

"I doubt Brain would have come back to this area of his own accord," said Holmes. "The Babbacombe Building Society and this account seemed to cover more or less all the money we think he might have had, so no reason to come here, and every reason not to."

"That must mean that Ernshaw's men got to him before we did. How on earth did that happen? We were only hours behind him at one point and, according to you Ernshaw's men broke down on the A303 two days later. Unless they were a bluff, and Ernshaw already had him."

Neither man was to know that Sir Arthur had switched trains for Winchester and stayed in the town for a few days before taking to the road to hitchhike north from there. Little Alf had been towed into that city by a breakdown crew who finally worked out that the plug leads had been switched. They got the car running and charged for numerous new parts. Little Alf grumbled, but then had the unbelievable luck to find their quarry standing at the roadside with his thumb in the air. Sir Arthur completed his last major journey in the ample boot of the Cortina whilst his little case of banknotes rode in style on the back seat.

22. Autopsy

Holmes asked Lionel Dee to formally identify Sir Arthur's body. In the absence of any family he was the person who seemed to know him best. Holmes was not aware of Tracey Mulligan's closer long-term acquaintanceship.

Lionel was happy to oblige, and attended the antiseptic mortuary that evening. He had mixed feelings as whilst he detested the man he did not wish him dead. Grant De'War accompanied Lionel and confirmed the identification. He had no such fellow feeling, and was going to meet up with several ex-Goose Green Co-op members afterwards to celebrate.

John Dillon also had mixed feelings when he heard the news. For himself it was the result he would have wished, especially the details of the missing fingers and facial re-arrangement. But he was aware that there was virtually no chance for Tracey to recover her money. If Ernshaw had done the deed, as seemed likely, then he would not honour his agreement to pass on any surplus, as it would be an admission that he was involved. She would not be a happy girl, and with the demise of Sir Arthur there was little reason for her to continue meeting him. He would miss that. Their relationship had been strictly one of mutual vengeance on Sir Arthur, but he considered that they had become friends.

The eventual post-mortem showed that Sir Arthur had been dead when he went into the water, and that death had been around four am Monday morning. The injuries to the man seemed to pre-date death by several hours.

Later that week Dillon met Holmes in *The Squinting Badger*. Holmes was drinking a half of mild. He only drank pints when on overtime and expenses. The two men swapped a number of stories and eventually got round to current cases. Holmes asked Dillon if he knew anything about the Hardcastle Polish Company. Dillon shook his head, then added that he had heard that the fraud squad might find Ponsonby worth watching. A contact of his in the casino business said he thought the man was a heavy gambler and owed money to some unsavoury characters.

"Ernshaw?"

"No, a syndicate that takes bets on boxing matches. And possibly arranges illegal fights in empty warehouses down in Millwall Dock."

"Interesting. What do you know about the factory owner, Sebastian Hardcastle?"

"Not much. He lives in Streatham. He only works three days a week as he is not in the best of health."

"Stomach?"

"No idea. Why do you ask?"

Holmes outlined his suspicions, but without saying how he knew what he did. Dillon frowned and sucked his teeth. Then an idea struck him.

"If Ponsonby is trying to knock off his uncle and you get enough evidence to arrest him, who would look after the factory in his absence?"

"Couldn't say. The only man there with a business brain was Fothergill. But I was there on the day that Ponsonby fired him."

Dillon nodded. He had heard what he needed to know, and an idea was growing in his mind. He made his excuses and left.

An hour later, Dillon was sitting in the *Star of the East* with Tracey Mulligan having what could have been a last meal together, and going over the facts and conclusions.

"Looks like I can say goodbye to my money, John. I don't think taking on Ernshaw is a sensible option. Not without something up my sleeve."

Dillon took the opportunity to take her words literally, and sat back admiring what she did have up her sleeve, and between the two sleeves as well. She grinned at him as she noticed what he was doing and sat more upright to improve his view. Eventually Dillon broke the silence.

"I agree. But think back to Christmas. What did you want to do then?"

"I'd planned to invest in the factory, as you very well know."

Dillon smiled.

"What if I could find a way to further your plan, without too much further capital?"

"But how?"

"DC Holmes thinks Ponsonby is trying to poison his uncle. If Ponsonby was out of the picture do you think you could run the factory?"

Tracey gave him one of those knee-weakening smiles and flicked her hair back from her face.

"I'd need up to date sales and staffing figures. And find some way to get Hardcastle to take me seriously. You know the problem John, and I hear he's a bigoted old man with Victorian attitudes to women in the workplace... Do you have a plan?"

"It would need working on to bring all the strands together at the right time. If Ponsonby was arrested at the same time as Hardcastle became aware that a business study had already been carried out to turn the company around, and Ponsonby had hidden it from him, then who do you think Hardcastle would appoint to run it in his absence?"

"But there's still the problem of his attitude to women."

"Maybe not, provided you show you can do the job better than he can. In the end what matters to him is money."

Tracey took a sip of the house white, grimaced at the taste and then let a grin slowly spread out from her pursed lips to both ears.

"I wonder if we could teach Piggy how to use a photocopier?"

On Friday evening, Piggy let himself into his flat and threw his jacket on the lounge settee. He was beginning to enjoy living by himself. The place was a little untidy, but not excessively so. His wages did not run to many extras to clutter the place. But it was home and, with his mother away, a place of his own. What little spare money he had, he set aside for the day when he would have to find rent on the flat.

He was mashing some potatoes to go with the Kennedy's sausages he had brought in with him when he heard a knock at the door. He wondered why they did not use the doorbell, but went to answer it without fear, as he was now under the protection of Big Ernie. People who previously looked down on him now had an entirely new attitude that included a certain amount of grovelling and toadying.

He opened the door to find both John Dillon and Tracey Mulligan standing there.

"I hope we are not interrupting anything, Piggy," said Dillon with a grin.

Piggy returned the grin. "No, I'm on my own. Just cooking my dinner."

"I think you've been holding out on us, Piggy. But never mind. It was none of our business what you did poking around the factory for the police, until now!"

Tracey spoke in soft silky tones, but Piggy could not miss the undertone of sarcasm, nor the fact that she knew much more than he had told her.

"It was Mr Holmes. He got me to look around 'cause he suspects Ponsonby of summat."

"And that's why we are here. It seems to me that all honest citizens are duty bound to help the police where they can, and I'm sure that you have become a most honest citizen of late."

"I don't understand. I've done all you asked, and now they have found Sir Arthur there's nothing else I can do."

"Oh, but there is, Piggy. And it's to all our advantage for you to do it. I see a bright future for you. In charge of the storeroom at

Hardcastles before Christmas and who knows what dizzy heights in years to come."

"You're kidding me. Harry Derry don't retire until March next year, and there are dozens of people more likely to get his job before me."

"But Mr Derry may retire early, say at Christmas, or perhaps move to a new department on a higher wage. That would help his pension. Besides, without Ponsonby there, the new manager may think you are worthy of promotion."

"What new manager?"

"Sorry, I should have said New Owner."

Piggy looked from Dillon to Mulligan and back several times, but had no idea what they were talking about.

"On the other hand, if you're not interested we can stop right now. You've been extremely helpful to us and to show my appreciation I could have a word with the magistrates and get your Mabel let off with a caution."

Tracey smiled as she spoke, and Piggy went white.

"You wouldn't!"

"But I must. I owe you a favour for all you have done, and I can think of nothing else you would like."

Piggy did not have to think long to come up with something else, but he realised it was not an option. Fleetingly he wondered if she realised the effect she had on men. But the thought was gone in an instant, forced from his mind by the prospect of Mabel at large, with the emphasis on the word large.

"What do you want me to do?"

"Tomorrow morning you're to come over to the probation office and we will teach you how to use some office equipment."

"I'm working tomorrow morning."

"Well never mind. Tomorrow afternoon will do. I'll have some sandwiches made up so you can come straight from work."

"Yes!" Piggy said meekly.

"Oh, and Piggy we really are grateful for what you have done. I almost forgot to give you this."

Tracey reached into her handbag and brought out a little plush box.

Piggy opened it and gazed at the pair of silver cuff-links and matching tie-pin.

"See you tomorrow!" said Dillon as he closed the front door behind them.

Piggy stood for some time before moving. He had mixed feelings. The lovely Tracey still gave his body peculiar feelings whenever they met, and only friends give each other presents. Deep inside he still knew that his life was not his own yet, despite it being much better than he could have dreamt on that day when he was released from Brixton.

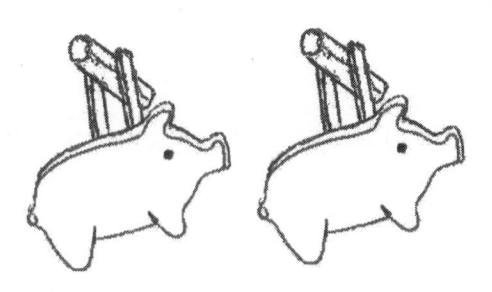

He returned to his cold mashed potatoes and wondered how to revive them. He was still wondering when he heard another knock on the door. Piggy rushed to open it hoping for a few more minutes with Tracey, but to his disappointment it was DC Holmes.

"I hope I'm not interrupting anything, Piggy."

"No, Mr Holmes," said Piggy miserably.

"I need your help, Piggy. I think Ponsonby is up to something serious, but can't get the evidence without your help."

"What can I do?"

"I need a legitimate reason to get in that locked room, and to do so without Ponsonby knowing I'm coming."

"But how can I help with that?"

"You can start by drawing a map of that corridor and describing what is in the rooms either side of it. Does he go to visit his uncle or does the uncle come to the factory?"

"I don't know. I'll ask around."

"Do it carefully, Piggy. If Ponsonby were to get wind of anything I would not give much for your chances. Remember that this is a man who would murder his own family."

Piggy shuddered. "How do you propose to get in the room, Mr Holmes?"

"You're going to set fire to the room next door! I'll let you know when, but I suggest you think about how you are going to go about it. I'll be in touch."

Holmes smiled at the jaw-dropped Piggy and turned to leave.

"Goodnight Piggy. Enjoy your dinner."

At the front door Holmes paused and sniffed the air.

"You've not taken to wearing perfume have you, Piggy?"

Piggy did anything but enjoy his dinner. He decided not to attempt to revive the mash and ate it cold. He plastered it with liberal quantities of 'Daddies Sauce' but it did little to improve it. To compensate he followed it with a tin of peaches that he had been saving for Sunday. He had no idea why he was saving it, other than he had the notion that Sunday dinner should be special. But sadly the peaches failed to improve his enjoyment of his evening meal. He found himself reflecting nostalgically about cauliflower cheese in the mess hall at Brixton.

Saturday morning at work was a time to tidy up and catch up on any backlog of orders. Piggy clocked in at eight-thirty, and Harry Derry arrived an hour later. As they worked, Piggy chatted about the factory in general and worked the conversation round to who really owned it.

"Do we ever see him? I wouldn't want to run his toes over with the trolley without recognising him." Piggy laughed as he spoke but waited anxiously for Harry to reply.

"He comes in once a month, last Friday in the month and takes any profits that haven't been spent on wages and materials. He spends an hour in the boardroom going over the books with Ponsonby and then leaves."

"Must be nice to have a rich uncle to give you a posh job. I bet he has a big house and all."

"Don't know about that, but he has a place at Streatham and another in Gloucestershire."

"I wish I had a big house. Don't think I'd invite Ponsonby to it though."

Harry laughed. "Nor does Hardcastle. From what I hear he's not been out the factory for weeks. No I tell a lie. We saw him at that boxing match. But that car of his has not moved for some time."

Piggy nodded but did not reply.

"That reminds me, young Reg. I didn't thank you properly for that. I never expected to go out to dinner afterwards. Best grub I've had in a long while, even if it was Italian. I never knew you moved in such circles. I'll have to mind my manners around you."

"It's not me. It's my Mum. She knew Ernshaw when he was an honest motor trader."

"From what I hear there was nothing honest about his motors. Clocked back and rusty bodies filled with paper and sawdust was what I heard."

"I don't know about that. Long before my time."

The morning passed quickly and at noon they closed the store and clocked out. Piggy headed for the probation office where he found both Dillon and Tracey. Apart from them the building was empty.

Over a lunch of corned beef and spam sandwiches they set about teaching Piggy how to use a photocopier. In particular they emphasized the need to leave the machine looking exactly how he found it, with the same amount of paper and toner and switched on or off as before.

After lunch Tracey reached in her handbag and brought out a strange looking device.

"It's a camera. A Minox B. You'll have to use it for anything that you cannot get in the photocopier. We'll have a practise this afternoon."

About four-thirty Dillon decided that Piggy had learnt all he could about the equipment and left him to Tracey to describe what it was he needed to copy. He nipped out and returned about five o'clock with cod and chips for three.

As Piggy bit into the hot battered fish he hesitated for a moment. Tracey noticed immediately.

"Is there something you want to tell us, Piggy?"

"Mr Holmes wants me to set fire to the factory."

Both Dillon and Tracey adopted his mouth open pose, and stared at him.

"I don't think he wants a big fire. A bit of smoke really, enough for him to come in with the fire brigade and accidentally find what's in the locked room."

"Best that you tell us all, Piggy."

"He's sure that Ponsonby is poisoning his uncle, but can't get the evidence without getting into the room. So he needs the fire to have an excuse to break in."

They completed their meal in silence, wiping their oily fingers on the outer wrapper, thus de-oiling them but smearing them with newsprint.

"When does Holmes want you to do this?"

"Don't know. He'll tell me when he's ready."

There was little more to say, other than that Dillon would let Piggy know when they were ready for him to do his bit. They needed a plan to get Ponsonby out of the way. They locked up and went their separate ways.

Piggy wandered slowly home, where he found one of Big Ernie's thugs waiting for him.

"The boss is holding a surprise party for your mother tomorrow night. You'll be picked up at seven."

Piggy nodded. He noticed the subtle change in the man's demeanour compared with earlier visits. Being a future stepson of Big Ernie certainly improved his health prospects.

Piggy nodded and went up to his flat. It was quiet and secluded inside and he planned to stay there as long as he could. But it was not to be. As he boiled the kettle for a mug of tea there was a knock at the door. A heavy knock.

Piggy cautiously opened the door to see Keith Longman and two equally ugly friends standing outside. Piggy froze. Running would be useless as they blocked the only exit.

"I know it's short notice, Reg, but I've got a spare ticket for the boxing, and since you are almost family I thought you might like to come along."

It took Piggy a while to take in what Keith had said. He forced a smile and muttered about having plans, then shrugged his shoulders and reached for his jacket.

"Are you not boxing tonight?" asked Piggy as they walked down the stairs.

"Not tonight. I hurt my hand last time and it's taking its time healing."

As he spoke Longman thumped Piggy on the back. Piggy presumed it was a friendly gesture, but one he would not want repeated too often, even from an injured hand.

Longman's tickets were not for the comfortable second row that Big Ernie had previously given him, but a hard bench at the middle of a back row. When they arrived, Longman introduced Piggy to a number of family members. Piggy was relieved to see that Mabel's grandmother was not there. It was obvious that Mabel had spread a somewhat different story to the actual facts, and cast Piggy as a romantic who went down on one knee to make his matrimonial offer.

It was equally obvious that no one blamed Piggy for her subsequent remand. Piggy was being accepted into the ranks of a family that he had no wish to join. Apart from Keith Longman there were several other cousins who engaged in violent sports. Sitting on the bench there were nine uncles, aunts and cousins in all, each yelling their heads off as they encouraged their favourite competitor to do bodily harm to his opponent. Two hundred years ago this family would have had season tickets for front row seats at the hangings on Tyburn Tree. One bright spot was when Piggy spotted Ponsonby on the other side of the ring in the company of a somewhat under-dressed woman. He made a lavatorial excuse during the third bout and slipped outside. There was no sign of Ponsonby's car anywhere.

After the last bout, Keith suggested they adjourn to a kebab house up the road. Squashed between two of Mabel's muscular cousins at a rickety table, Piggy sat quietly as they ate shish kebab and salad. The presence of so many sharp pointed sticks in the hands of his betrothed one's relatives made him nervous. He also found it strange that no one mentioned Mabel or her current incarceration over the whole evening, other than at his initial introduction.

Eventually they spilled out on to the pavement of the Old Kent Road and went their separate ways. Piggy found himself walking with Benny and Dennis, two of Mabel's cousins who lived near him.

"You're a brave man, Reg, but maybe Mabel will settle down now she has found the right bloke. The last one who trifled with her got a broken arm before he fled somewhere," said Dennis.

"No, that was the one before, Dennis. The last one spent a month in hospital with head injuries," interrupted Benny.

"I thought that was the little Greek bloke. No! I tell a lie, there was another between them two. What was his name now? Bert Howard! Bert Coward more like. I've never seen a man cry so much as he did when he heard she got off with a fine and was looking for him."

As they walked, Dennis and Benny continued to entertain Piggy with similar stories about the string of miserable wrecks that littered the wake of Mabel's love life. Piggy became more and more fearful with each step. Finally they came to a junction where they parted company, and Piggy scurried home. As he locked the front door of the flat behind him he wondered if the council could provide something sturdier than the thin plywood and glass construction that struggled to keep the wind out, let alone a determined Mabel.

Next morning Piggy was woken early by the telephone. It was only as he picked up the receiver that Piggy remembered that there was not a telephone in the flat. He stared at the object in his hand and wondered if his memory was playing tricks, or if he was still asleep and having yet another odd dream.

"Hello!"

"Hello Reg, is that you? Of course it is. Nobody else would be there at this time."

"Mum?"

"Of course, dear. Wasn't it nice of Ernie to install a telephone for you. Now we can chat whenever we want to."

Piggy sank into a chair as he listened to his mother. Until that moment the flat had been a haven from the outside world, but even that was now taken from him.

"There's someone at the door, Mum. Bye. I'll see you tonight."

Piggy put the phone down and sighed. Then he remembered that the party was supposed to be a surprise. Life was never this complicated in Brixton. He got dressed and wondered what to do with his day. He decided to go out before his mother rang back to remind him what a nice man Big Ernie was, or ask why he was seeing her later that day.

At lunchtime he found himself in the Old Kent Road and bought himself a takeaway kebab. He was almost getting to the point where his hunger was satisfied and he was beginning to speculate about what kind of meat it was, when the blue J4 van stopped alongside him.

"DC Holmes has been looking for you, Piggy. He says to tell you to meet him at the station tomorrow at six pm."

"Yes, Mr Walker."

* * *

Mrs Swinton's engagement party was a lavish affair. Petty criminals from as far away as Lewisham and Deptford attended to pay their respects to Big Ernie. Piggy's mother was showered with gifts, many of which would make the top ten of that week's stolen property list.

At about ten o'clock Ernshaw drew Piggy to one side.

"It's about time you met a few of the boys, young Reg. When the guests have gone we'll have a little chat in the pool room."

An hour later Piggy noticed most people were drifting off, and Bald Peter motioned to Piggy to follow him. In the pool room there were a dozen or so men one side of the pool, with Big Ernie sitting on a chair opposite. As they approached Ernshaw beckoned to Piggy to join him on his side of the water.

"Gentlemen, I want to introduce you to my future step-son, Reg. Young Reg has only recently returned from a spell in Brixton and I want you all to make him feel welcome around the manor."

There were nods from assorted dangerous-looking characters as they weighed up the new member of the family.

"Now to business." continued Ernshaw, "Knosher, what happened to that jewellers we were casing?"

"He went bust the day before the blag, gov. We turned up in the motor and rammed an empty window."

Ernshaw shook his head sadly.

"What is the country coming to? It makes it hard to make an honest living these days."

Several others reported their own exploits of the previous week, including one who had burnt out an ice-cream van depot. Piggy guessed that Ernshaw was fulfilling his end of the bargain with his Italian dinner host of the previous week.

"Now Reg. You go off with Charlie here and tell him what you can about the factory. You can start with where they keep the wages overnight, and what time on a Friday that they pay out."

Piggy was stunned. He had not expected Ernshaw to include him in his activities, certainly not so soon. Six months ago he would have jumped at the opportunity to conspire with such renowned villains. But to his surprise he found the idea distasteful.

23. Piggy in the Middle

Straight from work on Monday, Piggy walked round to the police station and asked to see Holmes.

"You're early Piggy. Come through."

Piggy followed Holmes into a small bare interview room.

"I see you were up at the arches last night. I don't think your probation officer would be happy about that."

"I had no choice Mr Holmes. It was Mum's engagement party."

Holmes looked at Piggy for some time before speaking.

"No choice indeed! But you need to tread carefully."

Piggy nodded glumly.

"You know I'm not a grass, Mr Holmes. But they are planning something. I'm trying to go straight. Honest I am."

"What are they planning?"

"A wages snatch at the factory."

Holmes said nothing for a while, but then he got up and went to the door. He stuck his head out and beckoned a young PC.

"Get me two teas from the canteen lad, and see if you can find some biscuits."

"Well Piggy, you are in a pickle. You had better tell me all, and we will see what we can do."

Piggy related his previous evening's events and Holmes listened patiently. The tea arrived as he was finishing his tale.

"How far is the safe from the locked room we are interested in?"

"It's two doors away."

"So," conjectured Holmes, "if the gang made a mistake and went for the wrong room, and if, purely by chance, a uniform PC happened to be passing at the time, then we might catch them and have a look at the room at the same time... would save creating our own reason for a visit."

"But I think they want to take me along. To make sure I'm committed."

Holmes shook his head.

"You'll be committed all right, if uniform recognise you. Even if you do escape at the time. We need to keep you out of the building somehow. When are they planning to do it?"

"They've not said yet. But I think it's probably on a Thursday night. Hardcastle comes and clears the takings on the last Friday of the month, so the most money would be in the safe the night before."

"Hmmm, that gives us three weeks!"

The two sat in silence for a while before Holmes got up.

"You'd better slip out through the yard. We don't want you being spotted leaving do we? Call me when you hear something more definite."

"That's easy Mr Holmes. Big Ernie installed a telephone in the flat so Mum and I could chat."

Holmes frowned. "Best not to use that phone Piggy. You don't know who might be listening in, or being given a log of your calls. Ernshaw may not trust you as much as you think."

Holmes's words sent a shudder through Piggy. He knew of the demise of Sir Arthur, and like Holmes, he was in no doubt about who was responsible. He had no wish for a similar fate.

Piggy left through the yard and into the quiet street behind. Then he made his way to *The Flatulent Fox* where Mabel's family did much of their drinking. Oddly he now felt safer surrounded by her pugilistic relatives who only a short while ago he went out of his way to avoid. He found Dennis and bought him a drink. He steered the conversation on to boxing, about which he knew virtually nothing, but his interest was in when the next bout was arranged at the *Thomas A'Becket*. The next night when he could be reasonably sure that Ponsonby was out of the factory.

"Wednesday week. It's an ABA eliminator round. If Keith's hand is okay, then he stands a good chance of winning."

That was exactly the information that Piggy needed, a high profile evening. Ponsonby was bound to attend. Piggy made his excuses and left the pub. It was a good walk down the Old Kent Road to Peckham Hill Street and Piggy bought a bag of chips to keep him company. As he turned off into the less well-lit road by the library he looked around cautiously. He noted each potential bolthole as he passed it and was glad when he came out on the busy Camberwell Road. By the time he reached the safety of home he was drenched in sweat, yet felt chilly.

Piggy changed his damp shirt and made himself a mug of tea. There was not much to eat except a packet of Vesta curry. He settled down in the lounge and began to read the instructions on the packet. Ten minutes later he gave up and tossed the packet on the seat beside him. As he got up to turn the television on the doorbell rang.

Piggy frowned. Most of his recent visitors had ignored the bell-push and thumped on the flimsy door. He answered the ring to find Tracey standing there. He also saw Mabel trundling along the walkway towards him.

"Yes Miss? What can I do for you?" he said in as loud a voice as he could without it being obvious, meanwhile frantically swivelling his eyes towards the approaching hulk.

Tracey glanced to her right at the approaching fiancée and then replied in a voice loud enough for Mabel to hear.

"Have you found Jesus?"

"What?" said the slower witted Piggy.

"Have you let Jesus into your life? We of the Church of Jehovah have found great peace and we wish to share it with you. Joining our congregation can give you utter calm and tranquillity, as well as ensuring an everlasting spiritual contentment."

At this point Mabel came within arm's length of this, to her, unwelcome visitor.

"Bugger off. He's mine. If he wants tranquillity he can have it in bucket-loads, just for the asking: starting right now."

Tracey turned to Mabel and gave her a beautiful smile.

"Hello Madam! Can I interest you in eternal life? You look like a soul that has suffered its share of torment."

Mabel snarled and raised her right fist.

"I can see you are busy. Perhaps if you find time tomorrow, you may wish to attend one of our services. Our church is by the town hall, and the six o'clock service is popular."

She turned her head to Piggy as she said, "six o'clock," and then stepped back as Mabel wedged herself between them. Moments later she was looking at a closing door. But a quick thrust with her foot halted the swing.

Inside, Piggy quaked as Mabel pushed him towards the bedroom. Obviously she was in no mood for small talk or preliminaries.

"I am so sorry for doubting you, my love. I should have realised when you got a job that you were serious about starting afresh."

Piggy had forgotten that Mabel was scheduled to attend court that morning. He was also puzzled as to what idiot of a magistrate could have possibly let her out to walk the streets.

"How did you get on?"

"Don't tease me, darling. You know very well that it was you who got Big Ernie to ask Mr Florribund to defend me. I was annoyed at first when you did not show up in court to watch, but Mr Florribund explained that your presence might imply that I associated with criminals and so prejudice my case.

He was wonderful. He spoke of my broken home and my unhappy childhood and said that I was trying to put my life in order. He told the magistrate that I had recently got engaged to a responsible young man with a steady job, and a custodial sentence would severely set back my rehabilitation. He said that I promised to join AA and was looking forward to making wedding plans. One of the magistrates was so moved she had to wipe away tears."

"AA? I didn't know you could drive... But what was the result?"

"I got a suspended sentence. So we are free to make our plans, and I must make it up to you for doubting you, even if I was drunk."

At this point she pushed him backwards onto the bed and seemed to topple herself on top of him, banging her head against his as she fell. Things went black and for a moment her voice floated away into the distance. Then Piggy knew no more.

24. Peace at Last?

Even before he woke up properly, Piggy knew he was not in his own bed. The sheets felt too crisp and there was a distant hum of activity and the occasional squeak of rubber soles on varnished wood floors. Faint smells of ether, iodine and perfume mingled in his nostrils, each competing for his attention. He kept his eyes shut as he let his mind test each part of his body: legs were okay, arms were okay, chest hurt like hell each time he breathed in, head throbbed in time to his pulse.

He cast his mind back to try to remember what had happened. He remembered Tracey at the door. Then he remembered falling backwards with a great weight on top of him. Little details began to return and he groaned.

"Nurse! He's coming round."

It was his mother's voice. He opened his eyes and looked about. There beside him was his mother. Behind her was a hospital locker with a vast array of flowers ,and beyond that were the clean bright walls of a single bed side ward.

"Where am I?"

"St George's, Hyde Park Corner. So much nicer than the local hospitals. But I don't know why they brought you here. It's much further for me to visit and it's costing Ernie a fortune to park on the ambulance bay downstairs."

"How did I get here?"

"Bit of a mystery that. Apparently that nice Jehovah's Witness lady said she heard a crash and looked in the window to see you pinned under a collapsed Mabel. Mabel's in King's College with a nasty bump on the back of her head. She cannot remember what happened either. It was lucky that nice lady was there. She phoned for an ambulance and the first one brought you here. Then a police van turned up and took Mabel to King's. She's in the secure ward there. Something about breach of bind over conditions. I'm afraid that it looks like she may be away for a while.

Silly girl really, after all the effort I put into persuading Ernie to get Florribund to defend her.

There's one thing I don't understand. The bed was broken, but if that was where you fell then you cannot see it from the front door window."

Piggy's mum prattled on for half an hour until a nurse came in and suggested that she leave to let him get some rest. Piggy had his eyes closed at the time and was just making the odd murmured response to let the world know he was awake, but he recognised that silky seductive voice and that perfume. He opened his eyes to see a face framed by heavy black-rimmed Buddy Holly glasses with neatly bunned blonde hair and a smile that made his knees go weak. Laying down he was not sure how he registered the state of his knees - he just knew it. She placed her long manicured red nailed fingers on his wrist as if to take his pulse. If she had done so it would not have been a typical resting rate.

"He's very weak. Come back tomorrow. He will be a lot better then."

Mrs Swinton unquestioningly obeyed the voice of authority and picked up her empty shopping bag. At the door she smiled at her son and frowned at the ridiculously pretty nurse who was wiping his brow with a wet sponge.

"If that don't put his blood pressure up I don't know what will," she muttered to herself as she squeaked along the polished corridor.

"I'm sorry Piggy. I never meant to hurt you."

"You didn't. Mabel fell on me."

"Only because I coshed her!"

Piggy stared at Tracey. It was pointless asking how she managed to be standing in front of him in a crisply-starched staff nurse's uniform. There was probably a surgeon somewhere liberally splashing on the Yardley Black Label in anticipation of an exotic evening.

"You're not badly hurt, only bruised, but if we exaggerate your injuries then it will solve your Mabel problem for a while. I've had a word with Ernshaw and now he knows the truth about Mabel, he agrees it was a mistake to let your mother persuade him to get Florribund to represent her."

"You've had a word with Ernshaw?"

"Yes. He was most reasonable after he read the copy of the file I gave him. If it became public, then he would be joining Mabel in secure accommodation. Well, not joining, but sharing the experience anyway. He's begrudgingly admitted that he may have made an accounting error and now finds he has a sum left over that he has no right to. Not the full sum I lost, but a good proportion of it."

Piggy's jaw dropped and she gently put her hand under his chin and pushed it back shut.

"But I still want you to get that information for me. Ernshaw has decided to bring the boxing match forward a week. Did you know he half owns the gym? Well, anyway he had to phone round the season ticket holders to tell them, and it's clear that Ponsonby will be attending.

You lay here and put it on a bit. John will pick you up about seven tomorrow and have you back in your hospital bed before midnight, with a watertight alibi. I think Ernshaw will be in to see you later. He seems to be anxious to speak to you."

Piggy grunted. He probably wanted the floor-plan of the factory.

She smiled at him and reached for the huge bunch of black grapes that sat in a glass bowl on the top of the locker. She broke off two and put one in his mouth before biting the other.

"Can you get a message to Mr Holmes? Tell him that Ernshaw has brought forward the boxing and say Ernshaw is after a floor plan. He will understand."

She nodded, kissed her finger and rubbed it on Piggy's forehead. She then left him alone. When she had closed the door Piggy squealed in delight.

Piggy was dozing later that afternoon when he became aware of the smell of coffee, and the noise of the occasional slurp. He opened one eye to see Holmes sitting in a chair beside him, filling in an expense sheet entry for refreshment bought for an informant.

"Ah, Piggy, awake at last. Some delightfully voiced woman phoned me and said we needed to have a chat. Didn't give her name, but if perfume could come down a telephone wire I bet it would have been *Evening in Paris*. A bit of luck you being in here. Seems you may be able to help me and safely establish an alibi for being somewhere else at the same time."

Piggy glowered at him. He was not feeling lucky. But Holmes ignored him and went on to outline a plan. Piggy was to provide Ernshaw with verbal directions to the room containing the safe. But, injured as he was, he could be forgiven for giving vague directions to Ernie's men. Both the door they wanted and the locked one were brown with a cream lower panel. All the other doors in the area were plain brown.

"Ernshaw is going to hit the factory at 9 o'clock tomorrow evening. He's not waiting for the end of the month. Ponsonby drinks Scotch when watching the boxing, and his second drink will be drugged. Fingers Fisher came in to see me earlier. They have chosen 9 o'clock because it is almost dark and less chance of being recognised by passers-by."

"How many?"

"Don't know! Fingers will probably drive. Then there would be someone to blow the safe, and probably another two to carry and provide muscle if need be."

Holmes grinned.

"Suppose that the Indian restaurant got generous and the Q car crew wanted to find somewhere quiet to enjoy a curry with a few bhajjis and poppadoms. That road behind the factory would be just the place. And what with all the car windows open to keep the air sweet, any unusual noise would be bound to be heard."

"They would need to be in place about a quarter past nine, Mr Holmes. Any earlier and they may be seen. I've heard that Big Ernie gets Bald Peter to take the dog for a walk round the area before a job, and they don't start until he gives them the nod."

Holmes nodded.

"It's a shame you'll miss all the fun, Piggy. What with you being in here. Still at least no one will doubt where you are, or why. Incidentally I hear they are moving Mabel to the infirmary at Holloway tomorrow. My guess would be than her latest arrest leaves you in the clear for a good six months."

Piggy nodded. He still had mixed feelings about Mabel, despite the bruised ribs. She was good around the house and the only woman who had ever been actually eager for his body instead of begrudgingly willing. Perhaps prison would give her time to lose both her drink habit and some weight, but somehow he doubted it.

"Well, I'll let you rest. I expect they will have you up in a day or two."

Holmes put away his expenses sheet and stood to leave. Piggy closed his eyes, but if he hoped to be left to rest he was mistaken. Heavy steps resounded along the corridor, heralding the arrival of Keith, Dennis and Benny Longman. Holmes adopted the authoritative air of a doctor and cautioned his new visitors not to excite the patient, then he slipped out of the room.

The three new visitors ignored the stern advice. They were in an ebullient mood. Keith's hand had healed well, and both he and Dennis were on the bill for Wednesday night. Despite the fact that Mabel was about to serve her stretch in Holloway, they still saw Piggy as a family member in misfortune. They deposited magazines, about boxing naturally, and a crossword puzzle book on his locker and enquired after his health. Piggy milked it for all he was worth, mindful of establishing his alibi for the following evening.

Eventually they left to spend the rest of the evening in the gym, parting from Piggy with wishes for a speedy recovery. Piggy closed his eyes again in hope of some peace and quiet.

Wednesday passed slowly for Piggy. In some ways it was like being in prison, despite the stream of attentive pretty nurses. But at six-thirty an orderly came in to say he was being sent down for X-ray.

Piggy became alarmed until he saw the man anxiously looking out of the window.

"Car's here," he said. "Hop on the trolley."

The man wheeled him out and into a lift. Half a floor down, he stopped the lift and reached under the trolley for a bag containing a boiler suit and a pair of plimsolls.

"When you get back, go to the rear entrance by the laundry cages."

The man restarted the lift and they went down to the ground floor where Piggy got out and the man pointed him towards a side exit. Outside stood the Morris Oxford. Dillon was driving and Tracey was in the front passenger seat. Piggy did not recognise her at first. She had her hair tied back in a ponytail and she was wearing a similar dark blue boiler suit to the one he had on. Somehow it looked nicer on her.

"We're not going to have much time, so I'm coming in with you."

Piggy sat and stared. This was something he had not bargained for.

At ten past seven they approached the factory. Dillon dropped them and drove off.

"Where's he going?"

"Too risky to stay here. He's going to park up by the phones at the bus garage. I've got their numbers and we'll ring when we've finished."

Piggy was not sure of this. He had always worked alone, and a female accomplice, no matter how beautiful and clever, was bound to be a problem.

They quickly found the stack of pallets on the loading bay and Piggy soon had the storeroom window open. Their first problem was squeezing Tracey through the narrow window that the pigeon chested Piggy slipped through without a second thought. But once inside they raced for Ponsonby's office and began to copy as much as possible. From there to Sales and finally Piggy left Tracey photographing staff pay records while he went to Tom Dawes's office to find a key for the locked room.

Piggy looked at his watch as he unlocked the door. A quarter past eight. The room looked much as it had before. One tin of rat poison was half-empty and there were only nine bottles of the peppermint cordial on the table. He raced along to borrow the Minox from Tracey and took a few photographs.

Before they left the way they had come in, Tracey picked up the phone on Harry Derry's desk and dialled a number.

It seemed like forever before John Dillon answered.

"All done!"

Once she had squeezed through the window Tracey made for the service road while Piggy put the pallet back on the loading bay. As he turned towards the road he saw a maroon car pass the entry in Gordon Road. It was still not quite dark and Piggy felt very self-conscious as he walked along the pavement towards it.

Tracey was already in the front passenger seat and Piggy resumed his familiar position on the back. John Dillon drove off and turned the lights on as he came to the junction. As they sped towards Camberwell New Road Piggy saw a man walking his dog: a short bald man with a large hairy dog. He ducked down in the back of the car as they passed him.

Tracey wriggled out of the boiler suit to reveal her more normal attire underneath. She shook out her hair and reached in the glove box for a perfume atomiser.

"Pass me those shoes, Piggy."

She smiled as she kicked off the plimsolls and slipped into her familiar red heels. At five to nine the Morris dropped Piggy at the rear of St George's Hospital. A man standing by the laundry bins dropped his cigarette and stamped it out before nodding to him.

As Piggy rolled off the trolley onto the floor of his single side ward room he thought for a moment that the porter had brought him to the wrong room. Someone appeared to be asleep in his bed. But a quick flick of the sheets revealed it to be just a row of pillows and a mop-head. The porter removed them and left.

Piggy climbed into bed and smiled. Yet again he had committed a crime and not got injured, and best of all he had a watertight alibi.

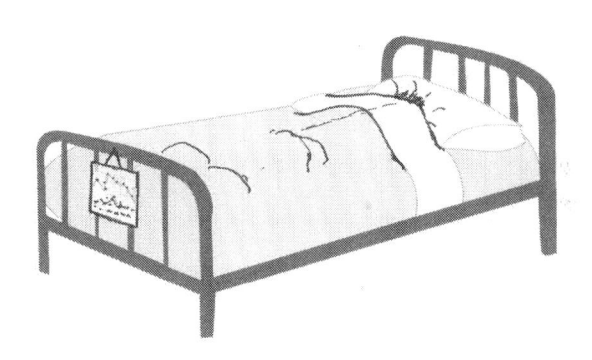

25. Caught in the Act

On Thursday morning, Mrs Swinton went to see her son in hospital. She was not happy. Big Ernie had been on the telephone most of the night and was in a foul mood, and she had to travel by bus instead of car. Ernshaw's driver, Fingers Fisher, was nowhere to be found, and apparently a business deal had gone wrong. She did not know any details, other than about the missing driver.

"Ee never showed up to take us home from the boxing. There we were, standing by the car with no driver. At first Ernie said he was doing a little errand for him, and he would be along in a minute. But he went into the pub to make a phone call and came back out in a foul mood. Eventually Bald Peter came and drove us home. But Ernie was up all night and was gone when I got up this morning."

Piggy listened attentively to his mother. Whilst she was talking that attractive blonde nurse came in and smiled at them both.

"Mrs Swinton?"

"Yes!"

"Doctor says that after he's seen Reg this morning he thinks he may be able to go home. Have you got some outdoor clothes for him? I'm afraid the surgical team got a bit carried away and cut his shirt off to check on his injuries without moving his arms too much."

The nurse smiled and left, leaving behind a residual trace of perfume. Mrs Swinton departed soon after to get Piggy a shirt and jacket, and the nurse returned as soon as she had gone.

Piggy smiled as Tracey re-entered the room.

"John tells me that Holmes had a busy night last night. It's amazing how much police work is a matter of luck. Apparently an unmarked police van was parked behind the factory while the crew ate an Indian takeaway and they heard an explosion. They called for backup and went in to find a mob breaking into the safe. It really was a stroke of luck. Apparently the mob broke into the wrong room first and that delayed them. If they had not done so the crew would have missed the explosion. They would probably have noticed the broken front door though.

Must have been quite noisy all round. The getaway van made a break for it and there was a long chase before they cornered the driver up by Rotherhithe.

Odd thing is that the police also arrested the factory manager for something or other."

She grinned and Piggy laughed. His laugh quickly turned to a grunt as the movement of his chest reminded him of his bruised ribs.

"I've got a lot to do today so I'll leave you in peace."

She turned and left Piggy to speculate on the events of the previous evening.

Shortly after Tracey's departure lunch was served. Piggy was hoping his Mother would return soon, but instead he got an unexpected visitor.

"Hello Harry! What are you doing here?"

"I thought I'd pop in in my lunch hour, young Reg. It's been chaos at the factory this morning. Somebody broke in last night, but the police caught them. And Ponsonby is nowhere to be seen. Probably at the police station helping them out. Hardcastle arrived just before I left so I can't stay long. Funny thing is I keep thinking I can smell perfume in the stores. *Evening in Paris,* like my old lady used to wear. I must be going crackers in my old age. I can smell it now as well."

"I didn't know you were married Harry," said Piggy, anxious to change the subject.

"Been widowed ten years now. She found a lump and kept quiet about it instead of going to the doctor. I never smell that perfume without thinking of her."

"I'm sorry Harry," said Piggy quietly, but he felt it an inadequate reply and the following silence embarrassed both men.

"Doctor says I should be able to go home later today. I'll be off for a few days but I'll see what I feel like on Monday."

"Nah, you take your time. I can manage for a while. What happened to put you in here anyway?"

"It's a bit embarrassing. Mabel fell on me."

"Your Mabel? I heard she has been arrested again. Not just for falling on you surely?"

"It's a long story Harry. She breached her bind-over conditions to come and see me. So when the police came with the ambulance they arrested her."

"You youngsters do make life complicated for yourselves. In my day courting was a much quieter affair, and a lot longer. It was four years before me and the missus were allowed to be alone together: not until after the wedding."

Piggy smiled. He wished that he could put Mabel off for four years.

"I'm not sure there will be a wedding. Mabel will be away for six months."

"You'd better watch yourself, Reg. The Longmans are a bit funny about their womenfolk. They might get it into their heads that you're to blame."

"That's odd as well. Keith, Dennis and Benny have been in to see me. All very friendly like. Seems Mabel is the exception to the rule. Perhaps they think she can look after herself."

Harry laughed.

"Do you know how the boxing went?"

"Keith Longman won on points. Don't know about Dennis. A mate of mine who works over at Goose Green was there and said there was a bit of a to-do afterwards. Your future stepfather was going around shouting at people. And Ponsonby was there too. I don't quite understand what happened, but the police took him away. Not sure why. My mate said they had to wake him up first and some tart was there with him shouting the odds. Bit of a lively night all round according to him."

Harry paused and looked at Piggy.

"I must be off. I'm not sure if having Hardcastle at the factory is better or worse than it being run by Ponsonby."

As Harry got up, he took one last deep sniff of Tracey's lingering presence, then shook his head sadly and left Piggy in peace.

26. Preparing the Final Account

Sebastian Hardcastle sat in the manager's office of the polish factory and belched loudly. His stomach was still painful, but his expensive Harley Street doctor assured him that he should make a full recovery. For three years he had suffered with his stomach and not once did he suspect the peppermint cordial that his nephew regularly presented him with was the cause rather than a palliative. The very action that had endeared the man to him was designed to eventually separate him from his mortal coil.

He still could not believe what that detective had told him, despite the evidence from the police laboratory showing rat poison in the bottle of cordial that his nephew had given him earlier that month. A really smart chap that detective. Fancy him walking past the smashed door, glimpsing the rat poison and bottles on the table, and putting two and two together like that. The man must have a razor-like mind and the eyesight of a hawk to have noticed that the full bottle on the table had the cap misaligned compared to those in the open box.

Hardcastle had elevated his opinion of the police force on the strength of it. They had caught a gang of safe robbers and saved his life at the same time by pure vigilance. He wondered if their diet contributed to their alertness. Having been summoned from his bed at 2 am, he had arrived to find some of the officers at the scene positively reeked of garlic and curry. He had the window open wide, and he could still detect a faint odour. He wondered if instructing the canteen to serve curry would increase productivity.

He also revised his opinion of his incompetent but thoughtful kin who presented him with a bottle of peppermint cordial for his dyspepsia each month when he collected the takings. But this was in a downward direction! As his only kin, or at least the only one with whom he bothered to have any contact, Sebastian Hardcastle took his betrayal badly. Ponsonby's few possessions had been gathered into two tea chests and dumped on the drive of the little house that he had once shared with his dim, but attractive, wife and two noisy children. He felt sorry for them, but not sorry enough to make a financial contribution to their upkeep.

From that point on Sebastian Hardcastle considered himself one of life's orphans. A man with no family and precious few friends.

"There's a man on line one to speak to you," simpered Ponsonby's secretary.

Hardcastle looked at her and groaned. She reminded him that his nephew was an idiot. He had clearly recruited the girl for her chest size rather than her brain size.

"Who is he? What does he want?"

"He didn't say."

"Did you ask?"

She fled in tears. Jason Ponsonby never spoke to her like that. Even last night at the boxing when he got excited and started shouting for Knightly to murder that Longman fellow he never spoke to her in that tone.

Hardcastle sighed and picked up the phone.

"Good afternoon, Sir. My name is Dillon from Executive Services. My company did some work for Strudwick's last year, helping them attain BS 5750 accreditation. At the time we were concerned with company efficiency within the production areas, and the management suggested that we might have another look after a settling in period. I know that our Miss Mulligan was particularly concerned that costs were not managed effectively.

I understand that there has been a change of management and perhaps the new owners might be more receptive to advice. Particularly in today's difficult financial climate.

I was hoping to send one of my team over to have a chat and see if we can help maximise profits for you."

Hardcastle had begun to lose interest as Dillon went through the script that Tracey had prepared, but the words 'maximise profits' got his full attention. In the short time he had been in the factory he had found that his nephew had hidden the true position from him. Whilst he had showed a dismal monthly cash balance he had failed to mention the growing bank overdraft. As far as Hardcastle could see, the place was leaking money faster than a sieve.

He reached for the desk diary. Most of Ponsonby's entries related to evenings out with one or other of the incompetent clerical staff, and the working days were mainly blank.

"I could see you next week Wednesday," said Dillon helpfully, "or our Miss Mulligan could spare some time on Monday."

"Monday at three o'clock?"

"Hmm, she would need to rearrange something, but yes, I'll ask her to come and see you then."

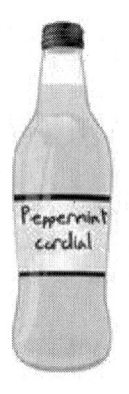

27. Knowledge is Power

Piggy lay on the settee with his feet up, milking his injury for all it was worth. His mother fussed around him, in between packing her summer clothes and a few personal possessions.

"Ernie says I can pick up a one year passport at the all-night post office at Gatwick, as long as I take the right documents. Peter is picking me up at nine o'clock for the night flight to Alicante."

"Does that mean the wedding is off, or are you having it in Spain?"

"I don't know, Reg. Ernie said that he had urgent business over there and it might take a while to sort out. Must have been urgent for him to fly off in the middle of the night without any luggage. I'm taking a case out for him. He said I can buy nice summer clothes out there, so I only need a small holdall of personal stuff for myself. I'll phone you in a few days when I know a bit more. I thought I might get bored if he was tied up with his business a lot, but he said I could always help Finger's mother out if I was at a loose end. She runs some sort of hotel for sailors down in the port."

Piggy smiled to himself. He guessed that his mother did not know the nature of the 'Hotel' that Ernshaw owned out there, but he was sure that he was not going to be the one to tell her.

"I should enjoy the sun, Mum. Seems daft going all that way just to work in a hotel."

The doorbell rang.

"I'll go Reg."

She opened the door to a man and a woman. The woman was smartly dressed and wore the same perfume as that attractive nurse that had looked after her son. She even looked a bit like her. The man was a little older.

"Are you Mrs Swinton? We are from the probation service. Reginald has missed an appointment and we need to see him to assess whether we should recommend him going back to serve the remainder of his sentence."

"My Reg has been going straight. He's found himself a job. He's just had a bit of bad luck and been in hospital."

"Ah!" said the man from over the woman's shoulder. "Perhaps that explains why he didn't see me yesterday as arranged. Is he in?"

"He's in the lounge. But you go easy on him. He only came out of hospital yesterday."

"Why was he in hospital?"

"He had an accident! Something heavy fell on him!"

"Ah! I'm sorry to hear that. All those packing cases at work, I suppose. It must take a time to get used to heavy lifting. Especially for someone like Reginald who is not used to working."

Mrs Swinton glared at Dillon. Berating her layabout son was a mother's privilege, not to be assumed by strangers. She ushered them to the lounge. If Reg wanted to give them more details then it was up to him.

"Don't get up, Mr Swinton. Your mother tells me you have had an accident... We won't detain you Mrs Swinton. We need a few words with your son in private."

Mrs Swinton glared again as they paused and waited for her to leave the room. She left the door ajar but John Dillon leant back on it and heard the latch click as it closed.

"Well Piggy, Fingers bolted when the backup vehicles came, and once they caught him Holmes persuaded him that Ernshaw thinks he set them up. Fingers is terrified of being let out while the gang are looking for him. He's confessed to breaking into Hardcastle's office in Streatham. He's singing like a canary over at the Nick. Ernshaw's disappeared but word is that he is not pleased with Fingers. Ernshaw's mouthpiece Florribund came to arrange bail for Fingers, but he said he'd rather stay in the cells. I think he suspected that he might not last long on the outside. I do love it when thieves fall out."

Dillon smiled as he updated Piggy and settled in a battered armchair. Tracey perched on the arm and also smiled. She took an official looking brown folder from her briefcase.

"We have a meeting set up with Hardcastle next week. The papers we copied make grim reading. As things are, I doubt that the factory will last until Christmas. But I expect Hardcastle will try to give the impression that it's a thriving concern if we make a bid for it. I've asked Inland Revenue to do a spot audit."

She grinned as she spoke. When she had trained as a business analyst and worked in the City, she had dreamed of leading a takeover team, but a male-dominated industry had repeatedly confined her to minor roles supporting less able men. During this time, she made a number of useful contacts, and currently a tax inspector in Penge was anxiously awaiting the return of his best suit from the cleaners in time for an evening assignation.

"What I would like you to do," she said, "is tell me what you think of a few of the factory staff. If we put a proposal to Hardcastle we need to know how some will react. Let's start with your boss, Harry Derry. What other jobs do you think he could do there?"

Whilst they talked, Mrs Swinton popped her head round the door to say that Bald Peter had arrived to take her to Gatwick. As the handle moved slightly, John Dillon motioned with his hand and the conversation switched to stern probation officer lecture mode before the door had started to open.

"Don't keep my Reg up too late. He's only just come out of hospital and needs his rest," admonished Mrs Swinton.

"We are almost finished, Mrs Swinton. Now that Reginald has explained, and given the circumstances, I don't think he has too much to worry about. Probably a formal letter about keeping us informed."

John Dillon smiled as he spoke. A wide, deep smile designed to show off the benefit of having a good dentist. She stepped across to where Piggy sat and kissed him on the cheek before turning and leaving for sunnier climes.

"We need you back at the factory, Piggy. We need to know how Hardcastle is running the place."

"I was going back on Monday."

"Why don't you go in tomorrow to give them your sick certificate and have a chat with Harry Derry while you are there."

Piggy realised that this was not a suggestion, simply another order in the sequence that had dominated his life since his release. He nodded.

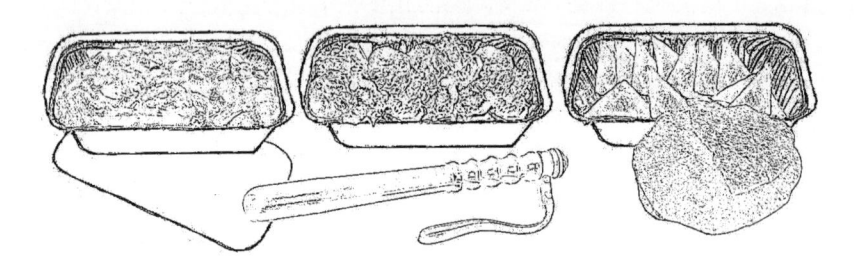

28. The Wounded Hero Returns

Next morning Piggy got up late. He was awake at dawn, but stayed in bed as a token gesture of rebellion against having his life dictated to him by others. When he eventually stumbled into the kitchen he found only mouldy bread and a tin of baked beans. Again he was invaded by mixed feelings about Mabel. He boiled the kettle and stood the opened tin in a saucepan of water to heat while he trimmed the bread. Once he had accomplished this the bread was too misshapen to toast or pour beans on, so he ate them from the tin with a spoon.

At the factory Harry Derry was pleased to see him, but busy doing the work of both men.

"I could sit and paste some labels if you like?"

"If you feel up to it I'd be grateful. It's been mad here ever since I came in and found the place swarming with policemen."

"What happened?" Piggy asked with what he hoped was an innocent tone.

"A gang tried to break into the safe. Must have been really incompetent as they got the wrong room at first. They smashed down Ponsonby's private storeroom door. And when they did finally find the right room, they used so much explosive on the safe that a passing police car heard it."

"Wasn't Ponsonby here?"

"Nah, he went to the boxing."

"So it was early evening, not during the night. They must have done a fair bit of damage. I bet Ponsonby is not a happy bunny."

Piggy was finding it hard to maintain that innocent tone of curiosity.

"A most unhappy bunny. The police have arrested him."

"What? Do they think he was in on it. Fiddling his uncle?"

"Nah. I've a mate who's son is a rozzer. Word is he was planning to do his uncle in."

"No! I don't believe it. Bit of a snide but not a murderer. Besides, I would have thought he would have been more likely to snuff his missus, since it was she who threw him out."

Piggy shook his head in disbelief. Having mastered his innocent tone, Piggy decided blending in surprise and a little acting would be a nice touch, distancing him from any possible suspicion.

Piggy spent a happy hour with Harry. Pasting labels and chatting about how Ponsonby's arrest would affect the factory. Harry was of the opinion that any change would be for the better, to which Piggy agreed.

"I've heard Hardcastle is a mean man to work for, but at least he keeps the business going. I know you've only got a year to do for your pension, but I'm enjoying it here. I've been made redundant twice recently."

"Fancy a bit of lunch?"

Piggy nodded vigorously. He was going to have to do some shopping on his way home and a hot meal in the canteen would reduce his load.

As far as possible Hardcastle restricted the supplies to the factory canteen to his own product lines. The main course was invariably 'contract beef' in one form or another. Contract beef was a euphemism for old cows who no longer came up to scratch in the milking parlour. They tended to end up in the pie factories or as mince on a school dinner plate. Dessert was invariably cake that failed to come up to package standard, swamped in thin custard. Today was no exception, cottage pie and ginger cake.

Piggy pushed his empty bowl away and licked his lips for any stray crumbs or custard drips. Then, as the hot intake met his late breakfast of beans, he burped quietly.

"You'll be putting on weight if you eat like that. I expect your mother will have a hot meal for you tonight as well."

"Mum's gone off to Spain. Don't know when she will be back."

Harry looked at his young assistant. His life was never dull like his own existence of work, sleep, work with relentless monotony.

"Do you think Ernshaw is out there as well? My mate's son says an anonymous file describing a lot of his activities arrived in the post for Superintendent Hackman at Peckham Police Station, and they are anxious to talk to Ernshaw about it."

It seemed that Tracey was not best pleased by the miserly amount that Ernshaw thought he could give her to buy her silence. It was nothing like the balance left over once he had extracted his twenty thousand. Hackworth had kept her up to date on Holmes's findings at Babbacombe so she knew exactly how much Sir Arthur would have had on him.

"Couldn't say. I only saw Mum briefly when she came home to pack."

Lunch over Piggy stepped out into the road and headed for the Co-op. He was about to cross the main road by the bus garage when a rusty Transit van stopped beside him.

"Get in!"

Piggy froze as Bald Peter spoke. But a small voice inside him said that to run was to only delay the inevitable. He heaved open the passenger door and climbed in. Peter drove round into Peckham Hill Street and parked.

"The boss says you are in charge while he is away."

"What?"

"That's what I said when he told me. But he says that you are almost family, and that family is important. Personally I think he has been reading too many American Mafia stories. But you don't argue with him. Well, not if you value your health."

Piggy was stunned. This was either a very bad joke or else a trap to get him somewhere that he did not want to go.

"What exactly does he mean by in charge?"

"How would I know? He don't tell you anything unless you need to know, or he knows you won't be telling anyone else."

Piggy shuddered at the second option. Ernshaw was famous for telling his victims things they would never be in a position to repeat.

"I think he wants someone on site to tell him what's going on. Pass messages on and report back. That sort of thing. He thinks being family makes you trustworthy. The men will respect family."

"I wouldn't be there long once the probation service got to hear of it. And I doubt I could do much from inside Brixton."

"He's thought of that. You've got a new name. I've got it written down here somewhere. Now where did I put it."

Peter rummaged through the pockets of the worn leather jacket that he stole as a teenager to go with his first, equally stolen, motorbike.

"Ah, here it is. William Ernshaw," said Peter as he handed Piggy a driving licence.

Piggy stared at Peter in disbelief. As stand-in for Big Ernie he was to be called William Ernshaw. William bloody Ernshaw. That would soon get shortened, if that is the right word, to Little Willy; with all the connotations that the nickname implied. So much for respect for family!

"So, how do I stand in for him, keep the job the probation service got for me, live in accommodation approved by the probation service and run his crime empire all at the same time?"

Peter scratched his bald head. It was a futile symbolic gesture - there was nowhere on that pink desert for fleas or nits to hide.

"I'll drop you back at your Mum's flat and go back to the arches. Big Ernie might phone one or other place."

"Is Maria at the arches?"

"Don't even think it you randy little git. Standing in for Ernie does not include taking liberties with the hired help! Besides, she's as good with a knife as her mother ever was."

"I was hoping for a decent dinner," Piggy retorted indignantly, "Mum left the flat without any grub there."

Peter chuckled.

"Sorry boss. I thought you was getting ideas."

But Piggy did not hear him. Peter's remark had the opposite effect to what he intended and Piggy was fantasising about Maria. There was the added bonus that she was probably the one woman who could protect him from Mabel when she got out of prison.

"Stop at the Co-op. I need to do some shopping."

"We'd do better at the Cash and Carry. Big Ernie has an account there."

"And you expect them to see me as buying on his behalf?"

"Don't worry boss. I've been spreading the word all day!"

Piggy sighed. He had become used to being a pawn in other people's games. But it seemed he'd been transferred to a bigger board and reached the far side, only to find they were out of Queens and made him a King instead, with all the restrictions and problems that came with the job.

The Cash and Carry was a new experience for Piggy. As well as bulk cases of mundane items such as toilet paper and Brobat there were rows of freezers full of tempting goodies. Steaks, gallons of ice-cream and made up meals that made his mouth water just to look at them. But the fridge in his Mum's flat had a freezer section the size of an Oxo tin so he settled for a box of steaks to thaw and a bag of frozen oven chips along with more usual basics such as bread, jam and cheese.

The place was a members only outlet so at the till he fished out the new driving licence that Peter had just given him and began to explain that he was shopping for Ernshaw. The checkout girl raised her hand and snapped her fingers.

Piggy managed to control his alarm as a sallow youth came bounding along towards them. She whispered a few words to him and the boy grabbed a pair of brown bags and packed Piggy's groceries in them.

"Sorry Sir, we did not see your Jaguar in the car-park."

"It's the Transit over there!"

There was no mention of asking for payment. The boy grovelled, picked up the bags and ran to where Peter was holding a rear door open.

The checkout girl smiled, and Piggy returned the favour before sauntering out to where Peter was now holding the front passenger door open for him.

"Have we got anything besides this and the Jag?"

Peter laughed.

"Stock is changing all the time. If you want something that demands respect there's a dark blue roller."

"How about something that can go unnoticed?"

"We've got a few rep-mobiles. Grey Minx? Blue Zephyr? Any colour you like in Cortinas. Beige Vauxhall Victor? Good passion wagon the Victor. Bench front seat and a powerful demister for after."

Piggy ignored the ribald insinuation. Partly to maintain his dignity and partly for lack of a willing partner for such pastimes.

"Next time we meet bring the Minx."

Peter stopped the van outside the block of flats and sat with the engine running. Piggy waited for him to get out and get his shopping, but Peter made no attempt to move. Eventually Piggy turned to Peter and was about to speak when the bald headed man beat him to it.

"That back at the Cash and Carry was just for public consumption. As far as I'm concerned you are just Ernie's fancy piece's kid. Now hurry up I've got things to do."

Piggy heaved open the door and went to retrieve his shopping. Ahead of him was an empty flat, and an unknown length of time waiting before a steak was thawed ready to cook.

As Piggy pushed open the front door, he knew something was wrong. The kettle was boiling and there was the smell of cooking from the kitchen. Various thoughts went through his mind. Mum changed her mind and come back? Mabel escaped from Holloway? Tracey taken pity on him. Despite the last thought being the least likely he dwelt on it for some time before venturing towards the kitchen. As he opened the kitchen door he heard the lounge door open behind him.

"Dinner will be ready in fifteen minutes. However, the wine will not be chilled for some time longer than that. I presume you do not wish me to put ice cubes in the glasses. It is a vulgar practice."

Piggy turned to see Maria standing behind him, immaculately tied back hair, wrinkle-free stockings and an apron so newly starched that you could smell scorched Robin.

He began to wonder if he had the mental power to think wish fulfilment as she curtseyed slightly and motioned for him to go into the lounge.

"Reg, my boy. I've been worried about you. I expected you home half an hour ago."

Piggy's jaw dropped. There sitting in his favourite spot on the settee was Big Ernie.

"I thought you were in Spain!" he gasped.

"So does everybody else! That balls-up at the factory has cost me dearly, and that little runt Fisher had better hope I don't get my hands on him. Now close your mouth, there's no telling where those flies have been."

Piggy snapped his jaws shut, nipping the soft inside of his left cheek as he did so. He was not a religious man, but now he prayed fervently that Holmes, Dillon or Tracey did not pay him an unexpected visit.

"I want you to make a few phone calls while we wait for Maria's excellent Castilla y Leon."

Ernshaw's calls were all to get his hands on monies stashed away with trusted underworld bankers. He said that getting Piggy to make the calls reinforced his position as stand-in boss of the gang. Piggy thought it more likely to be to incriminate him and make it harder for him to try to opt out. By the time Maria announced that dinner was served he had arranged for five deliveries to the flat.

"My place is being watched and I can't trust anybody after that weasel Fisher has opened his mouth. Except you of course."

Dinner was wonderful, but Piggy could not enjoy it. Twice the door bell rang during the dessert and each time Piggy looked around for somewhere to escape to. He thought of trying to tie sheets together and climb down from the bathroom window. But it was a tiny window and had not been opened for years, certainly not since it was last painted. Fortunately both callers were met by Maria who subsequently brought packages in and packed them in the small attaché-case which rested open on the sideboard.

As the evening drew on Piggy, got more and more nervous. The fifth package arrived at about nine o'clock and Maria closed the case.

"Ring this number and ask Peter to come and pick you up. Say I've rung and want you to do an errand. Don't let him ask what the errand is, just put the phone down."

As Peter answered the phone the doorbell rang. Piggy froze. Maria got up and turned towards the door. He saw her reach into a hidden apron pocket and bring out a flick knife. He shuddered as she tucked it in under the bow where her apron strings met in the small of her back. As a perfect servant she always stood with her hands behind her back, making the knife ready to hand. She calmly went to the door while Piggy delivered Ernshaw's message to Peter in a decidedly wobbly voice.

There was a muffled exchange of voices across the threshold and then Maria came back with a stiff manilla envelope.

"Mr Florribund says you may wish to use the enclosed documents at the airport, Sir. He thinks that perhaps your current alias may be compromised. He'll post the contents of the bank box on to your address in Spain on Monday."

Piggy breathed a sigh of relief. Ernshaw misinterpreted his action as an expression of concern for himself.

"Now then lad. There's no need to worry about me. I've got friends at Gatwick and at the first sign of danger they would whisk me onto a cargo plane. Not so comfortable, of course, and probably a bit inconvenient if we land elsewhere. But my people out there can handle such inconveniences."

Twenty minutes later Peter arrived and stood beside the Minx in the car-park.

"You'd better go down and get him to come up for my bags."

"No point in me going. He's made it clear that he will only attend me for show in public."

"Maria. Be a good girl and pop down. I think I saw a grey raincoat and headscarf in the hall. Best that you put them on to avoid prying eyes."

She gave an almost imperceptible curtsey and left. Two minutes later an out of breath Peter arrived for the first of the cases. As soon as he left Ernshaw turned to Piggy.

"I'm afraid that you will have to put up with Maria for a while. She cannot go back to the house yet and she is far too recognisable to fly with me. I have a contact who works for Fred Olson, so she can sail out of Millwall on the weekly Canaries cruise. Perhaps you can assist her. She will have a lot of luggage."

Piggy was beginning to believe the wisdom of the saying '*be careful what you wish for*'. Maria was totally without emotion and would probably win an inscrutability contest against a Chinese master of the art. He had no idea of her opinion of him and the little he knew of her related to her ability to fight and kill chickens. Suddenly being alone with her in the flat sounded like a bad idea.

Peter came puffing back for the last of the cases and Ernshaw bade them goodbye. As he left, he passed Piggy a rather full manilla envelope.

"You'll need some dosh for expenses. Spend it wisely."

The envelope was open at one end and Piggy could see it contained a considerable amount of money.

Maria closed the door behind Ernshaw and came to stand beside him at the window to watch as the car drove away.

"Thank gawd for that!"

Piggy looked round. She was untying her apron and taking the pins out of her neatly tied hair.

"Strewth Piggy boy, put the kettle on," she said as she shook her hair free of its tight little bun, "I'm gasping for a cuppa."

Piggy's jaw was becoming accustomed to dropping at the slightest provocation, but this time it beat previous records; deeper and faster to the extent that it locked and needed a supporting hand to return it to a more photogenic pose.

"Well get a move on, I've got a throat like the bottom of a parrot's cage."

Piggy needed no further prompting. He bolted for the kitchen.

"Got any chocky biscuits?" she called.

"Sorry, no! I'll get some tomorrow."

"How about a bit of bread and jam?"

"Yes. I picked up some on the way home. In the bag in the hall."

"Bring some plates in, Piggy boy."

When he returned, she had put a Mother's Pride and a jar of Bulgarian plum jam on the coffee table. She had unbuttoned the top three buttons of her dress and removed the detachable white collar. She had her feet up on the coffee table and a hand rolled fag in the corner of her mouth. She grinned at him.

"You're a star, Piggy boy. Gawd it's hard work keeping up that servant malarkey." She reached in her pocket and brought out her knife. She tossed it to him and to his surprise he caught it.

"Do me a favour and make me a sandwich. I'm knackered."

She laughed at Piggy's puzzled expression.

"Mum's from Stepney. She was up the duff when Dad buggered off. He was a waiter. She only went out to Spain to try and find him. She met Ernshaw when I was a nipper and worked his clip joint for him. She was always handy with a knife, and she learnt to fight in the mud wrestling ring. It was better money than waiting tables or bar hostessing. I used to practise with her. "

Piggy was not sure if he was relieved or more concerned. Not only was she a fearsome fighter, but a Jekyll and Hyde character as well.

He sat down in the armchair opposite and pressed the button on the handle of the knife. The blade shot out and locked with a snap. He made four sandwiches and put two on a plate for her. As he did so the kettle started to whistle and she leapt up to head for the kitchen.

"Tea or coffee?"

"Coffee please! There's only condensed milk and I don't like it in tea."

She came back with two mugs and put one down in front of him.

"Do you have to go out to Spain?"

"Well, Mum's out there and it's a good life living in a posh house on rich grub. Don't know how much longer I can do it though. The food's getting to me. I had to let out that dress last month."

Piggy took this as an invitation to admire her figure: from where he sat there was absolutely nothing wrong with it.

"Don't look at me like that. I'm not after a fellow. Well, least-ways, not at the moment."

"Sorry!"

"That's okay Piggy. I suppose you've been starved of female company for a while anyway. From what I've heard there was only that hulk Mabel, and it was your mother who encouraged her. When she moved in with Ernshaw she got him to run her round in the motor and gave her a door-key."

Piggy frowned. He liked the girl opposite him, but he wondered if her perfect servant was an act or if she had a split personality: and if the latter was the case then were there more than two of her. He made a mental note to wedge a chair under his doorknob when he went to bed.

Next morning when he got up the flat was empty. On the kitchen table was a flash of coffee, a basket of fresh rolls and a jar of jam. As he sat and reached for the rolls he spotted the note stood resting on the kettle.

"Gone to get a bit of shopping.

Back in a while. Maria x

And there, at the end of the note, was the tiniest 'x'.

29. Tying up Loose Ends

Piggy did not wait for Maria to return. He added a post-script to her note and headed off for the probation service office.

"Late for my parole appointment.

See you later, Reg"

He wondered about adding an 'x', but he was still in two minds about her so he decided not to.

He dashed across to the probation office, but being a Saturday it was shut. He swore under his breath and wandered along towards the Town Hall. Tracey's office was somewhere around there, but it was a bit vague. He hoped to spot her, or perhaps for her to see him hanging around.

Some hundred yards before the Town Hall a Hillman Hunter stopped beside him.

"Get in Piggy!"

He turned to see DC Holmes at the wheel.

"I'm supposed to meet my probation officer, Mr Holmes."

"I'll only keep you a minute."

He got into the passenger seat and Holmes turned off the R/T. The car still reeked of curry.

"We are very pleased with you Piggy. In one night, I got a safe cracking gang and prevented a murder. We are still doing the paperwork, and Fingers is being very co-operative. By the time we're done we'll have cleared up half the outstanding crimes on the books. And I've not forgotten your part. I said I'd remember and I will. It's a shame we cannot give you a commendation. Might not be appreciated in some quarters, or should I say arches."

Piggy squirmed in the seat.

"I might be in trouble, Mr Holmes. The maid from Ernshaw's home is at my place. Mr Dillon and a friend came to see me the other day. It might get me into bother if they did that while she is there."

"Do you want me to arrest her?"

"I don't think she's done anything wrong, well not in this country, but she could blab to Big Ernie."

Holmes thought for a moment.

"I'll give Dillon a call and put him in the picture. I suppose you are here to speak to his friend?"

Holmes grinned as he spoke.

"I don't know where she is. She meets me by the Town Hall sometimes."

Holmes's grin broadened and he started the engine.

"Come on, I'll show you."

Outside the Town Hall he stopped the car.

"See that window over there with the sign 'Executive Services'. You get to it down the side alley."

Piggy joined Hardcastle in his rising admiration of the police force. Holmes seemed to know everything about everything.

"Before you go. Do you know where Ernshaw is?"

Piggy shook his head. It was almost true. Apparently Spain is a big place.

As Piggy stepped out of the car a familiar voice spoke to him.

"Are you looking for me, Piggy? And Mr Holmes. So nice to see you again."

"Why, Miss Mulligan. What a pleasure to see you. So you know our little Piggy. Perhaps we should have a chat."

Tracey pushed Piggy back in the passenger seat and got in behind him.

"Not here, let's find somewhere quieter."

Holmes drove them to an isolated back street. On one side was the canal and beyond it, watching them with bored eyes were Ernshaw's horses.

"Perhaps you could start, Miss, by explaining your relationship with young Piggy."

Tracey leant forward slightly, improving Holmes's view of her lightly clad torso and bringing her perfumed self closer to him.

"Mr Swinton works at the Hardcastle factory. My firm has been been in contact with Hardcastle with a view to doing some consultancy for them. I met young Reginald by accident and he has been helpful in telling me a bit about the factory."

"Industrial spying?"

"Certainly not. As you know we consultants charge by the hour. Getting some background about Hardcastle saves me time, and him money.

The explanation was almost plausible, and Holmes was in an indulgent mood, but he could not resist letting them know that he knew there was more to it than she had said.

"Well, go carefully Piggy; I suppose there is no need for me to contact John Dillon for you now."

"No, Mr Holmes."

As Piggy stepped out of the car, he realised he had inadvertently confirmed the link between Dillon and Tracey.

"Would you stay there for a moment, Miss... She'll be with you shortly, Piggy. Shut the door on your way out."

Holmes waited for the double click of the lock before turning more fully to speak to her. *Evening in Paris* struggled to compete with three day old curry.

"That's a nice perfume you are wearing Miss. *Evening in Paris* if I'm not mistaken.

She smiled.

"You have a good nose, Mr Holmes."

"Not really. You see I smelt it recently and since then I've spent some time at the perfume counter of Jones and Higgins identifying it. Would you care to tell me why I smelt it in the factory on Wednesday night?"

"Are you free for dinner next week sometime?"

The question caught him unawares. It was one he had wanted to ask for some time, but it sounded wrong coming from her. He did not pursue an answer to his own question.

"Yes. I understand the *Star of the East* is nice."

She laughed. "But you've eaten from there once this week. Give me a call early next week. I'm rather busy for the next few days but am free later in the week. I'm sure we can find somewhere more interesting to go. Somewhere more atmospheric perhaps."

She opened the door and swung her long shapely legs round. Her red heels clicked as they made contact with the pavement. Holmes already had his expenses sheet out to make an entry for that night before she closed the door behind her.

"Now, Piggy. What was it you wanted to see me about?"

Piggy explained his predicament about his house guest. She nodded and said she would contact Dillon. Holmes had driven off and they stood looking across the canal. Through a gap between a stable block and a shed they could see the imposing Georgian façade of Ernshaw's house.

The sluice gate had been opened to flush the canal and debris floated past at a walking pace. Piggy understood why Holmes had chosen that particular spot to park. Sir Arthur probably made the same final journey as the debris that was in front of them. Not that they were likely to ever prove it.

"Best you get back home so you can keep an eye on her, Piggy."

He turned and headed for the estate. As he approached it looked particularly mean and shabby in comparison with Ernshaw's mansion.

30. Business is Business

On Monday afternoon, Tracey presented herself at Hardcastle's at ten to three. She had prepared well, and probably knew as much about the factory's financial state as Hardcastle himself. The tax inspector's report was most revealing. She also had a good idea of the abilities of his staff, which was probably more than he did. She had spent Friday night in the company of Stanley Capes, Gloria Ford and Roos Wouters and was confident that she had done her homework. She had almost caused a family row on Saturday afternoon when she turned up unannounced at Henry Fothergill's home to pick his brains and see if he had found a suitable position yet.

Ponsonby's top heavy secretary sniffed as Tracey presented herself at the outer office of the management suite. Apart from two smashed doors in the corridor outside, little had changed since she had visited the factory a year before. She carefully chose a chair that would result in Hardcastle seeing her the moment his door was opened and sat down to wait.

"Good afternoon, Mr Hardcastle. Thank you for seeing me. I hope you are well."

She approached his desk and turned the visitor chair through forty-five degrees before sitting down. Hardcastle stared at the woman who now sat demurely, yet showing a delightful pair of crossed knees below a short skirt, and a tantalising glimpse of lace-covered breast within her loose fitting, low cut blouse. She took her time opening a hard covered foolscap notebook. Then she looked up and smiled.

"Say your piece young woman. I'm a busy man."

"Naturally Mr Hardcastle. But call me Tracey. Everybody does."

She simpered slightly, playing on the dumb blonde stereotype to lower his guard.

"Well then, Tracey. What is it you think you can do for us?"

"When I was here a year ago, Sir Arthur seemed to have his own fixed agenda, and my team were concerned that it was not in the best interests of the company. If I may be frank, much of the work here is boring. Sending staff on complex courses only makes them dissatisfied with their lot. The net effect is that you spend money, yet have a negative effect on productivity."

"Agreed!" Hardcastle had no intention of spending money on courses, or Christmas parties or anything much else.

"The Russians have devised a system of internal competition in some of their factories. The workers are in teams which have goals, and they compete with each other for a small monthly reward. You need to keep detailed production costs at the team level. As well as rewarding the more productive, it allows you to identify the less productive, and take corrective action."

Hardcastle mulled over her words for a while. His idea of corrective action normally involved a P45, but he was having trouble concentrating on what she said. Much as he enjoyed gazing at her face he found his eyes kept dropping towards that one open button on her blouse. He struggled heroically to keep his mind on business.

"Smart idea. Sack the slackers as a lesson to the others, eh?"

"Not necessarily. There might be valid reasons for the difference in work rate. Slower machines, poor lighting or heating, bad practices that have crept in over time. You need a proper work study before making changes."

Hardcastle paused for thought again. He shut his eyes to eliminate distractions, but that only made things worse for his mind interpreted the closed eyelids as permission to wander off into fantasy. He forced his eyes open again and concentrated on the oak panelling of the wall behind her.

There was a lot of sense in what she said. He was about to offer her a consultancy, when his lifetime of hard business practice finally regained control of his mind. There was no need to employ consultants when a free chat could give him what he wanted. Maybe a time and motion man for a few weeks, but not fancy consultancy prices.

"You're a sensible young lady Tracey. But I don't see what you can do for us. We are jogging along quite nicely without outside help."

"Oh! I'm surprised that you say that. My understanding was that you were running at a three and a half percent monthly loss and that the factory could bankrupt your whole business empire within two and a half years, or close within eight months if not subsidised by your other interests."

Hardcastle stared at her. She was not simply decorative or as gullible as he had assumed.

"Where did you hear that nonsense?"

"It's common knowledge. Your posted quarterly accounts make interesting reading if you probe into some of the subsidiary elements. I must say that your nephew was quite inventive when it came to finance. I can see why your recently fired accountant had difficulty deciphering the morass of figures. But then he was not aware of the full extent of your bank loans."

She smiled at him. Mr Wilson at the bank had been eager to exchange information about an obnoxious client for an evening of pure delight.

"That's slander, young lady!"

"No. Fact. Ponsonby was increasing borrowing each month to feed you a small cash return. Currently your debts amount to fifty two percent of the value of the business. If your bank manager, Mr Wilson, were to call in the loan, then you would go bust. Currently the factory carries debts of about half the site value, and staff redundancy costs would bring its total worth down to virtually nothing. My guess, after all debts are paid, it's worth less than thirty thousand pounds. Much less."

Hardcastle sank his head in his hands. He knew he had met his match, and every minute that he prolonged the meeting would result in more and more concessions to her. It was as if she could see into his mind and understand the information stored there better than he could himself.

"What do you want?"

"As my colleague said on the telephone, we can help you. We can either do a profit share deal, or else take a fixed fee. Either way we would need to install our own management team and have a free hand to do things our way. Frankly we couldn't do worse than your nephew has done. The benefit to you would be a share in a profitable factory, and free time to concentrate on your other interests. I am sure that while you spend time here here are other areas which are neglected.

Besides, I think that you should ease up while you recover from the effects of your nephew's evil intent."

Hardcastle stayed slumped. This woman had walked into his office and given him a more accurate assessment of his position than he had managed to get in the six months since he bought the place. Buying the factory had been a disaster. He had thought he fleeced a bunch of innocents, but found he had bought a lemon. His nephew had put people's backs up wherever he went and now he had no effective management at all.

On top of that, she was now giving him health advice. And good advice at that. He looked her in the face and smiled a weak smile. Anyone who knew him would realise the significance of that smile - probably the first for many years.

She reached into her briefcase and drew out two sheets of paper.

"I'll leave you with these. They are the two options I've just outlined. Naturally I'll have to make a more detailed study before we have an agreement. But I'm sure that with intelligent management we could return to a healthy profit within a year or so. Personally if I was in your position I would consider selling out. It would give you enough money to look after yourself without the worry of managing a failing factory."

She stood up and turned to go. The slight draft from the window wafted her perfume across the room as she did so. It was a nice smell, one Hardcastle had faintly smelt earlier in the week, but could not remember where. It certainly softened the implication of her comment about intelligent management.

After she had gone, Hardcastle called his secretary and told her to hold all his calls. He sat and reflected on life in general, and Tracey Mulligan in particular. If he had met someone like her when he was a young man, his life could have been very different. Poorer perhaps, but in other ways infinitely richer. Now, in a lonely old age with no friends and cut off from his only relative, he succumbed to sentimental flights of fancy. More free time, regular business meetings with the delightful Tracey and a slow digestive improvement as a result of fine police-work combined to make a sudden and marked change in his philosophy.

He opened his desk drawer and took out his chequebook. He would start with a substantial cheque to Ponsonby's wife, and an invitation for her to bring her two adorable children to lunch on Sunday. Even if he cut off his nephew she was still a relation, and perhaps a good nature compensates for an empty head. Things were going to be tough for her, so perhaps she might like to move in to his rambling Victorian villa. If he had enough contact with the children at an early age then perhaps he could shape their minds and make a decent heir out of one of them.

Two days later Hardcastle phoned Executive Services. He wanted to negotiate the sale of the factory. Tracey took the call and when he had hung up she phoned Mr Wilson, her favourite bank manager. She was about to offer him a deal with fringe benefits he was unlikely to refuse, or get offered anywhere else.

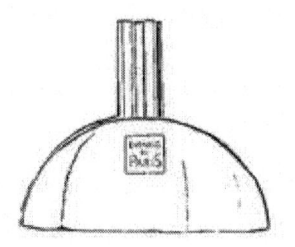

31. Piggy the Protector

When Piggy had returned to his mother's flat that Saturday morning, he had been unsure what he would find. In the event he found Maria in a pair of slacks and tunic top singing an Adam Faith song and scrubbing the kitchen worktops.

"Hi Piggy. I'll only be a minute getting these bloodstains off."

He watched her for a moment. It was only the cockerel that Ernshaw had got her to kill, but given her association with that man he was sure she would be as happy in her work if it was something more sinister.

"I guess it's a bit boring in the flat for you, not being able to go out and being cramped in these few rooms after all that space at Big Ernie's."

"Don't fret so, Piggy. I've not had time for myself for months. I've got magazines to read and you've an interesting collection of records for a young man. When I've cleaned the bath I'm going to have a long hot soak and you can bring me a mug of tea. Nothing like a bit of music and attention to make a girl go all soft and gooey."

Piggy glanced at the record deck where Mabel's do-it-yourself seduction kit still sat on the turntable then back at Maria. She studied that worried look in his eyes for a while then she burst out laughing.

"Jeez! You're so easy to wind up, it's almost a crime to do it."

He smiled. He was still having difficulty believing that this was the same prim, perfect servant that stood so unobtrusively in the background at Ernshaw's.

All that week Maria stayed in the flat. Each evening when Piggy returned he would find she had cleaned something unexpected and had a hot meal waiting for him. As the week went on he became increasingly comfortable with her presence. He began to forget about the prim maid, and enjoy the company of the down-to-earth energetic girl he was sharing his home with. On Saturday morning she was up before Piggy, as usual, and had made breakfast when he finally rose.

"Could you help me? I want to wash my hair and have some photos taken. But I don't want any of Ernshaw's gang to see me afterwards."

Piggy nodded. He did not understand what she wanted him to do yet. But she had been serious as she spoke.

She disappeared into the bathroom and he heard her sing as she cleaned the bath to a higher standard than Piggy or his mother ever attained.

"Come and give me a hand!"

Given her earlier comments about having a bath, Piggy was not sure what to expect. But as he stepped into the room he saw her standing in front of the mirror with a towel round her shoulders and a pair of scissors in her hand. Much of her long black hair lay in clumps on the floor.

"I can't get to the back. Be a pal and cut it for me."

He took the scissors from her and gingerly snipped at the strands.

"Buck up, Piggy boy! Otherwise we will be here all day."

Warming to his task he stepped closer to her and spread his fingers through the thick locks before cutting away to a similar length as the sides. He enjoyed the contact and lingered over the task, snipping individual stray hairs one at a time. As he lifted and cut he could see that deep down in the roots her hair was actually a mid-brown.

"I dyed it this colour 'cause I thought it added to the Spanish maid image. It will need a wash to get it out, and another to lighten it afterwards."

She giggled at Piggy's surprise.

They spent an hour in the bathroom, an hour in which Piggy stood and poured water or massaged in shampoos and potions. Always close and making occasional light bodily contact between them. They chatted about trivia and life in general and he enjoyed her company.

He began to wonder if his new status as an employed person would open up an improved social level for him. A level that included such girls, rather than the pub pickups that had mainly been his companions of late.

Eventually she lifted her head for a final rub with a towel and then shook it like a dog just out of water. She giggled as the droplets splashed his face. He wiped himself dry and stood admiring her. She was now a slightly boyish crop-haired blonde. A pair of cotton buds to bleach her eyebrows and the transformation was complete. The general impression was of the sort of girl who cycled everywhere and was good at tennis.

"When it's dry I need to pop down to the photo booth in Woolworths. Then I can get a new passport. Have you got a Fred Perry or something I can borrow? All my clothes are a bit too girlish."

He nodded and went off to his room. He returned with a soft pink Ben Sherman.

"Will this do?"

She looked at it and then at him. There was no need for words but he felt obliged to explain.

"My mother bought it for me."

She took it and held it up against him.

"Mothers can be strange animals."

A little later, she left the flat to get to Woolworths while they were quiet during the afternoon football on the telly. On the stairwell she passed Bald Peter puffing his way up. He never gave her a single glance as she hopped down two steps at a time.

Peter thumped on the door and Piggy nervously opened it.

"Big Ernie says you are to get rid of Maria. If you need a hand I can bring the Transit round to dump her out by Erith."

"What do you mean, 'get rid of her'?" asked Piggy incredulously.

"He says she knows too much and he can't take the risk. If you don't have the stomach for the job, then the Garman brothers will do it, but it will cost you."

He turned and walked away. He stopped about ten feet away and turned back.

"Big Ernie says for you to be in at ten o'clock Monday night. He'll ring to see if it's done. I suggest you make sure it is."

He held up a hand and pointed an index finger at Piggy. Then he slowly closed the other fingers as if squeezing a trigger. Piggy was left in no doubt as to the meaning of the gesture.

Half an hour later there was a gentle ring at the doorbell. Maria had returned with her strip of photographs and a big bag of shopping, including a selection from the pick and mix.

"I've had a visitor."

"Yes, I saw him but he didn't recognise me. What did he want?"

Piggy looked deep into her enquiring face. Her hazel eyes flickered as she returned the gaze.

"He said Ernshaw wants you dead!"

She had not expected that, and she went white in the face as he spoke.

"The bastard!"

He nodded.

"And he wants me to do it!"

"Double bastard... What if I run now. He'll never find me. I've got friends who work the hotels in Malgrat. It's way out of his area."

Then she paused and looked back at him.

"Oh! But he won't like that. You'd be in trouble! I've seen what happens to people who fail him."

The pair of them went into the lounge and sat down. Neither spoke for a long time. Finally Piggy broke the silence.

"There's this policeman who owes me a favour."

"Say that again!"

"There's this policeman who owes me a favour. I helped stop a murder and he got the credit. He's a very clever man. I'm sure he will have an idea. I'll slip out to the call box down the road and give him a bell."

Maria slowly moved her gaze from Piggy to the telephone by the window and raised her newly blonde eyebrows.

"He reckons that one may be bugged."

She sighed and wrung her hands together. People do not generally wring their hands together, despite what novels might imply. But she did. The fingers went white and the skin on the backs of her hands creased under the pressure. Eventually Piggy got out of his chair and sat beside her on the settee. He put his arm around her shoulder reassuringly, and she gripped on to him. He could feel silent tears soaking through the front of his shirt, and she smelt of bleach.

Finally he eased himself away from her and promised to get back shortly. Then he hurried down and out of the estate towards the post office. Glancing around to make sure he was not being watched he stepped into the phone box and dialled Peckham CID.

Holmes was not there. He had gone off duty at noon, and was not expected back until Monday. Piggy left a message for him to contact him urgently. He walked dejectedly back to the flat.

To cheer Maria up, he suggested that they go out for the evening. Somewhere well away from Peckham where there was not the slightest chance of them being recognised. She had changed her appearance considerably, but as Little Willy, stand in for Big Ernie, numerous local places had been put on alert to treat him kindly. Bald Peter had described him far and wide, and he had already had strangers nodding and forelock touching as he went about his daily life.

Separately they made their way to the bus stop and took a 36b to Victoria. Piggy remembered a cartoon cinema behind the station. But it had been some time since he had been that way, and on arrival they found it to have converted to a cinema club specialising in continental films, especially Swedish with subtitles. Piggy did not initially notice the change of name as they joined the queue outside.

While queueing a few minutes two things occurred to him. Firstly, he had never had to queue at a cartoon cinema before. It was a continuous loop of shorts designed to fill an hour or so before catching a train. Secondly, most of the other customers were elderly men in long grubby brown macs and plimsolls. He bade Maria hold their place in the queue while he went forward to investigate the programme. The blowups of stills from the film that lined the foyer, with large areas discretely blacked out, looked like no cartoon he had ever seen: except perhaps on the wall of the gents at *The Squinting Badger*. As he came back sheepishly a few minutes later the queue had condensed around her so there was physical contact on all sides. He glowered at them and pulled her out onto the blank pavement.

Feeling embarrassed and decidedly pink of face he explained the change. She laughed uncontrollably and threw her arms around him. They decided to go to the fish shop in Wilton Road while they laid plans for the rest of the evening.

The fish shop had a take away section one side of the fryers and a restaurant on the other. It was always busy and even in the summer with all doors propped open the glass frontage was always steamed up. It had a busy welcoming feel.

After haddock and chips for two with tea and bread and butter, Maria was still giggling about the cinema. It was gone eight o'clock. A bit too late for a West End show, so they decided to be tourists instead. They begged some spare crusts of bread from the fish shop and headed for St James's Park. They fed the ducks and pelicans and wandered round the perimeter of the lake. As the evening wore on, she started to hold hands. Initially while she walked, childlike, along a low wall and then more regularly as they wandered up Whitehall looking at the floodlit buildings. They passed the lonely horse guards, at this time of day unmounted but in polished breastplates with swords held to attention, before dropping into The Clarence public house at the top of Whitehall.

The portly landlord and his diminutive wife were tidying up and awaiting the after-theatre rush, so the place was quite quiet except for a few die-hard drinkers. A tray of sandwiches stood on the bar under a glass case to justify the establishment's late refreshment licence, and a yellow labrador lay in a corner with a rag doll in its mouth. It was dark and snug in the bar and they made their drinks last as long as possible before stretching their legs again around Trafalgar Square.

Maria was about to paddle her feet in the fountain when two huge policemen appeared behind them.

"I shouldn't do that if I was you Miss. About a thousand pigeons go in there, and I mean go in the lavatorial sense."

She turned to the voice and smiled.

"Thank you, officer."

Piggy instinctively turned his face away, but they had no interest in him. There was a vagrant sitting drinking Tenants Extra on the wall of the shrubbery and two unattached young ladies on the corner by the stone built police box. The two giant law enforcers had a difficult choice to make between duty and pleasure.

Eventually Piggy decided they would go home before the theatres turned out, and they made their way to the bus-stop at the top of Whitehall. It had turned a little chilly and she tucked her arm under his and snuggled up close as they waited. Piggy was delighted. She was now nothing like the servant he had met at Ernshaw's. She was more like the girl four doors away that he had admired as a young teenager, but was too shy to speak to.

Maria got off the bus by the flats and Piggy stayed on to the request stop beyond and walked back. He had a spring in his step as he walked. He had not enjoyed himself like this evening for a long time, if ever. He wanted to get back to the flat, and her, as quickly as possible. He was about to put his key in the door when a stern voice came out of the dark.

"This had better be important, Piggy! You've ruined a most promising evening for me."

He spun round to face the voice.

"And who was that I saw going in a few minutes ago?"

"Oh, Mr Holmes. Am I glad to see you."

He opened the door and ushered him in.

Maria had heard the noise outside and was standing in the hall with her right arm behind her back. Piggy guessed that the hand was not empty.

"It's all right Maria, this is Mr Holmes."

Holmes looked at her for some time. He had made enquiries at the arches in the past, but was having difficulty equating the girl before him with the memory of the maid at those premises.

"This had better be good, Piggy," he said, still irritated at being called away before his evening with Tracey.

Piggy ushered him into the lounge and motioned for him to take the armchair whilst he and Maria sat on the settee. She sat much closer than she had on previous occasions and he could feel the warmth of her hip against his.

"Big Ernie wants Maria dead, and he wants me to do it."

Holmes looked from Piggy to Maria and back again before answering.

"So she should run. She's made a good start with her changed appearance and could be away tonight. What's so urgent that you need me?"

"Because if I do run then they will probably kill Piggy instead."

As Maria spoke Piggy turned and gazed lovingly at her. He realised that she had several opportunities to leave during the day and he would have had no way of finding her.

"So you need to die," said Holmes in a matter of fact voice.

"Pardon?" said Piggy.

"No. Listen. Maria needs to appear to be dead. And if you are to stand a chance of survival, then you need to appear to be the cause. I presume Ernshaw wants one of his trustees to verify the event."

Piggy nodded.

"So we need to stage her death. And we need to convince Ernshaw's men of it. Make a pot of tea Piggy I need to think."

Piggy got up and went out to the kitchen.

"I see Piggy has realised that you are fond of him. That could be a problem, as he must stay here because of his parole terms and you must not. But I'll see what can be done."

Piggy returned and waited with one ear on the kettle.

"Does this block have communal hot water?"

"Yes, when it works. Seems to be fine in the summer and packs up in the winter. The boiler is too small... But what's that got to do with anything?"

"I can't help remembering something my Dad told me. He was a soldier during the war and helped free a concentration camp. The Germans were desperately trying to destroy the evidence as the Allies advanced and the stench from the ovens was horrendous. After the war he took to farming. Pig farming. And they were hit by foot and mouth when we were kids. The carcasses were burnt and the stench brought it all back to him."

Piggy looked blank and Maria frowned.

"So we need to convince Ernshaw that you have disposed of the body without his men seeing it. A big joint of pork incinerated in the boiler would do the trick. One whiff of the smell should convince anyone who comes close. If you were to ring Peter and say you've done her in, but she has some metal possessions to dump somewhere he would come round, smell the stink and report back how clever you were to dispose of her.

When did you cut your hair?"

Maria was surprised by the question.

"Why?"

"Because we need some forensics to start a murder enquiry."

He smiled, and the smile became a broad grin.

"Have you got any metal possessions?"

"A comb and a silver hairbrush."

Holmes looked around the room then held his hand out to Maria.

"And that knife tucked in the back of your slacks... Sorry Piggy. You are going to lose that radio."

"But..."

"It's got a serial number and my enquiries will turn up Maria as the purchaser."

Maria patted Piggy's hand and glanced at the brown envelope on the sideboard.

"Never mind, Piggy. You can afford to buy another one."

Holmes softened his tone as he turned to face Maria. "And I'm afraid you are going to lose all your other possessions... And there must be something in it for me."

"I've got some money..." Piggy began.

"Don't be daft. I mean someone has to get arrested."

Maria smiled. "How about catching a bent solicitor trying to beat the foreign currency regulations by post? And a lead to where Ernshaw is at the same time?"

Holmes chuckled. "Florribund?"

She nodded and his chuckle turned into a snortle. He had seen many a villain walk free as a result of that weasel.

They sat and drank their tea as Maria told of the fake documents and Florribund's message. Piggy noticed that she was careful not to say how or where she learnt of Florribund's intentions. Holmes then asked Piggy to repeat exactly what Peter had said.

Holmes drained his cup while he listened. Then he stared at the few traces of leaf in the bottom and smiled again. Things were getting better by the minute, and he made a mental note to add 'refreshments for informant' entries into his expenses to explain how he got the information he was going to use over the next day or so.

"Okay Piggy. Here's how it's going to happen. Maria you're coming with me tonight. Say goodbye to Piggy and get ready. Leave all personal stuff that any of the gang have ever seen, even if only for an instant, and enough clothes to convince them you are where they are no longer of use to you. And say goodbye to Piggy whilst I go and make some arrangements."

* * *

Superintendent Hackman was not happy at being woken after midnight. Especially since it was Holmes asking for permission to set up a multi-car surveillance for the next day.

"I thought you were off until late turn on Monday."

"Yes, but this is urgent."

"It better be!" said Hackworth as he mentally totted up the cost of giving the detective unlimited overtime on a Sunday.

"What's the case?"

"It's that murder enquiry that we suspect Ernshaw of. There's a possibility that they may be moving evidence tomorrow, and if we don't stop them then it will be lost forever."

"Go ahead," he sighed. "I'll phone the duty officer and okay it."

"And I think I might be arresting Florribund on Monday morning."

"Good solid evidence? I don't want him getting off and making us look like idiots."

"How about red-handed posting a wodge of cash to Ernshaw in Spain."

"Do that and you'll be a sergeant before Christmas. But take it easy on the expenses. You've already used up more of my budget than the rest of CID put together."

Holmes put the phone down and smiled. Then he picked it up again. He was going to enjoy the next two calls.

"Hello. Milly?"

"Who is it?"

"Terry!"

"Terry? Oh, Terry Holmes! I've missed you. Can you come down?"

"I'm sorry Milly. Not for a bit. But I need really big favour ."

"I thought we'd done that already, several times if I recall," she giggled.

"No. Not that, although it will give me an excuse to come and see you often. I want to send a witness down to stay with you and I don't want anyone to know where she has come from. I'm about to ring Martin Rudge to see if he can go to pick her up."

"Her?"

"Yes, she's mid-twenties and very handy about the house. If you get guests then you can safely leave her to look after them."

"The way I looked after you, do you mean?"

"God no! She's a maid from a big house. She can wait on tables, do housework and is an excellent cook. And woe betide anyone who attempts to try it on with her."

"All right, my lover, but you come and see me soon. When is she coming?"

"Should be early morning."

"Okay, but you owe me for this, and I won't wait forever. I'm a passionate woman who needs her man."

"Stop, Milly. You'll make me desert my post and come down right now if you carry on like that."

"That's the intention, my boy. And don't you forget it."

Holmes was reluctant to hang up, but he still had calls to make and things to do.

His next call was to Martin Rudge. He had no idea of Rudge's home circumstances and he was cautious when a woman answered the phone.

"Hello?"

"Is Martin there?"

"He's in bed. Who's that calling at this hour?"

"It's a friend."

"Some friend waking people at this time of night."

"It's urgent. Tell him it's Holmes."

There was a long silent pause punctuated by the sound of footsteps and a hammering sound at a door.

"Go back to bed Mum. It's probably work."

"He said he was a friend."

"Yes, and he's also a very clever detective... Hello, Terry?"

"Sorry to call so late, Martin, but I need help. I've got a witness who I want protected, but not officially as I think there are leaks that would put her and others at risk. I've spoken to Milly and she will put her up. But I want to get her there without leaving a trail."

"You want to meet somewhere?"

"No. I want to put her on a train at the last minute and get you to meet her. But not at the local station. Somewhere far enough away to confuse any attempt to trace her."

There was silence for a while as they both thought.

"Has she much luggage?"

"No, only a small bag."

"Get her on the newspaper train to Taunton. I'll set off straight away and be there to meet her. What does she look like?"

"About five three with short curly blonde hair."

"Tell her to get off the train and go to the ladies' loo on the platform. Wait until the guard blows his whistle and then count to a hundred before walking out to the car-park. I'll come alongside her as she reaches the kerb."

"Thanks Martin. I owe you. I should be down in a few days."

"You mean down to see Milly," he laughed. "You know, I don't think she's looked at another man since your visit. Twice she's phoned me to ask if I knew if you were coming this way."

Holmes rang off and made his way back to the flat. Maria was ready, standing in the hall with a duffle bag over her shoulder. She wore dark blue slacks and a white windbreaker.

"Hmm. That looks a bit too visible, and probably a bit cold for what I have in mind. Piggy can you let her have a heavy jacket of some sort? And a Benny hat or something."

He thought it better not to let on that she probably had a cold sixty mile motorbike ride ahead of her.

Piggy fished around while Holmes outlined his arrangements. He returned with a donkey jacket and a navy sea-scout beret. He'd never been a scout. He had found the beret in the pocket of an off the peg raincoat. Off the peg in the café down Walworth Road. Maria pulled a face as she saw the offered garments.

"No time to argue. Put them in your bag and change on the train. We haven't much time. I'm putting you on the train to Taunton."

Maria took a tearful farewell of Piggy. Obviously their relationship had developed more than either had realised in the last few days.

It was starting to rain as they pulled in to Victoria Station. Holmes left her in the car while he bought a single to Taunton. As he handed it to her he noticed the gold ring on one finger.

"I need to borrow that for a few days. I'll make sure you get it back."

She struggled to pull the ring from her finger as they walked to the platform. Holmes glanced at the clock. The train left in three minutes time. As they waited, he told her how she was to be met and what her destination was to be. She raised her newly bleached eyebrows in surprise as he gave her the details, but said nothing.

He stood by the barrier until the train cleared the end of the platform, then he returned to his car. There was a lot to do! First step was to knock up a friendly butcher on his way back to Peckham. Next was to supervise Piggy bagging up Maria's possessions in pillow cases. He carefully added a few strands of her cropped off hair to each bag and slipped some more into his pocket.

Time was against him as he entered Peckham police station, to speak to the duty officer and raid the evidence store. He remembered a box of incendiary devices seized in an arson case. The case was still on-going but they would not miss one. Finally he went home to bed and set his alarm for eight o'clock.

DC Holmes groaned as the telephone woke him. He glanced at the bedside clock. It was a little after six-thirty.

"Hello!"

"Morning Terry. I've got Martin and his passenger here. I thought I'd let you know you're missing one of my special breakfasts. You remember them, don't you?"

He certainly did. It was a 'morning after the night before' special.

"You've called me to say you are cooking breakfast?"

"No, my lover. I'm letting you know what you're missing and at the same time telling you that they arrived safely. Hang on, Martin wants a word."

"Terry? It went like clockwork. I met her on the bike with mud covered number plates and we came over the tracks across the Quantocks for a few miles to make sure she was not followed. She's in the bath washing the mud off and warming up, but she's fine."

Holmes grinned to himself. The thought of them riding the trials bike across woodland and moor at night with mud flying everywhere was so remote from his image of the ice-cool uniformed maid. But it was certain nobody could have followed them.

"Thanks. I'll call you tonight and give you an update."

He hung up and looked at the clock. No point in trying to get back to sleep, so he got up and made breakfast. It was a cold miserable offering compared with what he knew Milly was preparing for her guests.

32. Deception

At ten thirty on Sunday morning, Piggy went down to the boiler room, threw the leg of pork into the furnace and went back up to the flat to phone the number Bald Peter had given him.

"'Oo is it?"

"Hello Peter. I need a bit of help. Can you bring a motor so we can get rid of some stuff?"

"What!"

"Bring the van and get here as quick as you can!"

A curious Peter arrived to find a blood splattered Piggy standing in the lobby of the flats with a bucket of hot ash beside him and three stuffed pillow cases behind him. The door to the boiler room was open and a foul smell drifted out through the doorway.

"Jeez, what's that God awful smell?"

"It should clear soon. It's only the remnants in the boiler."

"What?"

"It's a small boiler so I couldn't do it in one go. I had to chop up and keep digging out the ash. Do you have any idea how long it's taken me?"

Piggy carefully kept to the script that Holmes had coached him in. Implying without actually saying that he had disposed of Maria.

Bald Peter looked at Piggy with eyes glowing in admiration. Who would have thought that he could be so coldblooded and matter of fact about it. If Peter had been asked the day before he would have put his money on Piggy chickening out and getting the Garman brothers to do it.

"What do you want me to do, boss?"

"This bucket needs dumping. She had a lot of metal fillings and I'm not poking about in the ash to find them."

"Sure, boss. I'll dump them in the dock."

"And those bits in the pillow cases have all got metal stuff and glass. Can you put them in Big Ernie's crusher?"

Peter nodded.

"No. I mean can *you* do it. I don't want anyone else involved. Least who know the better."

Peter smiled. Exactly like Ernie would have handled it. Perhaps the rumours about Piggy's parentage were true.

Peter got in the Transit and backed it up close to the doorway.

"That ash could make a bit of a mess."

"You can sweep her out later," replied Piggy, pleased with the ambiguity of his reference to the van in the female gender.

Peter laughed and heaved the bucket up onto the floor of the van. He packed the pillowcases round it and Piggy obligingly pushed one particularly grubby pillow up tight against it to steady it.

"Right! You had better be off. I've got a bathroom to scrub out and saws to dump."

The picture that Piggy's words conjured up made Peter shudder. He silently shut the van doors and drove off. Out in Camberwell New Road, a Hillman Hunter watched him pass from a side street and gently pulled out to follow at a distance.

"Mike Delta, we are off and should be in action in about five minutes. Let the fire brigade know now."

Holmes put down the microphone and smiled. He was going to enjoy this.

Precisely five minutes later as they approached Rotherhithe, smoke began to seep from the van. Peter pulled up and stumbled out, gasping and coughing as he came. As he opened the driver's door smoke billowed out to form a little cloud that rose slowly like a red indian smoke signal. A passing traffic division motorcyclist stopped to assist and a fire engine arrived within the minute.

"Good job we were passing. We were just going back to the station after a false alarm," said the leading fireman to a stunned looking Peter, as he watched his crew axe their way into the back of the van and douse the smoke.

Holmes had watched from some distance away. Now he drove up close and parked beside the fire engine.

"Anything I can do?" he asked the well-briefed traffic officer.

"Dunno guv. This pillock was driving around with hot ash in an open bucket."

Holmes peered into the back of the van. The dousing had washed a lot of the ash out, leaving larger lumps exposed. Mainly the bag of dog bones that the butcher had provided.

"Is that bone?"

The traffic officer went back to his bike and put on his gauntlets before carefully selecting a large charred piece of bone from Piggy's leg of pork. As he did so, Holmes leaned into the van and dropped a lock of hair on the floor.

"Looks like a bit of a femur to me," said the traffic officer in an authoritative voice after examining the object.

He then scanned around the floor and spotted the lock of hair. Picking it up he turned to where Peter was standing and coughing a few feet away.

"Is this yours, sir?" he politely asked the shiny domed Peter, to hoots of laughter from the watching firemen.

"Have you got an evidence bag on you guv?"

As the traffic officer dropped the hair into a bag quickly offered by Holmes, Peter glanced round him. Policemen seemed to have arrived from all directions in the last couple of minutes. A J4 was parked a few yards up the road and the driver was talking on the radio. Bolting was not an option.

"Well, well! Peter Smith, otherwise known as Bald Peter. And what brings you out of your pit on a Sunday morning. Early service at St Olav's perhaps?"

Holmes raised his eyebrows quizzically, but did not really expect an answer. Meanwhile the traffic officer had lifted the bonnet of the van and was looking inside.

"Interesting vehicle this. It seems to have two different VIN numbers, and I'm sure Ford don't use Chrysler vee eights. I think I need to see the log book, if its got one."

"Can you get it towed in to the pound at the Elephant? I'll take our friend here into Peckham for a chat."

"Righto, guv, then I'll go back to Trio Place and do a few searches."

PC Walker appeared and escorted Peter to the back of the J4 and locked him in. In order to remind the world that they were busy keeping the streets safe whilst honest folk were still abed, the driver turned on his blues and twos as they drove away.

With all the excitement over the assembled officers went their separate ways. Many, on overtime after a night shift, plodded their weary way home.

* * *

In the little interview room, Peter was thinking hard. He had been put in a cell the day before and left there all day and night. A TD Inspector had briefly interviewed him on the Sunday afternoon, and as a result had rushed off to get a warrant to search The Arches. Holmes had said that he would be interviewed after they made further enquiries, and left him to reflect on his position. If only he had had the sense to douse the ashes before he drove off, he thought.

However, unbeknown to him such action would have done no good. The incendiary device in the pillowcase had enough flammable material and plastic packed round it to ignite, regardless of anything else. Piggy had practised a number of times until Holmes was satisfied that he could trigger the device through the grubby pillow slip.

Holmes entered the room and nodded to the uniform officer present to leave.

"You seem to be in a bit of trouble Peter. We are looking for a young lady who may be a witness to a murder we are investigating.

Name of Maria. She worked for Big Ernie Ernshaw. But then you know that. Would you care to explain to me what my forensic team are finding in the back of that van?"

"I know nuffing."

"Come, come, Peter. We catch you fair and square transporting human remains and you know nothing? Well, I know something. I know you are going to be breaking rocks on Dartmoor until well beyond pension age if you don't start telling me what I need to know. Or would you prefer accommodation at the seaside? I'm told Parkhurst is nice at this time of year."

"Honest, Mr Holmes, I just fetch and carry. I don't know anything else."

"Fetch and carry for who? Big Ernie seems to have disappeared, or was it him in the bucket. The hair looked a bit long for him. Who's giving the orders now?"

There was a knock on the door and a young PC entered. He had a small gold ring in a plastic bag which he handed to Holmes.

"It was in the ashes. Looks like it fits a small adult. Dr Hitchcock thinks probably female. It's a Spanish design."

"That looks like the sort of thing that the missing maid would wear. Have a look through those bits in those pillow cases, constable. I think I saw a framed photo of her there. See if you can see her hands."

Peter squirmed. They clearly had enough evidence to prove it was Maria.

"Little Willy Ernshaw asked me to pick it up. Honest I was only doing a bit of driving."

"So you were only dumping it for someone else?"

"Yes!"

"So we are not looking at murder, only concealing a body and preventing registration of a death?"

"Yes!" said Peter eagerly.

"Whose?"

Peter looked up at Holmes. He realised that he had already said enough to convict himself. He also realised that the young PC was still in the room, and writing furiously in a little beige pocketbook.

"I'm not saying nuffing more without my brief."

"Mr Florribund?"

"Yes."

"You might have to wait a while, old son. He's in a cell down the corridor waiting for *his* solicitor to get him out. He was stopped at the post office trying to send a bundle of cash to an address in Spain."

Peter looked around the room for inspiration, but none came. Holmes waited for a minute then turned to the young PC.

"Find Mr Smith a nice sunny cell. He will be with us for some time."

Holmes left the uniform PC to attend to Peter's accommodation. He would have another chat with him after the man had time to realise the certainty of his fate. A gentle hint that they could go easy about transporting a body should get him singing about Ernshaw's activities as loudly as Fingers Fisher. If Peter was really co-operative then he might consider bail at a later stage. Then he could claim expenses for informant's refreshments whenever he interviewed him.

33. Piggy Swinton, Murder Suspect

Piggy was glad to get back to the dull routine at work on Monday. He had no idea if Maria was safe or what had happened after he had watched Peter drive out of the estate. On Sunday evening he had feasted on bread and cheese. He had several steaks in the fridge, but still had the stench of incinerated pork in his nostrils. He went in to the factory early and had swept up and tidied away all that he could before Harry arrived.

"I've never had a crime boss working for me before. I'd better watch what I say or else I might end up in a bucket as well."

Piggy started to protest, but then saw Harry trying to suppress a smirk.

"It's really not like that. I can't say much now, but someday I'll tell you all."

"That's all right, Reg. I know you couldn't chop up a body. You couldn't even throw away that half-eaten mouse that Tom here left on the floor. Anywise, we have other things to worry about. There's two coppers parked a van outside and came in as I did. Asked me where the Personnel Office was."

"Probably about the robbery attempt. Returning someth..." Piggy tailed off as Tom Dawes led two uniformed officers into the store.

"There he is!"

Piggy recognised PC Walker and was about to give him a cheery greeting when he saw him extract a pair of handcuffs from a little pocket in the waistband of his trousers.

"Reginald Swinton? I'm arresting you on suspicion of the murder of Mary Fluke, otherwise known as Maria Gomez."

Piggy's jaw, now used to dropping at the least provocation, was already in the lowered undercarriage position before Walker finished speaking. He meekly held his hands forward and allowed himself to be cuffed and led away.

It seemed to Piggy that Walker deliberately went the long way round, past as many of the factory workers as possible as he escorted his prisoner back to the van. Outside he stood on the pavement for further public scrutiny for what seemed like an age before being placed in the vehicle. All sorts of strange ideas flitted through his mind on the short journey to the station, including the possibility that Holmes had killed Maria and neatly framed him. After all, the man was clever.

Piggy sat alone in the interview room for half an hour before a grinning Holmes pushed open the door and brought in a tray piled high with bacon sandwiches and a flask of coffee.

"Sorry about that Piggy. I knew that Ernshaw would have difficulty believing that you did Maria in, so I thought it would be a good idea if we let him think we suspected you. Let me relieve you of the bracelets and help yourself to some grub. Incidentally Maria is safe and secure with a friend of mine in Devon. I'll arrange for you to visit her in a week or two."

"Jeez, you had me worried for a minute. I thought you was fitting me up."

"Really, Piggy. Surely you can trust me. After all we've done together."

"I wanted to, Mr Holmes, but when those cuffs went click I could have died."

"Never mind. I'll have to keep you here long enough for Ernshaw to think we've given you a good grilling and you've beaten us. But we'll keep you well fed and watered and you can help me clear up a few details to pass the time."

"How will he know I'm in here?"

"A good question, and one I often ask myself." It reminded Holmes to check out the switchboard operator. "I asked Walker to make sure as many people as possible saw him bring you in."

Piggy nodded at Holmes's explanation for his circuitous route to the van, and reached for a sandwich. For the rest of the morning and most of the afternoon they went over things that Fingers had spoken of. Piggy had forgotten that his past prison mate was residing in a cell along the corridor and dictating his biography to a team of eager detectives. Eventually Holmes leaned back, tilting his chair on the back legs as he did so, and closed the folder he had been annotating.

"Let's leave it at that, shall we? I'll pull you in again in a week or so, for the appearance of it, and to make sure that Ernshaw thinks we suspect you. I've got enough on Ernshaw to put him away for good if he comes back, as long as I can keep tabs on my witnesses, so you should be in the clear. Best that you walk back to work."

Piggy got up and was escorted out. It was almost four o'clock by the time he got back to the factory. On the way in he met Tracey coming out. She smiled, a smile that destroyed his powers of concentration for the rest of the day.

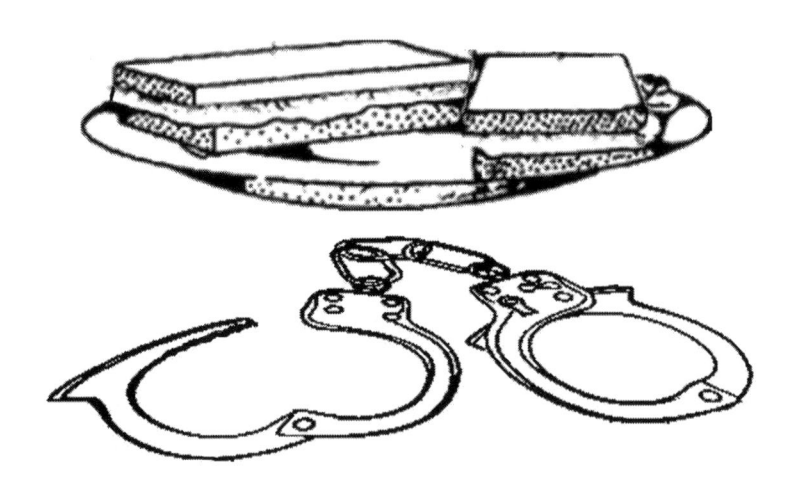

34. All's Well that Ends

On Wednesday afternoon, Hardcastle circulated a memo to heads of departments. He was retiring from active company management and had sold a forty-nine percent share in the factory to a business management company called Executive Services. They would appoint a new factory manager shortly, and the staff would be informed in due course.

Harry placed the memo on the table so he and Reg could read it together. Piggy read it, then burst out into uncontrollable laughter.

Harry looked at his young assistant, and waited until Reg stopped laughing and composed himself.

"Come on then, young Reg... Share the joke."

"I think you are going to enjoy working, Harry. You may even want to consider staying on after retirement age."

"How do you work that out?"

"I think I might know who our new manager might be. And she has quite a different approach to Hardcastle."

"Do you, by George, and what makes you think I might want to stay on? Did you say *she*?"

"Yup! Trust me. Life can only get better. You once told me your late wife wore *Evening in Paris* and the smell brought back memories."

"So?"

"Nice memories?"

"Of course! Me and my Lizzie never had a cross word in all the time we were together."

"I think you should prepare yourself for a lot of memories, Harry."

Despite all Harry's attempts to get him to explain himself Reg would not say a single further word. He just grinned and occasionally giggled throughout the rest of the day.

Piggy had a lot to grin about. Big Ernie was out of the country and unlikely to come back, except at the request of the Metropolitan Police. A request he would decline if he had any say in the matter.

The few members of his gang not in the cells had fled from Peckham. Ernshaw had managed to get a message to him from his cell in Morocco saying, in his words, 'since that idiot Peter had messed up disposing of Maria's remains, then Piggy should keep a low profile.'

He had a large brown envelope of money that he had put away for a rainy day. And best of all, over the coming Bank Holiday, Holmes was giving him a lift as he drove down to Devon for a long weekend.

Suddenly all was right in Piggy's world.

---- **THE END** ----

About the Author

James Court was brought up in Hove, Sussex, on the slopes of the South Downs overlooking the English Channel. His grandfather worked in agriculture and as a child he spent many a happy summer in rural Huntingdonshire, stacking sheaves of wheat and barley alongside his grandfather.

After a working life spent mostly in London he retired to the rural North Downs fourteen years ago, where he again found more time to indulge in his passion for books. For the first time since his youth he also now has time to write items longer than short stories and technical journals.

James writes humorous novels and *Mulligan's Revenge* is a sequel to *Strudwick's Successor*, the first in a series of stories set in Peckham, South London.

He also writes about rural life, especially about the 1700s

His rural novel, *The Whitedown Chronicles,* which is set in post-war Kent, has been published. Its sequel is currently under final revision.

December 2015

Printed in Great Britain
by Amazon